soulmates

Also by Jessica Grose

Sad Desk Salad

soulmates

A Novel

JESSICA GROSE

WM

WILLIAM MORROW
An Imprint of HarperCollins *Publishers*

SOULMATES. Copyright © 2016 by Jessica Grose. All rights reserved. Printed in the United States of America. No part of this book may be used or reproduced in any manner whatsoever without written permission except in the case of brief quotations embodied in critical articles and reviews. For information address HarperCollins Publishers, 195 Broadway, New York, NY 10007.

HarperCollins books may be purchased for educational, business, or sales promotional use. For information please e-mail the Special Markets Department at SPsales@harpercollins.com.

FIRST EDITION

Designed by Leah Carlson-Stanisic

Illustration by Hans Jeitner/Shutterstock, Inc.

Library of Congress Cataloging-in-Publication Data has been applied for.

ISBN 978-0-06-239157-5 (hardcover)
ISBN 978-0-06-264322-3 (Australia/New Zealand edition)

16 17 18 19 20   RRD   10 9 8 7 6 5 4 3 2 1

*To Michael Winton, for growing with me
for all these years*

Soulmates

Dana

I was waiting for coffee at the bodega down the street from my office when I saw his eyes blazing back at me from the cover of the *New York Post*. The cheap metal prongs of the newsstand were blocking the headline, and most of his face, but the eyes alone tipped me off. I hadn't seen my husband in five years, but I would recognize those limpid brown headlights anywhere. Making sure that none of my fellow lawyers were in the shop watching me pick up a tawdry rag, I walked three steps to the newsstand and, breath quickening, took a copy.

Ethan's face had thinned out since I last saw him. There were severe hollows in his cheeks where there was once a downy roundness from one too many weeknight beers. In the photo he had a full beard, and his curly dark hair, which he had always trimmed close to the scalp, now fell in dreadlock-style tendrils across his brow. He had aged considerably in just a short time, but not badly. He had a smattering of sexy crow's-feet ringing his eyes, the kind you get from hours spent outside. His skin had taken on a tan, faintly leathery quality.

It took me a minute to realize he wasn't alone on the cover.

She was there, too. Amaya's clean olive skin still glowed as if it were backlit, the product of a diet based primarily on kelp. Her dark-blond hair was pinned back in a dancer's bun. Both Ethan and Amaya had their hands pressed together as if in prayer.

The photo appeared to be a promotional image from one of their videos. Ethan and Amaya had made instructional videos for married people who want to be "cosmically connected through the ancient practice of yoga." Each video opened with Ethan and Amaya locked in a ball of intertwined arms and legs—some ridiculously complicated pose that made their limbs look like braids of lanyard. After they unfolded, but before the opening titles rolled on-screen, Amaya bowed to the camera and said slowly, in an even, condescending tone often used by preschool teachers, "We want to teach you how to share each other's consciousness. With our help, you can have the closest marriage."

I committed that line to memory after watching and re-watching every video on their YouTube channel—even the one that was just a dog nosing around a pile of sand. In those bitter months after Ethan left, I had a Google Alert for his name, and for Amaya's name, and then for their names together. The videos popped up about six months after they ran off together. At first I tried to figure out where the videos were made. It had to be San Francisco, right? Isn't that where people go when they leave their wives for yoga instructors? But I never could find any trace of Ethan or Amaya in my public records searches. There was no evidence of an apartment, or a new driver's license, or even incorporation data for When Two Become One, the name of their "company," according to the videos. Ethan had shut down his Facebook account right before he left me and never reactivated it. The videos were the only real thing I had.

Ethan's face looking up at me from the cover of the *Post* brought everything welling back up. I was so wrapped up in searching his new crow's-feet that I had missed the headline splashed in luridly enormous type across the *Post*'s front page: NAMA-SLAY: YOGA COUPLE FOUND DEAD IN NEW MEXICO CAVE.

I managed to slide the *Post* out of the metal rack without rattling it—no small feat, since my hands were shaking. I passed it across the counter to the clerk along with a dollar, turned, and walked quickly out the door. "Miss, miss! Your coffee!" I heard the clerk shout after me, but I no longer needed the caffeine.

I walked out onto Eighth Avenue and held my hand up over my eyes. The late-May sun—which seemed so cheerful when I left my apartment this morning—now felt oppressive as it bounced off the spotless glass of the office buildings. I briefly considered going back home and telling my boss, Phil, that I had eaten some bad oysters the night before and needed to take a sick day, but of course that wasn't an option. Phil is a forty-eight-year-old man who wakes up at 4:45 every morning to train for triathlons. Phil works eighty-hour weeks. Phil has 4 percent body fat, which he will find some way to work into the conversation within five minutes of meeting you. Phil refers to himself in the third person, and he never, ever gets sick. "Sickness is for the weak!" Phil says. If I were to call in sick, it would have to be from a hospital bed.

Staggering up to Fifty-Eighth Street, I wondered if there was some mistake. Maybe Ethan wasn't really dead. Maybe Amaya left *him* for some other poor sucker, and that was the body found in the New Mexico cave. She didn't seem like someone who valued a commitment overmuch.

I held on to this bitter fantasy as I rode the fourteen floors up to my office. I barely nodded at the receptionist, and mumbled a very curt "Morning" to my assistant, Katie, before scurrying into my office and closing the door. Katie is a competent recent college grad. She went to a local community college, but is a real go-getter and desperate to please me. She's good at her job but anxiously chatty, and I didn't want to risk being pulled into exchanging pleasantries with her. Not today. I sat down in my desk chair and, holding my breath, opened up the *Post*.

It took the search team more than a month to locate the bodies of Ethan "Kai" Powell and Ruth "Amaya" Walters in the rangelands of northern New Mexico. The lovebirds were reported missing from a swanky yoga spa called the Zuni Retreat, where they were instructors, on April 24. The owner of the retreat, John "Yoni" Brooks, notified local police a week after Powell and Walters failed to show up to teach their morning Aztec sun salutation class at 6 A.M. on the 17th.

Though the heights of the bodies found a few hours from Taos match the victims' descriptions, Powell and Walters were so badly decomposed after exposure to the elements that their identities had to be verified through dental records.

Details of the couple's deaths are hazy at this point, but a sharpened piece of obsidian was found in between the bodies.

That's as far as I got before my tears started dotting the photos next to the article—one of Amaya and Ethan wrapped in an upside-down yogic embrace, their arms entwined and their legs pointed up to the sky, plus smaller photos of Ethan from his college yearbook and Amaya from her pimply, brunette high school days.

There was no way Ethan was still alive. It's tough to argue with dental records. Though I had wished Ethan and Amaya dead nearly every day for twelve months after they fled New York, their actual demise gave me no joy. What I had really wanted was for Amaya to get a disfiguring facial fungus, or, if I'm really honest, for Ethan to get abandoned the same way I did. I never truly longed for their bodies to be splayed out, alone, in the rural Southwest.

But I still felt angry with him. Ethan and I had been together for a decade, since we were sophomores in college. We called each other "partner" in goofy cowboy voices. I thought we were a team, and I suppose we were—until we weren't. That's the thing I could never forgive him for, leaving me all alone to pick through the rubble of the relationship he detonated.

I had spent countless hours on the couch of a very understanding, maternally soft therapist to get myself over Ethan. Entire days went by now when I didn't imagine him standing in the vestibule of our apartment with a duffel bag on his shoulder, about to walk out of my life. He had written me a good-bye note that said he needed to go live with Amaya. "That is where my true self lies," he wrote. He didn't even have the courage to say it to my face.

But now I didn't know how to reconcile any of this. New Mexico? The Zuni Retreat? "Kai"? Dead? This wasn't at all what I had fantasized about Ethan's new life. So I called my sister, Beth. She's a graduate student in twentieth-century American history. She has been working on her dissertation for four years. She always picks up her phone.

"What's up?" Beth said sleepily. It was only nine, so she was probably still in bed, nursing her first coffee of the day.

"Ethan's dead." I tried to say this as calmly as possible, but I couldn't hide the hysterical edge to my voice.

"Wait, what?" Beth said, immediately perking up.

"He's dead. Amaya's dead, too. It's on the cover of the *New York Post*." I forced the words out between gulps of air.

"Holy shit," Beth said, almost in a whisper. She'd wanted him dead since he left me. She'd said it so many times. I wonder if some kind of vague guilt stunned her into uncharacteristic silence.

"That's all you have to say? My husband is dead."

I could tell Beth wanted to reply that Ethan wasn't really my husband anymore. I know how her mind works. But she took a long pause instead and said, "I'm so, so sorry."

That's when I started to cry. Really cry, not just that first sprinkling of tears that smeared the newsprint. Ethan's dimples from that sweet collegiate portrait started dissolving, which made me cry harder. I covered my mouth and tried to keep quiet.

When my tears had somewhat subsided, Beth cautiously asked, "What happened?"

"Their bodies were found in a cave in fucking New Mexico. Police don't know that many details yet. Some kind of sharp object was found near them, though." The anger I had worked so hard to quell came back up, bilious. This never would have happened if he hadn't left me.

"Oh my god," Beth gasped. "Do you want to come over here? I'll take care of you."

"I think I need to be alone right now," I said, surprising myself. "Besides, there's so much going on at work I can't take a mysterious personal day."

Beth sighed loudly. "I can't believe you give a fuck about work right now. This is important, Dana. You're allowed to deal with a monumental life issue."

"Well, we can't all be perpetual graduate students, Beth." My job had been my ballast for years. It paid me well, and it kept me grounded. Beth could never understand that; to her a job was meant to give pleasure.

Though she'd usually rise to this kind of bait, Beth said only, "Okay, okay. I'm here if you need me. Please call me to check in. I'm worried about you."

I sniffed out a moment of composure. "I'm okay. I'll be okay. I just want to know what really happened."

Beth was right. Staying at work turned out to be a futile exercise—but at least my face was there from nine to seven. I spent the entire day searching for any additional information I could find on Ethan and Amaya. There was similarly sensationalist coverage in the *Daily News,* and a few sober articles in the *Albuquerque Journal* and the *Taos News,* but not much else. It must have been a slow news day for the *Post* to lead with Ethan's story. I read everything I could about the Zuni Retreat, which seemed like a typical yoga spa for old hippies and young, rich Los Angeles types who posted Instagram pictures of sunsets in the desert accompanied by hashtags like #blessed and #centered.

I tried to Google the hell out of John "Yoni" Brooks. I had met him once, at a yoga class I attended because Ethan insisted. Yoni seemed sort of creepy at the time, but harmless. Apparently when you Google a common man's name and "Yoni," all you get is YouTube videos of home births and instructions about vaginal massage.

After I read everything, I felt like I needed to talk to someone else. I couldn't talk to any of Ethan's old friends, because I already knew that he hadn't been in touch with them since he left me. Besides, most of them had tired of hearing from me after my repeated calls and e-mails in those early days after his departure. At first they were sympathetic, but after several months of bombardment they all started avoiding me. When I would reach one of them, he'd find a reason to get off the phone as quickly as possible. One of them told me I was worse than his student loan collector. I can't say I blame him.

Ethan left me with so little information that I fell into a bad habit of analyzing the minutiae of his yoga videos with Beth— "But what do you think he really *meant* by showing that dog licking the sand? Is it their dog? A stranger's dog?"—until I could tell she was sick of it.

"You know I love you, Dana," she said, "but if I watch Amaya demonstrate the king pigeon pose one more time, I am going to throw myself out your window." We were having tea in my living room when she leaned across the couch and held my hand. "I'm the only one who can tell you this, because we're blood. None of it means anything. He's gone, and you need to move on."

I knew she was right, but I couldn't accept it. So I started keeping my evening meanderings to myself. I wanted some concrete explanation for why our relationship had fallen apart so swiftly, and I thought I would find it in the bits of digital detritus that flowed through my battered Dell. How did we get so far away from where we had been? Was there something in Ethan's voice that would help explain why he had changed so drastically? Something I could read in his body language, or the way he related to Amaya, or the angle of his grin, that would explain where the man I thought I knew so well had gone?

The searching proved fruitless, of course. Most nights I drank too much two-buck Chuck from the Trader Joe's on Fourteenth Street and passed out in the chair in front of my computer, head slumped to the side, And the more I watched Ethan in those videos, contorting his once stocky frame into a sinewy pretzel, the less I felt like I knew him—possibly had ever known him.

About a year after Ethan left I broke myself of the Google-stalking habit with Beth's help. In a silly ritual I read about in a women's magazine, we burned every photo I had of Ethan and me together. I legally changed my name back to Dana Morrison, so I wouldn't have to wince every time I took out my driver's license and saw Dana Powell staring back at me. Then I took a two-week vacation and went to my family's cabin in rural Minnesota. Even though I barely talk to my mom anymore, she allows me access. It's just a shack on one of those ten thousand Minnesota lakes, but we don't get Internet or cell phone reception there. The respite allowed me to go cold turkey on those last grabbing grasps at my husband.

When I got back to New York I stopped all my Google Alerts. I thought about filing for divorce. I had tried to reach Ethan via an e-mail address I found at the end of one of his videos, but he never responded. Maybe Amaya deleted the missives before he got to them. I'll never know. I didn't have the energy to hire a private investigator and make Ethan divorce me, so I let it sit.

And, when I thought about it, there was a reason to stay married: I didn't want to pay him any alimony. I've always made at least four times what he did. Before he found Our Lady of the King Pigeon he was working as a part-time copy editor for an advertising agency. He never loved the work, but he seemed to be content with it.

I checked the Web one last time before I left the office to see if there was any new information on the case. But there was nothing. I gathered up my things against the dwindling light pouring through the windows and headed downtown to the home where Ethan and I were happy, once.

Over the years I had developed a nighttime ritual to stave off thoughts of Ethan and our old life. I would come home from work and spend no less than thirty minutes but no more than an hour meticulously preparing a healthy meal. I would sit down at the kitchen table and eat my green vegetables and lean meats, making sure I chewed each bite at least ten times. At first I would actually count to myself, and the repetition would soothe me. But soon the *ten ten ten* became mechanically ingrained.

In those early days I would thumb through a hard copy of the *New York Times*, thinking that ascetic virtue could replace my unhappiness. But soon I shifted to reading the news on my laptop, then to the sale page of Shopbop, and ultimately to the mindless pleasures of early-evening television: local news, national news, *Access Hollywood*, reruns of *Gilmore Girls*.

By now, I still did the cooking and the chewing, but usually I turned on the TV the second I walked through the door. I liked to have it as background noise. Our apartment on the corner of Ninth Avenue and Thirty-Sixth Street was the perfect size for Ethan and me: one medium bedroom, a generous living room, a real kitchen, and even a small room that Ethan had used as an office, which we'd equipped with a pull-out couch for guests and a hideous ancient plaid chair he bought at an old lady's yard sale the summer before our senior year.

Ethan and I went to a small liberal arts college outside Minneapolis. We got jobs in town and stayed over the summer every year because we loved it there so much. It was late July, and we had passed the old woman sweltering under the relentless sun several times while running our morning errands. Each time we went by her, she was slumped deeper in her lawn chair. Our quiet street got very little foot traffic, and we'd seen only three or four people fingering her collection of 1950s-era suits and heavy mahogany furniture.

Though I felt sorry for her, we didn't need anything more for our apartment—we could barely fit a dresser in our tiny bedroom—so I didn't want to go to her yard sale and get her hopes up. But Ethan insisted. "She seems lonely," he said. "I just want to talk to her."

I watched from our kitchen window as he walked up to the old woman. She visibly brightened the second Ethan opened his mouth. She sat up straight in her rickety lawn chair, and as Ethan leaned toward her, she fixed her hair coquettishly, smoothed her floral dress, and cocked her head to the side. I could tell he was flirting with her, charming her with that aw-shucks Montana drawl that I found so irresistible.

After a few moments I turned away from the scene unfolding across the way and smiled to myself. When he opened the door twenty minutes later, with the yellow plaid monstrosity sitting in all its 1970s glory behind him, all I could do was grin.

I could not reconcile that man with the man who had left me. After I got back from Minnesota and cured myself of Googling Ethan, my final step was to get rid of that chair, setting it out with a sad thump late on a Sunday night so I wouldn't have to look at it again before the garbagemen picked it up early the next morning.

Now that I'm the only person who lives in our apartment, a hollow quality has settled over the once bright rooms that can be drowned out only by the soothing baritones of nightly newscasters. When I got home that night, I went over to turn on the TV after I set my briefcase down, but then I hesitated: I wanted to find out more about Ethan, but I was afraid to hear his name come out of a newscaster's mouth. I didn't think I could stomach moving images of the cave where he and Amaya were found, or actual footage of their body bags.

I decided to leave the TV off for the time being, but after a few minutes of trying to prepare a small, homely meal of bagged salad and a can of vegetarian chili, the sounds of the can opener cranking, the fridge door creaking open and shut, and the plastic bag rustling started to grate. I put my utensils down and paced the uneven wood floors.

I had thrown out almost everything that Ethan owned in the months after he left, but there were a few things that seemed too cruel to toss—mostly things that related to his mom. She had died in a car crash when he was fourteen, so I never met her. I had put everything I saved in a drawer in the spare room, and I went to go see what was left.

The first thing I grabbed was a photograph. It was in a cheap metal frame, but the image itself was lovely. Rosemary looked to be about seven months pregnant, and she was wearing a frame-hugging maternity dress that accentuated her protruding belly. The photo had the slightly brownish tint of lots of photos taken in the late seventies, and it gave her blond hair an almost reddish gleam. She was smiling at the camera, looking serene, and her left hand was supporting her stomach, like she was protecting its contents from the camera's eye. At the bottom of the picture, Ethan had written in ballpoint pen *July 1978*.

Looking at the picture reminded me of the heart-destroying discussions Ethan and I had about kids in the year before he left. Right after he split I thought about our phantom children all the time. I even had obvious dreams about babies dressed in frilly Victorian garb with blank spaces where their faces should have been. I thought we'd have children by now, at least one, maybe two. I pictured a little girl with Ethan's sweet expression and my light hair.

One thing Ethan and I had agreed on was that we wanted two children. Just like I have Beth, he has a younger brother, Travis, who is in the air force and stationed outside Doha, Qatar—or at least he was the last time I heard from him. I had met him only a few times, and though he tried to be a good sibling to Ethan, his efforts didn't always land. Ethan was a sensitive kid and he'd read his brother's concern as judgment.

Their dad's another story. He works for the Montana Fish, Wildlife and Parks department. An army vet who met Ethan's mom in San Francisco after the Vietnam War, he never knew how to relate to his striving, gentle older son. Ethan had zero interest in hunting, which was Ray's primary method of bonding with his boys. It didn't matter so much when Rosemary was alive. On weekends she would take Ethan to the nearest community bookstore and leave him there while she went about her errands. Ethan spent hours in a cozy chair in a distant corner of the shop, reading Jack London and Ernest Hemingway and Thomas McGuane and other bards of wide-open spaces while Ray and Travis would be out hunting deer, elk, or bighorn sheep, depending on the season.

In the months after Rosemary's death, Ray tried to take Ethan on a few hunting trips. But, Ethan told me, he always did something wrong. Make too much noise or get bored and stare up at the sky. Ray didn't get mad about this, exactly. He'd just turn silent and cut their trips short. Soon Ray would just go hunting with Travis or his buddies from the Montana FWP and leave Ethan at home. So Ethan would read whatever he could find around the house instead of whatever he could find at the bookstore. That's how he became an expert on indigenous flora and fauna. He could talk for hours about bears. I used to love the depth and oddity of his knowledge.

Looking at the picture of Rosemary, I thought about Ray. The way he looked proud and almost happy at our wedding. The sad, downturned lines at the corners of his mouth in repose, the ones I noticed the one time he came out to my family's house in Minneapolis for Christmas. Despite our difficult mother, Beth and I tried our best to include him, but our rituals seemed to make him uncomfortable. He left a day early, without any real explanation. Ethan looked crushed but never wanted to talk about it. "That's just how Dad is," he said at the time.

Ray and Travis had always done the best they could by Ethan, and he appreciated them for it. As much faith as I had lost in Ethan's integrity, I never thought he would cut ties with Ray or Travis. I knew that Travis had been in touch with Ethan—at least he was when we broke up. Travis called me all the way from Qatar about two months after Ethan left to lend me his support. Loyalty and a man's word were important to him, and he told me he didn't respect Ethan's choices. What he said was "I think that boy's lost his damn mind." It buoyed me for about an hour, but the brief elation of being right was no match for the misery of being left.

I started and deleted sixty-four e-mails to Travis, since I felt closer to him than I did to Ray. I wondered if Travis had even heard the news yet, if he was even still in Qatar. And what would I say anyway? *Hi, we haven't talked in a few years, but do you know what happened to your poor dead brother?* I couldn't bear to be the one to break it to him.

Fortunately, my attempts at composing a straightforward yet sympathetic e-mail were interrupted by my phone ringing in the kitchen. I walked over, picked it up, and saw that the call was from a 575 area code, which my phone helpfully told me was in New Mexico.

"Hello?" I croaked out.

"Is this Dana Powell?" a twangy male voice inquired.

"Dana Morrison. I used to be Dana Powell."

"You are married to Ethan Powell. Is that correct?"

"Technically, yes."

"Ma'am, this is Sheriff Matt Lewis from the Sagebrush County Sheriff's Office. I have some upsetting news." His voice got sensitive. "You might want to sit down for this."

"Spare me," I said, more harshly than I meant to. "I saw it all over the *New York Post*. What took you so long to contact me?"

"Well, ma'am, it took us a while to figure out that Ethan still had a wife. I was not aware the case had become news in New York City. We found your information among his personal effects and thought you might be able to aid us in our investigation."

I sighed deeply and sat up. I hated everything that I had been feeling since I found out about Ethan's death, but I wasn't a monster. I was a good girl. I would always cooperate with authorities. "I'm happy to help in whatever way I can."

"I appreciate that. Ideally we'd interview you in person here in New Mexico, but I understand if that's not feasible at this time."

I paused, my head spinning. Could I take time off from work? "It depends," I said.

"Well, let's chat now and we can go from there," Lewis said. "I'm going to need to ask you some difficult questions. I apologize in advance."

"I understand," I said, trying to stop my voice from quavering.

"How long were you and Mr. Powell together?"

"Ten years. Married for about three."

"And why are you living apart?" Lewis asked.

"He got involved with Amaya and left me." I tried not to sound bitter, but I don't think I succeeded.

"In that time, was Mr. Powell ever violent with you?" he asked.

I laughed out loud. Ethan made us get those useless no-kill mousetraps when we had an infestation at our apartment. When they didn't work—as I predicted—and I called the exterminator, he refused to speak to me for half a day.

"Ma'am? "Lewis said, his voice still even. "Can you answer my question?"

"I'm sorry," I said, pulling myself together. "No, no. He was never abusive toward me."

"Was he abusive toward others?"

"No. Never. Why are you asking me this?"

"Well, ma'am, one of the possibilities based on the evidence is that what happened to Mr. Powell and Ms. Walters was a murder-suicide."

"No," I said plainly. "That's not possible. What is your evidence for that?"

"I'm not at liberty to say. I don't want to jeopardize our investigation." Lewis maintained his monotone. "But we haven't officially ruled either death a suicide at this time."

"I don't believe that Ethan would ever kill another soul, much less himself. Are you investigating the possibility of foul play at the retreat?"

"We're looking at all angles right now," Lewis said, "but at this point we do not have anyone we're calling a suspect."

"I think you should be looking a little harder," I snapped. "How many murders does your department investigate a year?"

"Well, ma'am, this county only has about a thousand full-time residents. So this is the first one in quite a while."

"Maybe you should be handing this over to someone with more experience. Maybe the FBI or the New Mexico State Police. Because there's no way the man I love is a killer, and you'd know that if you did a little investigating." I tried to keep my voice calm, but it started to get louder. I slowed down my speech to make my point. "It. Is. Not. Possible."

Lewis sighed. "Listen. Between you and me, I do think there's something hinky going on at the retreat. But the guy who runs the place . . ."

"Yoni?" I offered.

"Yes. Yoni, John Brooks, what have you. Mr. Brooks has a

very expensive team of lawyers, and he's greased a lot of palms over the past few years among the people who run this county. Additionally, Mr. Powell and Ms. Walters died on unincorporated land and not at the retreat. As of yet, we have not been able to get a warrant to search the grounds, and we have not been able to interview Mr. Brooks or anyone else over there." I detected a bit of frustration in the sheriff's voice.

"You've got to be kidding me," I said. "How can you know anything about Ethan's life without seeing where he worked and ate and slept?"

"Well, ma'am, we can't get someone in there, at least not someone who is employed by Sagebrush County. But that doesn't mean a regular citizen couldn't stay there as a guest."

I thought I detected a little wink in the sheriff's deadpan. "Are you suggesting what I think you're suggesting?"

"I'm not suggesting anything," Lewis said, sans wink. "I'm just bringing you up to date on the current status of our investigation."

"I see."

"My number is 575-555-7849. If you find yourself here in Sagebrush County, or if you think of anything that might be pertinent to our investigation, please give me a ring."

I was so surprised by the sheriff's suggesting I should stay at the retreat that all I could do was say "Okay."

I looked down at my phone. I couldn't actually go out to the place where Ethan died, could I? I pictured the ample hair on his arms falling out and scattering in the desert wind, his body disintegrating and melding with the sand. My eyes blurred with tears and I doubled over. I cast the phone aside and sprawled out on the floor, crying so hard I thought I might throw up.

I stayed on the floor for a long time, even after I stopped crying. I turned on my side and propped my head on my hand, then started tracing the lines between the wooden floorboards. The physical occupation calmed my mind. Did I still love Ethan, present tense, like I'd told Sheriff Lewis? Even after all those bitter years, all those hours logged in therapy? Hadn't that affection been talked out of me?

Maybe it didn't matter. I moved my hand from the floorboards to the moldings, tracing the old-fashioned detail with my pointer finger, flicking off dust that my cleaning lady must have missed. I never would have missed that dust were I cleaning myself. *Ethan's gone now,* I thought, *so whether I love him, or I loved him, is irrelevant.*

I tried to focus on what did matter. Part of what made me a good litigator was my ability to zero in on the details that would help build a case, and the companion ability to discard the information that didn't help me. What mattered was that Ethan, even in death, was possibly being accused of a crime there's no way he committed. I knew it in my soul.

So what did I care? I cleaned the last mite of dust off the moldings and sat up. I looked around the apartment, which had seemed spacious when I left it in the morning but now felt like it was suffocating me with its familiarity. Despite everything that had happened between Ethan and me, I could not allow him to go to his grave labeled a murderer. That's not who he was. I wasn't someone who would have married someone capable of that. I needed to go to New Mexico.

I jumped up to my computer to make arrangements. According to the Zuni Retreat's website, the easiest way to get there was to fly into Albuquerque, rent a car, and drive. The sound of a babbling brook auto-played on the site, which was light blue and white and had perfectly lit photos of the serene, treeless grounds and the spare but luxurious rooms.

Those six-hundred-thread-count sheets didn't come cheap. If I wanted my own room, it would cost $400 a night. If I was willing to share a room with a total stranger, it was $225. If I was willing to sleep in a bunk bed in a big open room, European hostel style, it was $100 a night, but the website was clear that it "cannot guarantee a bottom bunk."

I opted for the room share. I didn't want to blow several thousand dollars going to some godforsaken corner of the desert filled with people who described themselves as "spiritual, but not religious." I figured I could handle one stranger for a few nights—I did it for a whole year in college. And it occurred to me that I would get a better sense of Ethan's life by mixing with the other people there as much as possible.

I booked three nights there, then the flights and the car. I looked at the clock—by this time it was about nine P.M. I called Matt Lewis. "This is Dana Morrison . . . Powell. I've booked a stay at Zuni. I'll be in Sagebrush County by tomorrow evening," I told his machine, leaving my cell phone number.

I called Phil to tell him I had a family emergency and would be out for the rest of the week. He picked up on the first ring and wasn't thrilled. "Dana," he said, "we're in the middle of this case and I really need all hands on deck."

I wasn't going to tell him what was going on, at first, because I didn't think it was any of his business. But after that insensitive dig I decided I just didn't care what he thought. "Phil, my estranged husband was murdered. I'm taking the rest of the week. If you have a problem with that, you can bite me."

With that, I turned my phone off, took an Ambien, and got into bed. As I drifted into the brief, trippy nether region before an Ambien-laced pass-out, I saw Ethan's face smiling serenely at me. Usually I would dismiss this as a drug-addled hallucination, but that night I took it as a sign that I was doing the right thing.

I woke up with a start and squinted at the clock, which read 6:07. That's when I woke up for work, and it took me a minute to remember that I wasn't going to work, that Ethan was dead, and that I needed to pack and get a cab to LaGuardia. I checked the weather for Sagebrush County's only town, Ranchero. It would be in the eighties during the day and the fifties at night.

I rifled through my wardrobe to find some appropriate clothes. I wanted to fit in at the Zuni Retreat. I searched for leggings and colorful tank tops, anything that resembled what those yoga girls had been wearing in their Instagram pictures from Zuni. I found a long wrap sweater that Beth bought me for Christmas a few years ago that had been languishing in the back of my closet.

That reminded me that I should probably tell Beth where I was going.

"Dana, are you okay?" Beth said before I could even say hello.

"I'm fine," I said tersely. I didn't want her sympathy right now; I felt like it would slow me down, make me sad instead of determined. "I'm calling because I'm going to New Mexico today so that I can talk to the police about Ethan in person." I didn't tell her my ulterior motive. Beth would lose it completely if I told her that I was going to creep around the retreat where Ethan had lived. Visiting his final home was about fifteen levels up from just Googling him obsessively.

"Why the fuck would you schlep all the way out there? Don't they have Skype?" Beth could sniff out the obsessiveness in this trip, of course, even with my trying to hide it.

"They think Ethan killed Amaya," I explained. "And I know that's not possible. That's not Ethan. I think it will be more convincing if I go out there in person and tell the police everything I know about who Ethan really was."

"So you're going to tell them that he's a coward who left you as soon as things got a little difficult?" Beth asked. She was always so tough on me.

"I knew you'd be like this," I said, trying to keep myself from yelling. Fighting with Beth always made me regress to our childhood dynamics of screams, tears, and threats. "I wasn't going to tell you I was going because I didn't want to hear this shit. But I didn't want you to worry."

Beth sighed and said nothing for a few beats. Then she said much more gently, "I get it, you're grieving." She paused again, then said, "And I guess I don't think Ethan could kill someone, either. But I just don't think this is the right thing for you to be doing in this moment."

"I understand where you're coming from," I said, trying to be conciliatory. "But it's something I need to do. I'm doing it for Ethan, but I'm also doing it for me. I want to know more about his last days. For closure."

"Okay."

"Okay?"

"I know that arguing with you isn't going to work, so I'm saying okay because I don't want to fight with you. But I want to go on record saying that I think this is a bad idea. I thought you were finally getting over Ethan, and now you're going to plunge back into all that old news. Are you sure you're doing this for closure, or is it because you don't want to think of yourself as someone who could have loved a killer?"

"Tell me how you really feel, Beth," I said, stung.

"I won't say it again. But I wanted to put it out there. Have a safe trip; call me if you need me."

"I will," I replied, and I even half meant it.

The Zuni Retreat was a little more than three hours' drive from the Albuquerque airport. Everything in the landscape looked bright and white and new. The desert sky was clear in a way it rarely is in New York or Minnesota, and the sandy hills reflected the sun so it was constantly blinding me. I kept adjusting and readjusting my visor in the rental car to keep the glare out, but it was mostly futile.

I was in a daze anyway. I kept turning Beth's words over while I drove, to the point where I imagined the proper, female British voice that came out of my GPS telling me, "This is a bad idea." But I snuffed down my doubts. I wasn't coming out here to obsess about Ethan. I was coming here to do my duty as a citizen and to help with an open murder case. There was nothing wrong with my wanting to make sure the Sagebrush County Sheriff's Office got a clear picture of the man Ethan was. There was something noble about it.

At least that's what I was telling myself as I saw the sign: ZUNI RETREAT: ALL SPIRITUAL TRAVELERS WELCOME. I made the turnoff. The road to the retreat was well-paved and wound through a small valley. I could see the dusty brown hills rising on either side as I drove along.

As I followed the road up to the retreat, I saw five young women walking in a line, all wearing lululemon. Their perky butts encased in black Lycra reminded me of the rich house-wives I'd see leaving SoulCycle on my way to work, with their huge diamond rings glinting in the early-morning light. Some of the young women here in New Mexico had their arms linked, deep in conversation. Others were just smiling gently at the horizon, where the late-afternoon sun was still beaming on the hilltops. I couldn't tell if they looked relaxed or lobotomized. Their identical demeanors made me anxious about fitting in, an ungainly ten-year-old on her first day of sleep-away camp. Did I have the wrong clothes? The wrong hair?

I parked in a lot near the main lodge, which was surrounded by three outer buildings, all of them done in a tasteful mission revival style: all courtyards and gentle arches. From the website I knew that one of the buildings was for guest rooms, one was for classes, and one was for dining.

As soon as I stepped out of my car, I nearly collided with a man. He was so close to me I could smell him. He had the clean musk of someone who had recently showered but didn't wear deodorant. I hadn't seen him walk over. It was almost like he'd been spawned by the asphalt, and this silent approach startled me. I registered his gender only because right before I bumped into him, I noticed his hairy toes sticking out of leather thong sandals. Even in the empty space here, I was momentarily claustrophobic.

"Whoopsie-daisy," he said. "Gotta watch out for you!" Then he laughed a pleasant chuckle with his mouth open wide. I could see that his teeth were blindingly white, like a reality TV starlet's veneers. Maybe they looked so bright because the rest of him was so tan. He had an unusual, attractive face, with hazel eyes that were slightly saffron-colored and thick, dark lashes. I wondered if he was part Indian, because his features suggested a perfect mixture of Eastern and Western forebears. His light-purple robe complimented his corporeal color scheme.

I stuck my hand out to introduce myself, but he had already started to bow toward me. "I'm Janus," he said. "I'm on staff here. Welcome to your first stay at the Zuni Retreat." He radiated a contented warmth.

"I'm Dana," I said. "How did you know it was my first stay?"

"I try to keep up with all of our students. Unless I am devoted to our children, I won't be able to help them progress. And besides, you're the only one checking in today." He grinned at me. "Let me help you to the Ganesha desk. We call our reception area the Ganesha desk because Ganesha is the Hindu god of beginnings."

I nodded. The lingo sounded ridiculous to me (*"our children"*?), and the theological references seemed to be a polytheistic muddle. But at least the retreat seemed to be offering a lot of personal attention for the expense. While it wasn't what I was really looking for, I imagined that personal touch was what the other guests were paying for, and what made them come back. "I'm just going to take my bag out of the trunk," I told him.

Before I could move, Janus waved his hand. "It's my pleasure to help you. Allow me." I watched him hoist my bag from the trunk in a swift, fluid motion, his defined arms flexing ever so slightly with what seemed to be minimal effort. "Let's go!" he said, cheerfully. "I can't wait to help you begin this journey." He carried my bag into the lodge and put it on a trolley near the entrance before bowing again. "Namaste, Dana. Have a blissful experience."

"Namaste," I said, bowing. The word felt strange in my mouth, but I guessed I'd have to get used to it.

When I turned toward the reception ("Ganesha") desk, I was startled. At first I thought it was Amaya standing there. The clerk had the same shade of dirty-blond hair and supple skin. But as I got closer I saw that her nose and mouth were completely different, though there was something similar around the eyes. I couldn't tell if it was an actual likeness or just a shared expression.

"Namaste," said not-Amaya, whose name tag read BAIKA. She put her hands in prayer pose and bowed gently to me. "Do you have a reservation?"

"Yes. Dana Morrison." On the plane to New Mexico, I had decided I wouldn't tell anyone that I was Ethan's wife. There was nothing I hated more than fake pity from random people. My name didn't connect me to him anymore, and I assumed he hadn't exactly crowed about the fact that he left me to be with Amaya years ago.

Baika touched a few keys on her computer, which looked like it had just been taken out of the box. In fact, everything about this building was clean and slick and new. It was decorated minimally—just a few prayer rugs and paintings of what appeared to be various yoga progenitors on the walls and a smattering of fat gold Buddhas lounging in corners. But the walls were painted a bright white, and the floor was a cool light-blue glass tile that must have cost a fortune. It would not have been out of place in a financier's bathroom featured in an architectural magazine.

"Excellent," Baika said. "Your bed is ready right now. Your roommate has already been here for a few days, and she's a return visitor, so she should be able to show you the ropes." She reached below her desk and pressed a series of buttons. "I've just notified someone to bring her to the front desk, so she should be arriving momentarily."

I fiddled with my luggage for a moment in an effort to avoid making small talk with Amaya's doppelgänger. I braced myself to see one of the lululemonites strolling down the hallway, but when I looked up I saw a woman in her fifties with a mane of wild, wiry gray hair coming toward me. She had a sweet expression and a fluffy stomach, the kind that mothers get after more than three children. "Hi, I'm Sylvia," the woman said.

"Dana," I replied, extending my hand to her.

"You guys will get along great!" Baika chirped. How the hell would she know? I wondered. But instead of barking at her I smiled back and said, "I'll bet!"

"Sylvia, why don't you give Dana a little tour," Baika said, her grin widening.

"My pleasure," Sylvia responded, and bowed to Baika. "Namaste."

"No locks?" I asked, following her inside our bedroom. I tried to sound breezy and jocular but it came out anxious.

Sylvia shook her head and laughed lightly. "Locks just close us off to each other. Trust me when I say they're not necessary.

"Here's your nest," she continued with a wink. I put my bag down on the empty bed. Sylvia's bed was closer to the door and had a purple batik draped over it. Other than Sylvia's homey touch, the room was quite bare. The sheets and the bedspread were a creamy off-white. I reached down and touched the pillow, which seemed a little lumpy considering how pricey the stay was and how fancy the photos on the website had been.

"I've been coming here for five years, since the retreat opened," Sylvia explained. "But I've been reading Lama Yoni's writing since the midnineties."

"Oh, really?" I knew Lama Yoni as the head of a yoga studio, nothing more. Certainly not someone who was powerful or compelling enough to inspire superfans who had been following him for decades. I thought Sylvia might elaborate on her experience with Yoni in this moment, and was trying to formulate a follow-up question, but before I could come up with anything that sounded casual, Sylvia said, "You can get settled after dinner. I want to show you the rest of the place before the mealtime gong is sounded."

"Sounds great," I said brightly, even though I was tired and hungry and part of me just wanted to lie down on that creamy coverlet until the next morning. But more than that, I wanted Sylvia to like me, and to treat me like any other eager visitor to the retreat. The more I played the part, the more info I could squeeze out of her.

I followed Sylvia across a stone walkway that seemed modeled after ones you'd see in Japanese gardens. The walkway was flanked by calm reflecting pools, one of which had flashy golden koi sliding against one another. Though she was probably thirty pounds overweight, Sylvia moved with a grace and ease that I almost never saw in New York. Her shoulders had no hunch to them, and her arms swung loosely as she walked. We didn't see anyone else on the path, and the air was so quiet that all I could hear was the trickling of the water into the ponds from some unseen source. It sounded like the rainfall setting on a white-noise machine, something they'd put on in a cheesy spa.

"Where is everyone?" I asked, my voice barely above a whisper so as not to disturb the peace.

"It's a rest period. Visitors are welcome to walk the grounds, but most people take the time to meditate in the silent meditation pod, which is in a yurt at the foot of the mountain." Sylvia gestured to her left, where I could see a dot of white off in the distance. "All of our most prominent teachers attend that particular meditation, but I never do." From her tone, I extrapolated that the visitors attending the yurt meditation were semipathetic brown-nosers.

We arrived at a building with big golden doors. "Gold is the color of success and triumph," Sylvia told me. "You should feel prepared for success and triumph in all your classes here at Zuni Retreat." She opened the doors and turned left down a long hallway. I could see a sunny central courtyard through a window directly across from me. "These are classrooms for yoga and movement," Sylvia explained, walking quickly. "These are lecture spaces, where our workshops are given." She stopped in front of a room that contained only a bright orange chaise longue. "This room is for mind/body integration work. It's not very popular these days, but I love it."

"Why isn't it popular?" I asked.

"The instructor, Lo, is in her sixties. She's been following Yoni's teachings since the seventies. And she doesn't have an Instagram account or a website or a public following, not like some of the other 'celebrity' instructors here." Sylvia spit out the word *celebrity* like an expletive. "Lo does her workshop just once a week, and only at certain times of year, because she's occupied with other matters the rest of the time. Some of the young ones around here find her methods a little old-fashioned, but she's doing the real spiritual work. They don't get it." I made note of Sylvia's reverence for Lo and tucked it away for later.

The fourth side of the building's rectangle consisted of one large, narrow room filled with bookshelves. Plush pillows in jewel colors—rich purples and dark blues—covered the floor so there was barely a path for walking. "Here is the library!" Sylvia exclaimed proudly. "I've done so much spiritual development here. It's probably my favorite place at the retreat." She took me by the hand and led me into the room. Her hand felt warm and well-moisturized. I tried to think of the last time I'd had an intimate touch with a human I wasn't related to, and I couldn't remember it. I took a deep, slow breath to keep myself from tearing up.

Sylvia walked purposefully to a group of shelves in the center of the wall. These shelves were painted red, while all the other ones were painted the same gold as the front door. "These are the books that have been generated by Yoni and by the teachers and students here," Sylvia told me. "Many of them were written in classes here, as part of the spiritual practice of the author." She dragged her finger over the spines, looking for a particular title. I had no idea how she was going to find anything, since the "books" were a messy jumble of photocopied pamphlets, leather-bound journals, just a few professionally bound books, and even one or two tomes made out of multicolored construction paper tied together with old, curling ribbons.

"Voilà!" Sylvia exclaimed after looking for just a few seconds. "I wanted to show you this. It's the pamphlet that got me interested in Yoni in the first place. They've bound it into a book since I read it, but back in the nineties it was just a xeroxed bunch of paper that my Berkeley mothers' group passed around in a brown paper bag. I call it the 'gateway drug.'" She chuckled, plucked the book from the shelf, and handed it to me with a flourish. "It changed all of our lives. Since this is your first time here, I really think you should read this as soon as possible."

I looked down at the slim volume. In Comic Sans font, the cover read *My Life's Journey,* by Geshe Yoni. I forced a smile. "Thank you for this. I'm sure it will be very helpful on my spiritual journey."

"You're very, very welcome," Sylvia said. She leaned forward and whispered, "You're not really supposed to take books out of this room, but I'll look the other way if you want to read this tonight in our dorm." She winked and pulled a green reusable grocery bag out of her pants pocket.

Gingerly, I accepted the bag and slipped the book inside. Even though I hadn't found anything suspicious about Lama Yoni on the Internet, it couldn't hurt to read his story from the horse's mouth, so to speak. "Thank you. I think I'll do just that."

Sylvia led me down another path toward the third and final building. "This is the dining area," she said, just as a gong started clanging in the distance. "And that gong means we have perfect timing! I'll let you find some folks your own age to eat with. You don't want to be stuck with a bunch of old birds at your first meal."

I followed her into the cavernous hall. We were among the first there, but other visitors began to stream in right behind us. Dinner was buffet style, and I passed several big, steaming cauldrons of what appeared to be different varieties of vegetable slop before ladling something that had firm squares of tofu sticking up from it onto my plate. After I finished serving myself I looked around the room for somewhere to sit.

Like in high school, the tables seemed to be divided into cliques. There were the older hippies, who were mixed in gender. They wore sloppy T-shirts and drawstring pants and the men had unruly beards. Some of them had that dazed, acid-casualty look in their eyes. There were younger people, almost exclusively women, most of whom were lululemonites. They all wore expensive yoga gear and had blowouts and chipping manicures. And then there were the off-duty yoga instructors, who were less polished than the lemonites, wore their hair in buns or dreadlocks, and dressed in ratty hoodies and cropped trousers. But despite their haphazard appearance, they were uniformly beautiful, radiating health and wellness.

I decided to go sit with a table full of the lemonites who looked like they were around my age. Feeling a surge of adolescent panic, I approached the table with a bright smile. The conversation halted as I took an empty seat. "Hi, I'm Dana," I said.

"Hi," one of them replied, monotone, without introducing herself. Her hair was the blondest of the bunch.

Everyone at the table spent another half beat sizing me up, and then, assuming I wasn't anyone worth knowing, they continued their conversation. I ate a bit of my tofu and as I felt the slimy texture slide down my throat, I glanced around. All the women had salon-straightened hair that fell smoothly down past their shoulders. Each wore perfectly applied natural makeup, so that they appeared to be wearing no makeup at all. They had enviably toned shoulders highlighted by flimsy T-strap tanks with the ubiquitous lululemon logo, patterned yoga pants, and Uggs. I've never understood that stylistic choice: If it's cold enough for Uggs, shouldn't it be too cold for flimsy tank tops? But looking at these women as a group made me realize the way they dressed was just meant to telegraph their belonging to one another.

Since they were acting as if I didn't exist, I had no guilt about eavesdropping on their conversation. "I feel, like, so centered after my class with Marcos today," one of the lemonites said. "He pulled me aside and congratulated me on my progress."

"Oh really?" another one, who had an unfortunately large mole on her left arm, shot back. "He told me I should be taking private lessons with him when we all get back to L.A. He says I'm really ready for the next big step."

This sent the first lemonite into a snit. "That's so awesome, Jenna. It's so good that you'll be able to get that extra one-on-one help you obviously need. Especially from a teacher as gifted as Marcos. He should really be able to help you."

The second lemonite was silenced by that burn and changed the subject. "Did you try any of the kelp juice at the beverage bar? It's sooooo good, and Sienna told me it will really get rid of any lingering toxins."

Off the rest of them went about their specialized diets and their lists of foodstuffs to be avoided at all costs. I zoned out after I heard the word *flax* for the sixth time. These lemonites didn't seem like people who would be helpful to know. They were obsessed with some celebrity yoga instructor. I doubted they had been here before, or would have taken classes with Ethan or Amaya. Not like Sylvia.

I didn't say another word to the table for the rest of my meal—not that they noticed.

Sylvia wasn't in the room when I got back, which was a shame, because I wanted to know more about her. I wanted to know if she knew Ethan or Amaya—it seemed highly possible, since she had been hanging around Yoni for years and had been to the retreat so many times.

It was only about seven thirty, but I was exhausted. It was nine thirty New York time and it had been a long day. I washed my face with water and a plain white washcloth. For the cost of our stay, you would think they would cough up a few vials of vegan cleanser or something, but no. At least I had remembered to bring toothpaste, and I brushed my teeth.

The sun was finally disappearing behind the hills outside my window when I turned off the lights and got into bed. The sheets were soft and felt worn in, but not in a creepy thousands-have-slept-here-before way. I turned on my bedside lamp, lay on my side, and opened up Yoni's manuscript. It was printed in large type, and the headings were in an amateurish-looking font, the kind that was used exclusively by an Apple IIe. On the first page was the title, huge and bright: *Capture the Sun: Buddhism and the Attainment of Wealth*. He used the byline Geshe Yoni Brooks; I assumed *geshe* was some kind of honorific, like *lama*. I wondered which Yoni preferred.

The introduction told a parable about a snake and a mouse. It was a little garbled, but the following line seemed to be the most important one:

> Because the snake was pure of heart and revealed his true intentions to the mouse, he was rewarded. The mouse understood his place in the ecosystem, and willingly, eagerly submitted to the snake. The mouse knew that when the snake had digested him, his body would fertilize the land and bring life to a new set of beings.

The whole book was page after page of these notions. That rich, powerful people (or crocodiles or lions or bears) merely had to be honest about their intentions in order to be spiritually rewarded, and the poorer and weaker would willingly go along with whatever their betters suggested. It was social Darwinism at its most unctuous, under a gloss of fake Buddha-speak. I figured that the beautiful surroundings at the Zuni Retreat were somehow funded by some crocodiles or lions that Yoni had managed to attract by flattering their spiritual vanity.

What was fascinating, and confusing, was that alongside the social Darwinism was a strain of radical egalitarianism that wouldn't be out of place in a freshman gender studies class. Yoni said that men should take their wives' names in order to dismantle centuries of the patriarchy, and he said that no spouse of any gender should control the other spouse's sexual life. "We don't own each other," Yoni wrote. He described how our sexual lives should be as open as our spiritual ones.

I put the book down and wondered if Ethan had read this pamphlet in the months before he left, and I wondered if it had permanently altered his views on our monogamous commitment. I searched my brain for any time we had discussed monogamy, but our marriage wasn't really something we talked much about in the abstract. At the time, I thought that was healthy—we weren't rehashing every single thing that happened, but rather were constantly moving forward with vitality, like sharks. Except in the end Ethan had surged away from me and toward Amaya, leaving chum in his wake.

I did remember one conversation we had during our senior year of college. We were living in our first apartment together, the one where Ethan dragged in that plaid monstrosity. He and I had been sitting on the green futon in our living room that we had inherited from the guys who lived in the apartment before us. No matter how many times I Febrezed it, the futon still smelled faintly of their mutt, Mary Jane, and of, well, Mary Jane. The sense memory was so strong that I could almost smell it now, in this clean, spare bed.

I was trying to gossip with Ethan about his best friend, Jason. Jason had been dating my friend Becca, and Becca had recently discovered that Jason was cheating on her with a sophomore. "Can you believe he did that?" I asked Ethan. "What a sleaze."

"Don't be so judgmental," Ethan said gently. "We don't really know what went on between any of them."

At the time, I liked that he said that. One of the things I had always appreciated about Ethan was that he wasn't ever bitchy. He accepted people as they were and didn't try to change them. I thought he made me a better woman, because he inspired me to be less knee-jerk. My instincts leaned toward moralizing, and he helped me think through situations before deciding those involved were somehow in the wrong.

But now that conversation took on a different meaning. Had Ethan had a flexible attitude toward faithfulness throughout our entire relationship? Would I have known that, had I ever bothered to ask?

I fell asleep before Sylvia returned to our room. I dreamed of grizzly bears baring their sharp teeth at me.

Sylvia was gone by the time I woke up. I figured she had slept in her bed because the batik throw had moved from the foot of her comforter to a chair in the corner of the room. I didn't know what time it was—there were no clocks anywhere, which I assumed was intentional—but my stomach burbled with hunger.

I checked my phone and it was seven thirty, which seemed like it should be breakfast time. I decided to walk over to the dining hall in the hopes of finding some food. I didn't want to waste time showering so I threw on black leggings, an old Twins T-shirt, and the sweater Beth had given me. Mornings were always cold in the desert, right?

I hustled across the cobbled path and opened the door to the dining hall to find it filled with people, some of whom were still lingering at the buffet table. The chafing dishes were filled with different kinds of what looked like gruel, so I chose one at random and slopped some onto my plate. There were also huge glass bowls of extremely fresh fruit, and I helped myself to a big portion, in case the gruel was inedible.

I looked around for someplace to sit and located Sylvia at one of the tables. I knew I wanted nothing more to do with the lemonites, and it was comforting to see a kind, familiar face. I sidled up next to her with my tray and said as I sat down, "I'm sorry I missed you last night!"

Instead of a kind reply, Sylvia shook her head gently and mouthed *No*. Then she pointed to a sign at the center of the table, which read PLEASE OBSERVE SILENCE DURING THE MORNING MEAL.

My face burned with embarrassment. I pantomimed zipping my lips, drawing my fingers across my face exaggeratedly, like a fool. As I dug into my gruel, which actually wasn't half bad, I vowed that I wouldn't make any more mistakes at the retreat. I had always been excellent at playing by the rules, a straight-A, type-A obsessive. I could learn the rules of this place like I had learned my torts, through hard work.

I ate slowly so that I wouldn't be finished before Sylvia was.

After she spooned her last bit of kiwi into her mouth, she put her spoon back into her bowl and bused her tray to a bin near the buffet table. Shit. Had I bused my dinner tray last night? I couldn't remember. Two demerits for Dana.

I waited a few beats after Sylvia had left, so she didn't think I was following her, and bused my empty bowl the way she had. When I got back to our room, Sylvia was sitting cross-legged on her bed with her eyes closed, chanting quietly to herself. I crept toward my bed and sat there pretending to reread Yoni's book while I waited for Sylvia to address me.

Several minutes went by before she turned to me. "I'm sorry about breakfast," she said.

"What's there to be sorry about?" I'd expected to get ha-rangued, which was what I was used to my mother doing when I made a mistake.

"I should have told you about our morning silence last night. That's my fault." She looked down at her feet as she said this, and her voice quavered slightly. She seemed to care—maybe a little too much—about her role as my guide at Zuni.

"It's really okay. I learned my lesson." I didn't want to have to comfort her over such a non-issue.

"It's not okay. The morning silence is a sacred time, and it's my fault that it was sullied." Sylvia looked like she might start crying. Her warm face crinkled up around the edges, so that it seemed like her eyes might disappear into the folds of her skin.

I didn't know how to respond. Sylvia wasn't like the lemonites, who seemed in it for the ego and for the hippie glamour of it. This was a deeply spiritual place for Sylvia, and I wanted to respect that, even though I knew that it was complete quackery.

"Why don't you tell me what we're doing next," I said to Sylvia, sitting down next to her and patting her hand. "That way this kind of thing won't happen again."

Sylvia brightened. "Of course," she said. "Midmornings are for our yoga practice. Classes start an hour after breakfast, and there are signs on each classroom door that tell you what kind of yoga is practiced in that room. If you want to take classes from the popular visiting instructors, you have to get there right after breakfast. But I like to take classes from the regular staff instructors here."

"Do you mind if I tag along with you this morning?" I asked. I figured "regular staff instructors" were the kinds who would have known Ethan and Amaya intimately.

"I would love it," Sylvia said, patting my hand as I had patted hers.

Sylvia's yoga class of choice was taught by Janus, who was encouraging without being annoying. After each instruction, he would let out some kind of exclamation, like "Right on!" or "This one will really release those chakras!" I found this charming, which surprised me. I didn't do much yoga, and I tended to prefer classes that focused exclusively on anatomy, not woo-woo about chakras. But there was something about hearing it in this place that felt right to me. And it wasn't like Janus ignored anatomy. In addition to his woo-speak, he did help me and other new students with our form. I noticed that he always asked for consent before touching someone. "I'm going to place my hands on your lower back, is that okay?" Janus inquired before adjusting my dolphin pose.

I felt refreshed after class, despite everything going on. On the way to lunch with Sylvia, I could feel my back unclench, releasing some of the physical tension that had built up over the past few days.

I followed Sylvia's lead walking into the dining hall this time. I sat with her and her table of middle-aged women, who talked about their experiences with different instructors at Zuni. "I don't like that Marcos character at all," said one woman, whose body was lithe like a teenager's but who, judging by her face and neck waddle, was probably seventy. "All those little girlies follow him around, but he doesn't know his asanas from his elbow!" The whole table erupted in huge laughs and I pretended to get the joke. I hoped someone would say something about Ethan without my having to figure out a way to casually bring him up, but no one mentioned anything. So instead I stayed silent and listened, studying the way these women interacted with one another, and tried to pick up what spiritual needs were being met by their repeated visits to the retreat. Maybe that could help me understand what Ethan had gotten from all this.

We went back to our room after lunch, and I checked my phone in the bathroom. There were a few texts from Beth, asking how I was, which I ignored. I was surprised that Sheriff Lewis hadn't responded to my phone call yet. I couldn't imagine he had much more pressing business than investigating a potential murder-suicide. I debated calling him again, but decided to hold off. I didn't want Sylvia to overhear my conversation and start asking questions.

When I emerged from the bathroom, Sylvia was waiting for

me. "In the afternoons, our time is less structured," she told
me. "I usually take a workshop, but as you saw yesterday, many
students go out to the meditation pod. You can also go back to
the library, which you might want to do today." She winked. I
figured she meant I should return Yoni's book before I got in
trouble for taking it out.

"The library sounds like a perfect place for me this afternoon," I said with a conspiratorial smile. I slipped Yoni's book
back into the green reusable grocery bag and set out for the
other building.

The library was almost deserted when I got there. One for-
tyish guy with a long ponytail was sitting on one of the pillows near the bookshelves, engrossed in a huge hardcover book
that he balanced on his knees. A few feet away from him was
a young woman with wiry hair pulled back into a messy bun,
looking at photographs of Indian men doing yoga poses. But
otherwise it was empty.

As I slipped Yoni's book back onto the red shelf, I glanced
at the titles of the books and pamphlets around it. They all
seemed to have some combination of the words *spiritual, enlightenment, centered,* and *blissful.* They were also all covered
in dust. It looked like the "enlightened" visitors to the Zuni
Retreat weren't much into book reading. Then I saw a volume
that stood out because it had none of those vague terms. It was
called *The End Is the Beginning: A Guide to Peaceful Separation.*
I slipped it off the shelf and looked at the author's name: Kai
Powell—Ethan's yogic name. I staggered back into the closest
pillow and started reading.

Ethan

DAILY AFFIRMATION: *Different flowers thrive
in different environments. What makes a sunflower
bloom is not what makes a crocus blossom.*

I'm writing this book to help other people recover from the pain of leaving a loved one. Sometimes we must acknowledge that our earthly bonds are holding us back from the deepest spiritual growth. The severing of these bonds is never easy or happy. But in the words of the writer Haruki Murakami, "Pain is inevitable. Suffering is optional."

The End Is the Beginning will cover the last several months of my relationship with my former partner, Dana. By hearing my story, I hope you, the reader, will take solace and come to a deeper understanding of why your relationship has naturally concluded. I want you to learn that one kind of demise can also be a different kind of renewal. It is natural, like the yearly progression from fall to winter to spring.

While my relationship with Dana was coming to a close, I began my spiritual nourishment with a guru named Lama Yoni.

You will hear more about his enlightened self as the story unfolds. My flower was also watered with loving kindness by a soul sister named Amaya. You will hear about her as well.

I want to start off on New Year's Day, which is a natural time of renewal. New Year's Day, 2007, was also when I started realizing my soul connection with Dana had begun to fray.

Dana slept in on New Year's. She was recovering from a blowout party at her sister's apartment. Beth's place in Brooklyn was full of some wonderful graduate students that Beth had met in her first year of school. I spent most of the night talking to a very kind bearded gentleman named Nikolai, who was studying loyalty review boards during the McCarthy era. We had a rousing discussion about neo-McCarthyism that lasted until after the ball dropped.

The party was pretty big, so I lost track of Dana while Nikolai and I were chatting. I found her after midnight, curled up in an easy chair while people swirled around her. The party was just starting to clear out by then, and she was sitting on a bunch of coats. Every time someone would come to retrieve his or her belongings, Dana would lean forward only slightly, so that the partygoer would have to yank his down jacket or her purse from underneath her.

Dana's face was blank, and she was clutching a red Solo cup of some unidentified liquid. She was taking huge sips of it and wincing slightly as the noxious brew went down.

"You're wasted," I said, in a way that I thought was nonjudgmental and accepting.

"I'm fine," Dana said. But I knew her. She held her liquor, in general, but she had certain tells: her eyelids droop, and her voice drops half an octave. "Did you have fun talking to your comrade, Nikolai?"

"He's a very insightful guy. I think you would have enjoyed some of his musings on today's Republican party."

Dana snorted. "Please. That guy is such a phony. He told everyone his name was Nikolai and that he was descended from some of America's real proletariat but Beth told me his real name is Nick Sampson and he grew up in La Jolla."

I sighed. "You don't have to be so judgmental. He was perfectly nice."

"Ooooookay," Dana said, drawing the word out in the way she did to signal that the conversation was over.

Instead of responding to Dana, I started practicing the deep cleansing breaths my Lama taught me to utilize during times of emotional stress. I tried to clear my mind of bad thoughts toward the outside world and focused on the sound of my own body.

"What are you doing? Trying to fall asleep standing up?" Dana asked sharply. My eyes must have closed without my noticing it.

"Nothing. I think we should go home."

"No, I want to stay," Dana said.

Part of me wanted to stay to make sure she got home okay. I didn't want my drunk wife wandering the streets of far Brooklyn by herself. But I wasn't in the mood to fight with her that night. I knew that the longer I stayed at the party, the greater chance there was that we'd get into some dumb argument. She was in no mood to compromise; she almost never was, but even less so when she was drinking.

My New Year's resolution, made just an hour before, was to leave behind the petty squabbles that had started ticking up in frequency. The year of the pig would be a new epoch for the Powells. Instead of insisting that Dana return home with me, I let her be. "Okay. I'm going to head out. I'll miss you in bed when I am falling asleep."

At first Dana scowled. But then her face brightened a little. "That's sweet," she said. Then she stood up to kiss me good night. Her kiss had more tenderness in it than most of her kisses had the year before. As cranky as she seemed, at the time, I took it as a good omen.

DAILY AFFIRMATION: *"Omens are a language, it's the alphabet we develop to speak to the world's soul, or the universe's, or God's, whatever name you want to give it."*
—Paulo Coelho

I'd been thinking a lot about omens at this point. I never talked to Dana about this—I knew she would snort derisively about it if I did—but I checked our astrological charts every day and compared them. She's a Taurus, but her moon is in Cancer, which means that she is both highly sensitive and excessively stubborn. I'm a Libra, and my moon is in Leo. I'm sensitive, too, but more malleable. I tried to look at our horoscopes to figure out which events in our marriage had been fated, and which ones we could control.

One of my coworkers had been instrumental in encouraging me to look more deeply into our lives and figure out how I could make positive changes. I worked the third shift at an ad agency doing copyediting. The agency was so big and there were so many pages of copy touting the benefits of the latest miracle weight-loss supplements and deliciously chemical energy drinks that they needed copy editors working around the clock to keep up with the volume.

I started this job in early 2006. I had been a bartender when Dana and I first moved to New York after college so Dana could go to a fancy law school. I was supposed to be making money at night so I could work on my playwriting during the day. I wrote a couple of short, semi-autobiographical plays that were produced in small theaters downtown. All my plays took place in Montana and involved a dead mother and a distant dad.

After three years I'd hit a wall, both with the writing and the tending bar. I realized I was just spewing the same small, sad story over and over again. And serving endless Jack Daniel's shots to depressed old guys who were avoiding their wives was sucking my soul. Dana was just finishing law school and since she would be making enough money to support both of us, she encouraged me to take a break from the bar and focus on my writing full-time.

At the time I didn't know it, but Dana's unyielding support had a time limit. When we turned twenty-seven, I'd been writing full-time for a year and hadn't produced a single play. The pressure to write was paralyzing. Then Dana started dropping hints.

"Both partners in a relationship should pull their own weight," she'd say.

Or, more pointedly, "Why don't you take a graphic design class? You've always been so artistically oriented and it's something you could do for work to supplement your playwriting."

And finally, after she came home one too many nights to find me sitting in my plaid easy chair, drinking a beer and reading Howard Zinn or Robert Pirsig, Dana said, "You need to get a real job."

I can't remember what I said to her in response. Probably just "Okay." I have never been into big blowups; I'm nonviolent to the core. But I was deeply wounded by her pressuring me about work. I do remember that I slept on the couch that night, totting up all the stray comments Dana had made over the past couple of months. They weren't addressed to me, but the subtext was glaring. Comments like, "Everyone in a household needs to make his own money." Or "I can't imagine sponging off someone else."

That was the first time I realized there was a fundamental misunderstanding between us. When we were in college, I thought Dana understood me, that she respected my art as an extension of myself. But it seemed like she couldn't comprehend that all of my studying was part of my process. Everything I read tilled the ground of my brain so that I could have a fallow space for deeper thought.

After that first entreaty for me to get a job, Dana didn't let up. She left the house before I was awake most days, and when I got out of bed I would find job listings already queued up on my computer. I didn't say anything, though I wish I'd had the inner courage to tell her to back off and let me do it in my own time. I just started setting up interviews.

I would trudge into various Midtown offices in the suit that Dana bought me and pretend to be eager about travel guides, or business websites, or pharmaceutical copy. After years as an unsuccessful playwright with an English degree from a liberal arts school, proofreading and copyediting were the only marginally lucrative jobs that I was remotely qualified for. I chose the job at the ad agency because it offered graveyard-shift work, and I thought that working at night gave me the best chance of playwriting during the day. It was also the only place that offered me any kind of job at all, but I tried to look at the positives of the situation and not the negatives.

Sometimes I want to go back to that moment and tell 2006 Ethan that he should fight back against complacency. That he should not take that job, because proofreading sentences like "Side effects may include clay-colored stools, decrease in urine output or decrease in urine-concentrating ability, and unpleasant breath odor" is soul-deadening work. But part of my current practice is about radical acceptance of circumstances beyond my control, so I have tried not to let myself wallow in regret.

And besides, if I hadn't taken the job at Green Wave, I would never have met Amaya, who has introduced me to Lama Yoni and a new way of living.

I met Amaya on 6/6/06, which in the Judeo-Christian universe has dark connotations. But in numerology, six is the most harmonious of all single-digit numbers. It can symbolize perfect balance, which now makes complete sense both physically and psychically. I believe that my meeting Amaya was in some sense preordained. She started work at Green Wave about a month after I did, and she told me later she was drawn to me immediately. She sensed that I would be open to Lama Yoni's instruction, and she was so right. Lama Yoni's yogic teachings have given me better balance in soul and body.

That's the only change Dana noticed in me when I started studying with Lama Yoni during the day—my body. She was working so hard she didn't get home until eight, at which point I was at Green Wave. She knew I'd started going to the occasional yoga class during the day when she was at work, but she didn't know how much of my life was consumed with my practice. Dana was happier assuming that I was plugging away on my latest play. She was also happier when my beer gut had been replaced with a burgeoning six-pack, and she was happiest about our athletic weekend sex. She wasn't able to see that our physical connection was fast becoming the only thing we had in common.

DAILY AFFIRMATION: *The universe is built on numbers. If I listen to those numbers, I can come to a deeper understanding of my life.*

Last year it was sixes that held significance for my fate. This year it's sevens: a number of creation, of generation. It was the twenty-seventh day of the seventh month of my practice when Lama Yoni took me into his inner sanctum for the first time.

I had been dutifully attending classes—usually Amaya's—at Yoni's Urban Ashram. I went to early-morning meditations, midday yoga, and afternoon indigenous culture study. But I'd never been allowed to see what went on in the back of the ashram, behind a wooden accordion door that stretched from one end of the front studio to the other.

But on the twenty-seventh day, after the meditations, I was sitting with Amaya, drinking cashew-apple-mint juice to recharge, when Lama Yoni approached us. He had never spoken to me directly before, but on that day he knelt down in front of my chair and looked me right in the eyes. There's no other way to describe my reaction in that silent moment: I melted.

The only other time I've had such a reaction to another man was when my mother took me to a town hall meeting in Bozeman that Bill Clinton held when he was president. He talked about protecting federal employees, like my dad, and about health care. Afterwards, I went up to shake his hand, and he gave me the same look Yoni did—one that said, *I understand, and I want to help.*

Without saying anything, Lama Yoni got up from his knees and walked toward the accordion door. Amaya gestured for me to follow Lama Yoni, and I did.

We stood in silence in the center of the inner sanctum on a small, circular purple rug. The room was all white—the exposed brick walls were even painted white. The only other color besides purple came from a small shrine with a golden goddess perched near a window. Lama Yoni stood five feet away from me and met my gaze. We stared at each other so long without speaking that I kept ascribing different motivations to Lama Yoni's actions. My thought process was something like: *Does he want to slap me? Kiss me? Is he trying to telepathically transfer some knowledge? Is this a test? What if I have to go to the bathroom? Oh god, I think I have to go to the bathroom.*

All this is to say: don't quickly dismiss a spiritual opportunity. After what must have been twenty minutes of this staring contest, my brain went to another plane. I felt like I was accessing some unused space that I could only find through true connection with a spiritual leader. I don't know how long we ultimately stood there, but I remained in prayer pose until Lama

Yoni broke eye contact. He bowed toward me so slightly he may just have been nodding his head. Then he walked slowly away, in large, deliberate steps, and sat down in front of his altar. Once his back was toward me I assumed it was my cue to leave.

Amaya was still outside the door when I emerged. She was drinking her juice and looking contemplative. It was a silent period at the ashram and so I didn't say anything to her, but, like Yoni, she gave me a subtle nod.

I left the building in a daze. I can't even remember how I got back to our apartment. But the same phrase kept appearing in my mind, like a mantra: God-shaped hole, God-shaped hole, God-shaped hole. It's a phrase I hadn't thought of since Methodist youth group. We weren't really religious, but I attended sporadically after my mom died because my aunt Mary was worried that I wasn't getting enough support at home. Our group leader, an earnest guy with a goatee and a guitar, would always tell us that going to church made us complete. It filled a vacuum inside us that would otherwise be empty.

At the time, I thought he was a moron, with his stupid facial hair and his Amy Grant songs. Jesus wasn't going to fix what was wrong in my life; he wasn't going to bring my mom back. But after locking eyes with Yoni, I finally understood what he meant. A void that I hadn't even realized existed felt brimming. I was whole.

Dana

I was still thinking about what I had read in Ethan's book while I waited for Lo to arrive at the mind/body workshop she was supposed to be teaching. I had been able to read only a small chunk before it got too painful. Was that really how he remembered our last New Year's together? Yes, I'd had a little too much to drink, but I'd thought we had fun. I didn't remember the tiff about Nikolai, or the discussion of how much I was imbibing. I remembered getting dressed that night in a silver sequined skirt and applying red lipstick. I remembered Ethan telling me how beautiful I looked. I remembered giving him that kiss before he left.

He didn't even mention the part of New Year's Day that we spent in bed together. We cuddled, and giggled, and ordered takeout from the Thai place down the block, and watched *A Few Good Men*—Ethan's favorite movie. He thought Aaron Sorkin was a genius. Ethan said Sorkin had been a struggling playwright doing odd jobs—he even delivered singing telegrams—before he hit it big. So Sorkin was also an inspiration. I remembered finishing that day much as I started it, asleep in Ethan's arms.

And yes, I had encouraged him to get a job. Aaron Sorkin might have had odd jobs, but they were still jobs! Ethan's account painted me like a bossy philistine who didn't care about his important intellectual work. When I started pushing him to get a paid position, it was not because I was coming home to find his ass sitting in that chair reading Howard Zinn or any other labor historians. I came home to him watching *Law & Order* reruns, playing *Call of Duty,* and once, memorably, hunched over his laptop with his fly open watching old episodes of *Saved by the Bell.*

He probably thought it served me right that he met Amaya at work. Wasn't I the one who forced him into it? I knew about Amaya before he left me, but I thought she was just his work buddy. I guess I had known that she introduced him to the yoga classes, but it didn't seem like such a big deal at the time. I was just glad Ethan had made a friend at work, and I was glad he was getting some exercise—and not only because it made his body fitter. Sure, I noticed the new muscles, but I wanted him to exercise so he'd live a long, healthy life *with me.* And what was all that zodiac nonsense? I had hardly heard him say anything like that when we were together.

To keep from seething I tried to take deep—cleansing?—breaths. Just because Ethan had misrepresented some facts, that didn't make him the kind of person who would kill his lover.

I was taking these deep breaths when Lo entered the room quietly, almost on tiptoe. She had warm amber eyes that crinkled when she smiled, and long, wavy gray hair that she wore loose and flowing. She was really petite—I'd be surprised if she cleared five feet, and her hair grazed the top of her hips. She looked like a very old child. The title of the class she was teaching was Reviving the Feminine Spirit: Empowering Women's Self-Renewal. I had no idea what that jumble of words meant, but I decided to take the class because Sylvia spoke so highly of Lo.

Lo sat down on a pile of pillows near the center of the room. She had perfect posture. "Namaste," she said.

There were only three other women in the class with me, all in their fifties and sixties. "Namaste," they parroted back. I mouthed the word along with them.

"I'm so glad to see you all here to do this important work," Lo said. "I see we have a new face among us old-timers here today." She smiled at me. "Please tell us your name, and what your intentions are for our work together."

"I'm Dana," I said. "My intentions . . ." *are to find out about my dead husband from you.* "Are . . . to become more centered and make sure that I leave here in better emotional shape than when I arrived." That wasn't even a lie, exactly.

That seemed to please Lo. She and the women around me all nodded approvingly. Lo cleared her throat and began the lesson. "Today we're going to focus on a mind problem that vexes many women of all ages: self-loathing." She had a soothing, somewhat mysterious alto, reminding me of Nico in the Velvet Underground, sans German accent. "When we do not love ourselves enough, it manifests itself in all sorts of bodily problems. The healer Habib Sadeghi says, 'Illness is what happens when women, the nurturers of humanity, forget how to nurture themselves.'"

My classmates were clearly enraptured. They all seemed to be tilted forward, as if leaning toward Lo would help them hear her every word better. "The antidote to self-loathing is self-care," Lo explained. "While our ultimate goal is to make positive change in the world, it's impossible to do so when our basic energies are depleted. As we are all individuals, we need different kinds of care to nurture our souls."

"Amen," said the woman next to me.

"As this is a sharing workshop, we will go around the room and release moments when we have denied ourselves care. Whether we recognized it or not at the time, self-loathing is the root of that denial. Sharing our stories will release the self-hatred, and allow us to make room for self-love." A sharing workshop? I thought, panicking. Did that mean I was going to have to speak? Shit, shit, shit. I wished Sylvia had warned me.

Lo turned to the "Amen" woman, who had dark hair and a strong patrician nose. "Nancy, since you've taken my workshops before, why don't you start?" I was relieved she hadn't picked me first. Maybe listening to Nancy's sharing would help me figure out what to say.

"Okay," said Nancy, who had a slight Southern accent. "Well, when my kids left the house, I was all set to enjoy myself. I spent twenty-five years being a mom first, and a woman second. Well, y'all, Goddess, she had other plans." She laughed ruefully. "Six months after my youngest left for school, my mom got sick. She passed a few months ago."

The room was completely silent as Nancy spoke. "When I was going through all that caretaking, I told myself that when it was over I would have time to myself again. I would get back to my yoga practice, which I had abandoned when Mom got sick. I thought I'd go get a haircut and maybe a pedicure. And I never get pedicures!" Nancy stuck her foot out to show us all the sorry state of her toenails, which were dry and cracking. "But I didn't do any of that. I just sat at home. I wasn't eating much, and I wasn't sleeping much, either. I felt like I didn't know what my purpose was anymore, without someone else to put first. I guess I hated myself a little for being so useless. My husband was the one who suggested I come back here, because he remembered how centered I was when I came here a few years ago, before Mom got sick. I guess this is my first act of self-care in a long time." Tears welled up in Nancy's eyes. She wasn't audibly crying. In fact, she was still smiling. She just let the tears fall.

"We're so glad you're here, Nancy," Lo said. "You need to be here." Then, barely pausing, she turned to me and said, "This whippersnapper is a brand-new student! Welcome, Dana. Can you tell us about a time in your life when you denied yourself care?" Lo's amber eyes fixed on mine with warmth and kindness.

What was I going to tell them? I hadn't been prepared for Nancy's legitimately moving monologue. I hesitated for a moment, but something about Lo's stare made me feel safe. Before my brain could make something up, I blurted out, "I haven't had an orgasm since my husband left me." My cheeks felt hot. Where had that even come from? I had never said those words before, not even to myself. And they were true. I wanted to crawl under the pillow I was sitting on and not come out until everyone had left the room.

But I was still looking at Lo's face. It wasn't judgmental or pitying. It was just open. Despite my embarrassment, the words continued to tumble out. "He left several years ago. Sex was an important part of my life then. But he left me unexpectedly, and I was shattered. I haven't dated anyone since then. Well, I went on one blind date because my sister made me, but it was such a disaster she never tried again." I let out a bitter little giggle. No one else in the room laughed. "But I, um, used to masturbate, even before my husband left. We had opposite work schedules and sometimes the mood just struck when he wasn't around. And I haven't really thought about it until now, but I stopped doing that, too." I stopped talking and held my mouth in a firm line.

Lo nodded. "You have literally been denying yourself self-love. I'm glad you're here. You need to be here."

Ethan

DAILY AFFIRMATION:
The most important love of all is self-love.

I would not have been accepted into the fold were it not for Amaya. She and Yoni have a special bond that can only come from practicing together for more than a decade.

Amaya met Yoni right after she graduated from a very progressive college in upstate New York. She thought she wanted to work at an NGO fighting for the rights of the indigent. But she spent three months in India and Bali and returned a spiritual seeker. She joined Yoni's Vikalpa commune, which was then operating in a Crown Heights brownstone but is currently on hiatus. She described it to me once on a break from our shift at Green Wave.

We were sitting in the barren, windowless break room, drinking green tea that Amaya had brewed in a hand-thrown ceramic teapot. Our supervisor had gone home sick for the night, so Amaya and I took the opportunity to get to know each other better. I remember that it was so hot outside that the sidewalks were still steamy even during the night shift. Amaya was wearing a nearly sheer white dress, and her hair was twisted into a high bun that managed to be both sloppy and elegant at the same time.

"We would get up at five and meditate for two hours in the nude at the commune," she told me. "Then all of us women would make the clean porridge we ate every morning."

I didn't really know what to say back. Because I hadn't yet come to see the unclothed body as the soul in its most pure state, I thought it was creepy that they were all naked. Because I hadn't yet learned about how each role a member of the community plays is of equal importance, I wondered why the women had to cook, and was curious about what clean porridge was. I ended up asking, "Didn't you get bored?"

Amaya smiled and sipped her tea. "When you're fulfilled, it's impossible to get bored, at least in the worldly sense. You are at peace with a blank mind." She always made intense, direct eye contact. She seemed sort of crazy. But also really, really hot. Looking back, I realize that things weren't great with Dana at that point. She was in her second year as an associate and she was working ninety hours a week. She was always afraid she'd burn out before she made partner, and that all her work would be for nothing. It's what drove her.

But I felt like she was always too busy to care about what was going on with me. I couldn't remember the last time she asked me how I felt about anything. And here was Amaya, sharing her spirituality with me, a virtual stranger.

"And what about you?" Amaya asked. "Are you a seeker?"

"What do you mean, a seeker?" It's funny to recall how ignorant I was about Amaya's enlightenment at the beginning.

"Are you interested in learning more about yourself and the world around you?"

"Of course," I said. "Who isn't?"

"You'd be surprised," Amaya said. "Most Americans are immune to the deep soul work that needs to be done to understand the world around us."

"Well, I've always been a really spiritual person," I said, unsure if it was remotely true but wanting to impress her.

"My guru, Lama Yoni, would love that about you. He has a whole philosophy about how good things happen to people when they follow the laws of karma," Amaya said. Then she closed her eyes and clasped her hands more tightly around her mug. She looked like she was about to say something else, but instead she got up slowly, nodded at me, and left the room.

On my way home from the office that night I couldn't stop thinking about Amaya. When I saw Dana sleeping peacefully in our bed, her lips slightly parted like a cartoon Sleeping Beauty, I felt guilty, but only a little. I was starting to feel the burgeoning of a spiritual awakening, and I owed it to myself to listen to those feelings and see where they led me.

DAILY AFFIRMATION: *Let the spirit fill up the empty spaces left by missing other halves.*

I took Dana out for Valentine's Day to our favorite restaurant. It really felt like old times again, and I know she was happy then. She got off work early, like she said she would, and I took the night off from Green Wave. That alone felt like an accomplishment for us. But I was already starting to feel like I was holding a crucial part of myself away from her.

Part of what helped that night was drinking. She hadn't noticed that I didn't have a sip of alcohol on New Year's, or that I had not been joining her in her boozy brunching. Because I wanted us to have a harmonious night, I split a bottle of wine with her at the restaurant, and since it's an Italian restaurant, I even gave up my clean eating for an evening to indulge in this Nutella calzone we always get for dessert.

Dana looked really beautiful sitting across from me in the tight red dress she wore every Valentine's Day. She's a sucker for tradition and doing things for old times' sake—hence the return to this particular restaurant and the dessert. She took solace in these rituals, and I was trying to apply my newfound discoveries from Yoni to our marriage. Lama Yoni would definitely approve of the idea of ritual giving people comfort.

I hadn't mentioned anything to Dana about the Urban Ashram at that point. I had been trying to think of a way to introduce her to everything I was learning, but I couldn't figure out how to do it without her saying something nasty. Dana has always been caustic, as long as I've known her. I remember when we first met, in our nineteenth-century lit class. Dana said she didn't like the main character in Jane Austen's *Mansfield Park* because she was "a weak little ninny." I wondered who that spunky blonde was, with her bob haircut and square glasses.

But that was long before I started my work with Yoni. It was starting to feel like another lifetime, in fact. Now all those sharp edges that seemed so bright and shiny when we were in college began to feel like razors, slashing up the meaningful work I'd been spending so much time on.

But during the main course Dana asked me how the yoga was going, and seemed to truly want to know the answer. "Can you do a headstand yet? That always seemed like the most complicated thing," Dana said.

"I can! It's not that hard when you put your mind to it," I said. "You should come with me sometime. I think you could get something out of it. You've been so stressed at work lately, I think it might help you unwind." I tried using subconscious persuasion techniques with targeted eye contact, which was something I had learned about in one of the classes at the ashram. The trick is to connect without intimidating.

Dana was a little drunk, and I could tell she was not in the mood to fight. "Sure. I could always use some de-stressing." Then she smiled a crooked little smile at me, and I wasn't sure she meant it, but at the time I accepted it. I knew she was in a good mood because she even let me pay for dinner, a gesture she didn't always make, since most of the money in our bank account came from her salary and we both knew it. She would usually say, "Why are you pretending that you're paying for dinner? We know who is really paying for dinner."

We walked arm in arm up First Avenue, and while we were waiting for the light Dana leaned over and kissed me, a kiss that made my experiences at the Urban Ashram disappear, for just a little while. We went home and had the best sex we'd had in months, maybe years. In that moment, I felt like our lovemaking had reached another level, not just physically but metaphysically. I was so pleased she'd agreed to go to a class at

Yoni's. Maybe she was really ready to understand the true me. But after she fell asleep, I remember that good feeling faded into a whole lot of nothing.

DAILY AFFIRMATION:
"You cannot plan the path of a glacier."
—Lama Yoni

At this point, though I still attended my classes at the ashram, I was trying to avoid Amaya between classes and kept our break room talks to a minimum. Things weren't perfect with Dana, but I had made a marriage vow to her. My parents' marriage was not the most actualized, and since my mom died my dad barely talks about her. I refused to repeat that pattern, especially considering the conversation Dana and I had the morning after Valentine's Day.

Dana woke up in a good mood, still beaming from our connection the night before. "I love that you're awake with me," she said. "It's been so hard since we've been on opposite schedules. We're like ships passing in the night." She leaned over and kissed me, then put her head on my shoulder. "Us being together and it feeling so good . . . it makes me start thinking about making some little Ethans together, watching them running around our apartment."

I pulled her closer to me and said, "Mmm." We were having a nice morning and I didn't want to ruin it with a prolonged discussion of our child-having prospects. I always figured we'd have kids someday, but since our marriage wasn't in the best place, I didn't think we should rush. I didn't want to risk bringing a brand-new soul into such a dark environment with so many conflicts.

I didn't even think we should plan. I've never been a huge planner. Dana was the planner, and I was usually happy to go along with what she envisioned. Like she'd say whenever we traveled, every marriage only needs one suitcase packer. But since I started studying with Lama Yoni, I had become concerned that her need for control was altering my natural stream.

Yoni once told a parable about the formation of the Panchchuli Glacier in northeastern India. While we were in savasana he described the hard snowpack accumulating year after year, compressing into a pile of forbidding ice and helping to create the Darma Valley. He talked about the compression pushing all the air out, so that the ice turns an otherworldly blue. He emphasized the fact that glaciers are always changing, that's their natural state. But you cannot plan the path of a glacier. It will shape-shift in a preordained way, at a preordained pace.

I knew that Amaya was in my life for a reason, but by that same logic Dana was in my life, too. And even though our bond was frayed, it would be moving that glacier to break that bond. I would need a loud and clear sign from the universe that my time with Dana was over.

After Valentine's Day, things were slightly better between Dana and me for about a week. But the following week we were back to our old inertia: I was asleep when she left for work, and I was at work when she finally got home. On the weekends, all she wanted to do was sleep and watch really ugly, soul-searing reality television. I kept trying to get her to come down to the Urban Ashram, but she kept finding reasons to avoid it. She'd say her ACL was acting up, or that it was too cold to go so far downtown. She knew she was hurting my feelings because she wouldn't look me in the eye when she gave me her excuses. I knew she thought yoga was boring, but she didn't care that this was important to me.

If our marriage had faltered a year earlier, I would have asked Dana to go to couples therapy to help us reconnect. But Lama Yoni believes that psychiatry stands in the way of our spiritual development, because it intellectualizes our instincts. I was sick of intellectualizing everything, like I'd done since I was a kid, so I was inclined to agree with him.

DAILY AFFIRMATION:
"Desire is the engine that runs the world."
—Lama Yoni

One morning Dana shook me awake at six thirty before she left for work. Her eyes were shining. "Hey," she whispered, her breath minty fresh. "I want to come to a yoga class tonight. Can you set it up for me?"

"Sure," I said sleepily. "What made you change your mind?"

"I know I've been really stressed lately and I haven't been spending enough time with you," she said. Then she kissed me sweetly before leaving. I was so grateful and happy that Dana was finally coming around. When I woke up for the second time I looked at her chart, and found that her transiting Venus was in strong trine with her natal Midheaven: in other words, the relationship energy of Venus was charging up her personality with more sympathy for others.

I called the ashram after I looked at Dana's chart and scheduled an eight P.M. class for both of us. Yoni was supposed to teach this class, and I wanted Dana to get the best of the best. I even remembered to e-mail her to tell her to get there fifteen minutes early. Dana was always annoyed with me for not remembering details like that. I hoped she'd give me extra points for being so responsible.

On the subway to the ashram, I was so excited I couldn't sit still. Yoni always said that one enlightened event can change a lifetime, and I was hoping that this might be one of those events. If I could start taking Dana to the ashram, I wouldn't need Amaya to fulfill those needs. It would take a while—first she'd have to get into yoga, and then I'd have to show her the spiritual stuff—but it would be worth it. Wouldn't I prefer to live an honest life, with my wife knowing all sides of me?

I walked into the ashram and waited in the lobby for Dana. I watched person after person walk into the class and set their mats down. I kept looking up at the clock that sits above the reception desk. Dana hates being late, so I couldn't imagine why it was 7:56 and she still wasn't there. I did some of my deep breathing exercises to calm down, then looked up at the clock again: 7:57, still no Dana. I started whispering a mantra to myself to keep tears from gathering in my eyes. Was Dana really going to let me down after all that?

At 7:59 she rushed through the door. From the look on her face I could tell she was in a dark mood. "I. Ran. Here. Subway. Stalled," she managed to get out while she put her hands on her knees and bent over to catch her breath.

"It's okay," I said, trying to retain my Zen bearings. "Yoni just really hates it when people are late. He says it disrupts the energy in the room."

Dana straightened up and shot daggers at me. "I'm sorry I was working hard all day and then the fuckups at the MTA 'disrupted' Yoni's energy."

This was not off to a good start. "It's okay. Why don't you change into your yoga clothes and we'll tiptoe in."

"Fine," Dana said before storming off into the women's wing of the ashram. She came back out a few minutes later and seemed to have collected herself a little more.

Yoni noticed Dana straightaway when we took our places in the back of the classroom. He kept making eye contact with her as we went through our opening poses. She was trying to deflect his gaze by looking in the mirror and correcting her form—she's a perfectionist in everything—but I could tell she was unsettled by his attention. When Yoni placed his hands on her hips to adjust one of her poses, she flinched like his hands were on fire.

During savasana, I kept my eyes half-open and watched as Yoni knelt behind Dana's head and massaged her temples while her eyes were squeezed shut. He started telling a parable about a burdened goat who was resigned to his life of servitude in Afghanistan.

"The goat was old, he was tired, but he knew he had to keep doing the job of dragging water up the mountain so that his owner's family could stay alive," Yoni said. I saw Dana's body tense.

"One day, the goat broke his leg. The owner sent his small son to put the goat down. But just as the boy was about to hack the goat's head off with a machete, he hesitated. This goat had served his family well—and now he was just going to die? Was this really the ending this noble animal deserved?" Yoni took a long, dramatic breath. "Yes, the boy decided. This was how the goat deserved to die. He stuck the knife right through the animal's back." Yoni thumped his hand on Dana's chest when he said this, pantomiming the goat's death. I heard Dana gasp.

Yoni smiled. "You will never get what you want in life by doing a job purely out of duty, rather than desire. Desire is the engine that runs the world. Namaste." He shuffled quietly out of the room.

As soon as the accordion door shut quietly behind Yoni, Dana sat up as if shocked by a cattle prod. She gathered up her stuff with such haste that she kept dropping her yoga mat. She ran out of the building before I had a chance to put my things away.

I caught up with her a block away. "What did you think?" I asked cautiously.

"I want to go home," she said. She looked like she was about to cry.

"Tell me what's wrong. What happened?" I wanted my voice to project comfort and loving kindness, but I ended up making her defensive.

"I don't want to talk about it. I want to get the fuck away from this place and I don't ever want to come back. Promise me I never have to go back."

"Okay, okay, I promise." I saw how shaken she was, and we rode in silence back to our apartment. I was so disappointed that she would never be returning to the ashram, I had nothing to say. Instead, I held her hand.

Dana

I hadn't thought about my interaction with Yoni since it happened, because at the time, it didn't seem like that big a deal. I had no idea until a few days ago that Ethan had run off to teach at Yoni's retreat, or that Yoni had been the leader of some bizarre commune before he became a slightly respectable yoga teacher. I just thought Yoni was your garden-variety creepy older yoga dude.

Furthermore, Ethan completely misread my reaction. I was angry at *him*, not shaken by Yoni's energy or whatever. That's why I ran off. I was not about to cry. I was pissed that he made me leave work early to meet him, and that he had given me a hard time about being late when I had made such a big effort. And I gasped when Yoni struck my chest because it was surprising. You don't expect someone to thump you in the middle of a yoga class. I had barely been listening to his weird goat story in the first place. I was zoned out thinking about the case I was working on.

Ethan's spiritual boner for Amaya became slightly less painful to read about as I went on. But not because I became inured to it. It was because learning his feelings about our marriage became more painful. I knew we hadn't been seeing that much of each other in the year before he left, but I thought we were just coasting along reasonably happily in the paths we had set early on in the marriage: I was the one who made the decisions, and Ethan was happy to go along with them. If I didn't take charge, it would take Ethan forty-five minutes to choose what kind of takeout we were having for dinner. He joked that my decisiveness kept him from starving.

But according to his book, those paths had become rutted, filled with potholes and cracks. He was right about the yoga. In the back of my head I knew he had been going a lot, but I dismissed it as unimportant, because I thought yoga was kind of silly. I didn't mind doing the hour-long classes at the gym that had zero spirituality and a lot of movement. That seemed physically useful. But spending at least ninety minutes every day listening to spiritual yakking and being forced to say "om"? I had no interest in that.

What's more, I barely thought about what Ethan did when we were apart. At work I thought only about work. At home I usually thought about work, too. If Ethan wasn't directly in my sight line, it was like he didn't exist.

My dismissiveness had started to get mean. I could see that now. And I could also see how I had stopped making him, or our marriage, a priority. I had been so angry with Ethan for leaving for so long, but I had never thought about my own culpability. Of course he should have gone to couples therapy with me instead of running off with Amaya to some yoga paradise. I didn't deserve to be left the way Ethan left me. But it was unreasonable to say my behavior had no role in our relationship's demise.

Sylvia wasn't in the room when I returned to it after Lo's class. I was still shaken by my unexpected outpouring. It was terrifying to think that my emotions were still so close to the surface that an old hippie could bring them out with just a tiny bit of prodding. I thought I had dealt with everything in therapy. That period of my life was supposed to be a discrete moment, now over. It had been put in a clear plastic storage box, appropriately labeled *Ethan,* and organized properly back on a shelf.

Trying to shake off the emotional tremors from class, I checked my phone. There were more texts from Beth, which I continued to ignore. There was also a voice mail from a number with a 575 area code, which I assumed correctly was from Sheriff Lewis.

"Hi, Dana," he said in a clear voice. "I'm glad you could make it here. I have some time to see you tomorrow afternoon. Please come by the station at three P.M. Call me back if that doesn't work and we can figure something else out." Then he gave me directions from the retreat.

I was glad the sheriff had finally gotten back to me. I only had one day left at Zuni after tomorrow, and I didn't think Phil would tolerate me missing any more work than I already had. I wanted to be able to help the sheriff when I saw him, too. So I resolved to work Ethan and Amaya into a conversation with Sylvia before the sun set this evening.

At dinner I sat with Sylvia and her friends again and listened to them chatter. I had learned their names by this point: the extra-fit seventy-year-old was Mae; the one who liked to wear her salt-and-pepper hair in two short pigtails was Raina; and the one with gargantuan, droopy breasts who nonetheless enjoyed going braless was Patty.

Their banter was soothing and funny. I pushed a chickpea around on my plate while listening to them talk about their husbands, children, and pets. Mae had three kids, two girls and a boy, all of whom were hard-charging professionals and none of whom called her enough. Raina had a daughter and a son, both in their midtwenties, and two cats that hated each other. Patty had one son and a beagle with testicular cancer. "He's only got one ball left!" she exclaimed, delighted by his perseverance.

I learned that Sylvia was on her second husband, and that she had four grown children. Most of her conversation at dinner had been about a particularly ungrateful son, who was in college. He wouldn't even open her e-mails, so she had taken to putting the entire body of the e-mail in the subject line so he would be forced to read it. Not that he wrote back anyway. "Have daughters, my dear," Sylvia said as she reached over and patted my hand. "They might cause you grief in other ways, but at least they respond to your e-mails."

I smiled wanly at her. It didn't feel like the time to get into my damaged relationship with my own mother, which seemed to have gone badly from the start. I gave her horrid morning sickness that left her dashing to the toilet all day, every day for the full nine months, a fact she never ceased to remind me of when she was irritated with me. No matter what a good girl I was—or continued to be—it was never quite up to snuff. When I brought home a ninety-eight on my math homework, the response was "Where are the other two points?" When I got engaged to Ethan, she gave me pursed lips and fake smiles. "He's a very nice boy," she said, "but is he really good enough for you?" I didn't speak to her for three months after that, and thought about eloping so I wouldn't have to mar my wedding day with her criticism. But I couldn't bring myself to do it.

"My daughter wants to come here with me next time," Raina said, beaming, interrupting my self-absorption. "Now that she's twenty-five, she gets it. When she was younger she just thought it was some dumb old thing Mom was doing."

"How long have you been coming here?" I asked.

"Five years, since the retreat started. Same with these other old bags." She smiled. I must have looked horrified, because she added, "I'm kidding. That's how we joke with each other. You'll understand when you're our age. We met the first year of the retreat and kept in touch, and we arrange our visits to overlap when we can."

"Sometimes life interrupts," Mae said, her eyes glossy.

"Mae's husband died last year," Sylvia stage-whispered to me.

"Jesus, Syl. We can still hear you." Mae's eyes went matte again.

"All Mae is saying is this place is really important to us," Patty said, her voice a lot more serious than it had been when she was talking earlier about Barney's one ball. "We've all had some real spiritual breakthroughs. It's a true testament to the staff. They're so much better than at any other retreat I've been to."

"That's good to hear," I said. Since we were on the subject of the Zuni staffers already, I knew this was my moment to ask about Ethan. "I was a little worried, because I overheard something strange about some of the staff members here."

All four of their faces dropped when I said that. Mae looked down at her plate and Patty shifted around on the bench. Finally Sylvia said, "Are you talking about the deaths?"

"Yeah," I said. "I heard something about two teachers dying. It sounded scary." I tried to sound ignorant and a little simple.

"You shouldn't be scared," Raina said firmly. "The teachers don't live here at the retreat, and I heard the two instructors who passed on had perverted Yoni's teachings. They were trying some very dangerous ancient indigenous rituals."

"Like what?" I tried to keep that touch of innocence in my tone.

There was an uncomfortable silence before Sylvia said, "It's really a shame." She shook her head gently. "I didn't know Kai, but many people I care about really respected his teachings. Amaya, on the other hand, she was a real gem."

"Oh," I said. I wanted to hear more about who Ethan had become. I didn't want to hear Sylvia say something nice about Amaya.

"I don't know how I would have gotten through Albert's death without Amaya," Mae added, solemn. "We worked through so much in her workshop on resilience, and she even called me and e-mailed me every day for a month after I got home from the retreat." Her eyes got glossy again. "Amaya was a true healer. She knew what to say and what to do with grief in a way my friends and family couldn't touch. My kids did their best, but Amaya really went above and beyond."

"Wow," I said, because that was all I could muster.

Ethan

DAILY AFFIRMATION:
New experiences create abundance in our lives.

I had been successfully avoiding Amaya, but shortly after Dana's bad experience with Yoni we ran into each other in the break room at work. She was sitting at the table, zoning out on a poster of Georges Seurat's *A Sunday on La Grande Jatte*. I considered trying to creep out backward without her noticing, but she looked up and smiled at me. "Hey, stranger. Where have you been?"

"Around," I said. I wanted it to come out as terse but I think it sounded flirty instead.

"Lama Yoni can't stop talking about you."

"Really?" I said, pulling up a chair. "What's he saying?"

"He told me he was really impressed with your focus and dedication. And that he wanted to see more of you at the ashram."

"Wow." I sat down next to Amaya to take it all in. "I'm really flattered. I didn't even realize Yoni noticed me."

"He wants to see more of you. I want to see more of you, too."

Amaya smiled at me again. And then she kissed me. I guess I should take partial responsibility for it. Maybe my body language was inviting her in. Yoni's always telling us we need to use all of our senses to communicate, after all.

I pulled off her gauzy poncho so that I could feel the beating of her heart pressing against mine. I felt our bodies merge for a moment, because I knew we were connecting on every metaphysical level in a way that Dana and I were not. I melted into this new consciousness, forgetting my physical self. Until Amaya started unbuttoning my jeans and it jarred me out of the spirit world and back into the natural world.

I came up for air and to my senses. "Stop. We can't do this."

"You're right," she said, pulling back from me. As entwined as we had been just a moment ago, she seemed unruffled by our souls' connection. I figured she was used to this kind of depth in her interactions. "You have already made a worldly commitment to your wife."

"Dana."

"Dana," Amaya said. She said my wife's name like it was a word in another language that she was learning phonetically. It made me feel even guiltier.

"I have to get back to work now," I said, more firmly than I felt.

"Me, too." Amaya leaned over and picked up her poncho. It floated back over her head, giving me time to admire her half-clothed body, and the fierce-looking butterfly tattoo on her left flank. It was black and red with sharp wings. "But Yoni really did say that. We would like to see more of you at the studio."

"I'm not sure if that's such a good idea."

"What happened between us just now is already forgotten,"

Amaya said. "Don't let our physical attraction get in the way of your spiritual progress."

I opened my mouth to protest, but I wanted to give what Amaya said full consideration. My time at the Urban Ashram had made me feel much better about my place in the world, and I didn't know if I was ready to give that up.

Amaya left the room before I did. I counted fifteen Mississippis before I followed her back out into the cubicle farm. I didn't want any of our coworkers to suspect the impropriety.

Even though she told me to, I could not forget what had happened. I kept smelling her on me, a musky, lovely scent. I decided to seek counsel outside the ashram for advice on the situation.

DAILY AFFIRMATION:
"The only way to have a friend is to be one."
—Ralph Waldo Emerson

I hadn't seen Jason in at least six months. I guess I didn't realize how consuming my time at the ashram had been. So I was pretty psyched when he e-mailed me about having lunch. It felt like my plea for someone neutral to talk to about Amaya was answered.

I met him at P.J. Clarke's, which is near Jason's insurance office. He's always been a levelheaded guy. Even when we were in college he was doing risk assessments of different bars, based on prior experience. "If we go to Fitzy's, there's a three-in-five chance we will get carded and turned away," he'd say. I thought he would be the ideal person to weigh in on my situation with Dana, since he's also known both of us since we were nineteen.

He was already there when I arrived, three minutes late. "Hey, man," he said, standing to give me a bro hug, with a requisite pound on the back.

I sat down at the table. "Hey. You're looking well." And he was: trim and bright.

"It's all this CrossFit I've been doing. You know about it? You have to flip tires over and shit. I love it." He paused to take me in. "You're looking pretty fit yourself," he said. "CrossFit? Biking?"

"Nah. A lot of yoga, actually."

Jason gave me a small, possibly mocking smile. "Yoga? Really?"

"Yes, yoga. It cleanses the body and soul."

"Okay," Jason said, his smirk lingering. The waiter came up and asked us for our drink order. Jason ordered a beer. "It's a Friday!" he said brightly. I could tell he wanted me to do the same, but instead I ordered a mineral water.

As soon as the waiter left, Jason seemed eager to plunge into the usual catch-up, small talk conversation, the kind we'd had so many times before. "So how you been, man?" Jason said. "It's been an age."

"I know. I've been really busy."

"Are you writing a new play? I loved the last one, *Elk Crossing*. I thought it was really your strongest work." I momentarily regretted putting my writing aside. Jason wasn't the kind of person who was into false praise, so I figured he actually meant it. But getting that burst of pride from Jason's compliment made me realize how ultimately empty my entire writing career had been—I was dependent on the praise and acceptance of other people to feel good about my work. With my work at the ashram, all my good feelings and confidence came from inside.

"Not really working on anything special," I said. "I've been taking other classes at the yoga studio. It's this place called the Urban Ashram. It's very time consuming. I'm learning a lot about the cosmos and myself."

"That's cool," Jason said. "Wouldn't have expected that from you."

"What do you mean?" I tried not to sound defensive. I concentrated on my yogic breathing.

Jason backpedaled rapidly. "Nothing, man. Just you never seemed particularly interested in that kind of stuff. How's Dana?"

"Well, that's part of what I wanted to talk to you about." I folded my hands in front of me to offset a twinge of anxiety.

"She breaking your balls about work again?" He leaned in, prepared to listen to the same old complaints from me.

"Not really. But this is kind of about work. Or I guess, a person at work." I met Jason's eye so I wouldn't look so guilty.

Jason was about to say something, but the waiter returned with our drinks and took our lunch order. He got a Cadillac burger with extra bacon. I got a market vegetable salad. Jason gave me considerable side-eye about this order but held his tongue.

When the waiter left he said, "Okay, so who's this 'person at work'?"

"This woman, Amaya. She's actually the one who got me into all the classes at the Urban Ashram. I've been learning about Buddhism, and ancient Indian rituals, and the seasons, and the importance of karma in our lives. It was a strictly platonic and spiritual thing at first with Amaya, but we ended up making out in the break room last week." Admitting it made me feel a little lighter, especially to Jason, who had always had a flexible moral fiber.

Jason's mouth dropped open. "Shit, dude. That's messed up."

"Really?" I said. "I thought you'd be into it. You were never Dana's biggest fan."

"Yeah, Dana can be a bitch sometimes—pardon my French— but she's your wife, man. And she's not a bad person. You took a vow. I was there when you did it."

"I know, I know. But she's been so cold to me lately. She doesn't seem to have any interest in my classes at the Urban Ashram, or in my feelings." I wanted to tell him how disconnected I felt from Dana on a spiritual level, and how connected I felt to Amaya, but I wasn't sure he'd get it.

"'Doesn't have any interest in my feelings'?" Jason mimicked. "Christ, dude, you've got to nut up. She's working ninety-hour weeks. Dana doesn't have time for your feelings. The last time I saw her she was barely sleeping, supporting your ass, and trying to make her career happen." His eyes were bright with anger.

"Whoa, whoa, whoa. I thought you'd be a little more understanding," I said. I wasn't sure if Jason could comprehend my spiritual development, but I thought he'd get that I was emotionally bereft and needed a brother-in-arms. This is one of Yoni's most important teachings: we are all only as strong as our least supportive comrades. "You know how hard she's been on me in the past."

Jason leaned back and the anger in his eyes dimmed. "Okay.

I know. She can be a bitch, like I said. But you know, she doesn't deserve this."

"But you cheated on Becca!" Even I could hear that my voice was rising.

"That was in college, and we were kids," Jason said, shaking his head like he couldn't believe I was bringing up Becca almost a decade later. "It's a whole different thing. You should know that."

I didn't say anything for a few seconds. The waiter came back with our food and Jason started in on his burger. "This Urban Ashram shit sounds weird, I'll be honest with you," he said.

"You don't know anything about it," I said. My yogic breathing was getting more intense.

"You're right, I don't," Jason said. "But I know lots about you, and the Ethan I've known doesn't talk about his 'spirituality' or cheat on his wife." He put the burger down and stared at me, hard.

"Okay," I said, digging into my salad. My commitment to nonviolence prevented me from really engaging here. Jason was obviously a nonbeliever. Lama Yoni always says that when you spot a nonbeliever, the only option is to go into neutral stance. "How's things going with you?" I asked.

Jason looked relieved at the change of subject. "Things have been pretty good, man. I started seeing this woman, Lily. Met her through my sister. She's super smart." He started describing their relationship and I tried to listen as best I could. But for the rest of our lunch I could feel the distance between us grow. We still bro-hugged at the end, though, like nothing had happened.

I walked down Third Avenue away from the restaurant and felt lonelier than I had in weeks.

DAILY AFFIRMATION:

My worth is not defined by what I am paid.

At this point I started wondering if I should quit my job. I hated it, and I would be more easily able to avoid Amaya if I found something else. In a moment of distracted contemplation, I floated the idea to Dana.

"What would you say if I wanted to quit my job?" I leaned over and asked her after her alarm went off. I had been awake since three in the morning thinking about everything. She hadn't had her coffee yet, so I knew she would give me her unvarnished opinion.

"I would tell you to go fuck yourself," Dana said. It was so over-the-top harsh, at first I couldn't tell if she was joking.

"Are you serious?"

Dana sat bolt upright, her face expressionless. "I'm completely serious. I'm not about to be married to some no-job loser. We're too old for this shit, Ethan. Grow. Up. Stop being such a pussy." She threw a pillow into my stomach, got up, stomped to the bathroom, and slammed the door.

I sat in bed, my mouth agape. When did she become so soul-negative? I just sat there until I heard her come out five minutes later. She'd washed her face, but her eyes were red.

"Ethan, I'm sorry I snapped at you. But I don't know where this is coming from. I thought we had a plan for our future."

I wanted to say *You mean you have a plan for our future,* but instead I told her, "It's okay. You're going to be late for work. We can pick this up later."

"Okay," Dana croaked, her voice shaky. "I am just really sick of going through this with you. We're at a good place to settle down, and I feel like you keep wanting to unsettle us."

I didn't know what to say to that. I was fundamentally unsettled in a way I didn't think she cared to understand. So I just gave her a hug and said, "I'll go make you some coffee."

DAILY AFFIRMATION:
*Moving forward in the face of uncertainty
is the definition of courage.*

My mind was ricocheting back and forth from week to week. After I saw Jason I was more determined about my study with Yoni—my problem was unsupportive brethren like him, not my newfound knowledge. Then, after Dana freaked out, I thought I wasn't going to go back to the ashram. Ever. I really wasn't. That week I thought, even though I had been learning so much from Yoni, I *had* made a commitment to Dana, and that commitment still meant something deep and abiding. When I thought more about Jason's reaction to my recent life changes, I went from defensiveness to ambivalence. Was my spiritual fulfillment worth making a break from everyone I knew and loved?

Amaya could sense my evasiveness; it was like she saw the chaos in my soul from afar. She cornered me in the break room on a Friday. I was reaching into the fridge for a Coke—one of the few perks of our fluorescent nighttime prison was free beverages. I was usually able to resist them because of my commitment to clean eating, but that night my spiritual mess drew me to all that sugar. Amaya caught me and poked me in the ribs.

"Indulging in a little high-fructose corn syrup? Not very Zen," she said, smiling at me.

"Well, we all have our vices," I said, guilty. "How are you?"

"Fine. Missing you at the ashram. Yoni keeps asking where you are."

"I've been busy, seeing old friends." I was trying to resist my new transformation, even though the deepest parts of me wanted to change. I was like a seedling struggling to burst through the chaos of tilled soil.

"Well, your new friends miss you," Amaya said. "Actually, Yoni wanted me to invite you to a special vernal equinox ceremony he holds every year on March twentieth."

"I'm not sure I can go," I said automatically. What a fool I was.

"I haven't even told you when it is. I don't think you understand the importance of this invite. Lama Yoni only asks one new person every year to this ceremony. It is a marker of acceptance at the ashram. Hundreds of students vie for this invite every year, and he's bestowing it on you."

"Wow," I said. I didn't think I had made that much of an impact on Lama Yoni. I felt like we'd had a serious connection through our eye contact earlier in the year, but I figured he had those sorts of connections with a lot of people. He's so open—it's like chemical bonds are at play, drawing others to him.

"So you'll come?" Amaya asked, looking me in the eye. "I'll write down the address." She took a pen off the counter, grabbed my hand, and scribbled an address on my palm.

"Herkimer Place? Where's that?"

"It's in Brooklyn. Arrive promptly at sunset. You can check the almanac for the time. Don't worry, you won't regret it."

Over the weekend, I convinced myself not to go. Dana was being really lovey and sweet. She agreed to watch *Samsara,* a documentary shot in twenty-five different countries that a fellow at the ashram said would really further my meditation practice. I told Dana I wanted to see it because I wanted to indulge my travel bug. Usually Dana is dismissive about this kind of thing, and with a flick of her hand would have said, "I hate that kind of shit." But that Saturday she said, "Whatever makes you happy, hon," and snuggled into my side as we watched it on my laptop in bed.

But as Wednesday rolled around I found myself checking when the sun was supposed to set that day, and looking up just exactly where Herkimer Place was, and plotting how I would get there, and somehow, almost outside my own volition, I was dialing my boss's number on my phone and affecting a throaty nasal growl to convince her I was sick and needed the night off. I knew I couldn't miss this opportunity for spiritual growth—it was so much more important than any of my capitalist commitments.

I left my apartment around six, knowing that the sunset was shortly after seven and not wanting to be late. On the A train out to Nostrand Avenue, I felt so many conflicting feelings about heading to an unknown—to me—corner of Bed-Stuy. The guilt of gentrification, the fear of danger, and the excitement of transgressing were all tumbling about in one anxious stew.

I got off the subway with a crowd, since it was the middle of rush hour, but as I neared Herkimer Place on Nostrand Avenue the group thinned. When I turned onto the street, it had a bleak, postapocalyptic feel. The buildings were mostly boarded up, and the shrubbery was limp and sad.

Number 8 was my destination. The door wasn't boarded, but the windows were covered with dark blackout curtains. The building looked at once sinister and industrial, like an abandoned factory that used to make doll heads, but not doll bodies. I started shaking as I lifted my finger up to the doorbell, which chimed softly.

Amaya opened the door. She was wearing a sheer white robe, through which I could see plainly that she wasn't wearing any underwear. I would learn later that underwear is only an unnecessary barrier, concealing the most sacred parts of our body from the natural world. I tried to keep my eyes level as she bowed toward me. Her hair was wrapped up on her head in an intricate woven pattern.

Without speaking, she turned away from me and started to walk away. I said, "Amaya, where are we going?" but she would not turn around and look at me. I followed her down a narrow, dark hallway, until I could no longer see the back of her dress. I heard the clomping of her shoes up stairs, and so felt my way gingerly behind her in the nearly pitch-black. Her refusal to look back made me feel like Eurydice. Would I be barred from the upper world if she turned around and saw my face? Finally I heard a door open.

I crouched on my hands and knees and felt my way upstairs and into a narrow tunnel. I was on the verge of hyperventilating, so I tried to practice some kapalabhati breathing to calm myself down while still moving forward. My head thwacked against a door handle, so I pushed down on it. The door opened up into a cavernous room where a group of figures were standing up against a multisided structure with a dome. It looked like something out of a kid's science museum, like there was something inside that would teach me about physics.

The domed structure was lit from the inside. I could see light projections of flowers and zodiac signs coming up through the dome, like in a planetarium. As I got closer, I noticed that each of the sides corresponded with a different sun sign. The only side that was empty was my own sign: Libra, the scales. As I got even closer, I noticed that the figures were only men, and that all of the men were naked.

The moment I noticed they were naked was the moment my mind and body split. I can't say more about what happened without violating the sacred bond I have with Yoni. But I can say that the experience changed the entire course of my life. Mentally. Spiritually. Physically.

Dana

The sheriff's office was in the middle of a barren, dusty street in Ranchero, Sagebrush County's only town. There were two other buildings near it. One was a tidy-looking trailer surrounded by plastic flowers stuck into the dirt. The other was a low-slung stucco house with the carcasses of at least two cars and three major appliances in its front yard.

Compared to those two heaps, the sheriff's office was palatial and kempt. It was a standard two-story brick municipal building, with wall-to-wall beige carpeting inside. There was a single receptionist in the otherwise empty waiting area, and she led me right in to see Sheriff Lewis. I sat at the sheriff's school marm-ish wooden desk in an uncomfortable but sturdy wooden chair, waiting for him while he was in conference with a man who seemed to be his deputy outside the fairly soundproof glass of his office. I could hear the pitch of their voices, but not the content of their conversation.

I had Ethan's book in my purse. It still took a tremendous amount of personal restraint not to throw it away, or just put it back on the shelf to languish in the retreat's library. I hated reading about Amaya's moves on Ethan, and how much he enjoyed them. And even more than that, I hated reading about how nasty I had been to him. I actually winced—my whole body retracted—when I read what I had said to him when he floated quitting his job by me. I couldn't believe I called him a pussy, but I knew it was true. In the years after he left, I had forgotten a lot of the memories that made me look bad—just as Ethan seemed to have left out a lot of the memories that made me look good when he wrote his book. Our memories have their own agendas.

In spite of myself I was starting to feel something approaching sympathy for Amaya. First of all, she was dead. It wasn't really productive to have total hatred for someone who didn't exist anymore. And I had to concede that she never promised me anything. She didn't even know me. I believed she really did help Mae through a terrible time in her life. I couldn't get a hold on who Amaya was now. After years of pure spite it was profoundly unsettling to have to reevaluate her.

For one thing, she must have seemed like a relief to Ethan after the way I treated him. She was so easygoing and so aware of his emotional life. But she also seemed insanely obsessed with Yoni, and she had been since she was barely of drinking age. I felt sorry for her; I wondered if she'd ever developed a sense of self outside of Yoni and his beliefs. Did Ethan like that about her? That her only demand of him was that he believe in the same spiritual claptrap that she did?

It was wounding to read about this vague naked party, even without any specific details. Group sex was something Ethan never mentioned being interested in. Not that I would have done it, but I did want to know about his fantasy life. I wanted to know him. Was that what he really wanted? Or was it just that he wanted Amaya, and this—not just the sex stuff, but the love of Yoni—was how he could get her?

The conflicting emotions had left me numb by the time Sheriff Lewis entered the room. "I'm sorry I kept you waiting, ma'am," he said, sounding genuinely contrite. He sat down and stuck out his hand. "Matt Lewis."

His hand was large, warm, and dry. "Dana Morrison. Formerly Dana Powell," I said. "I just want to emphasize up front, again, that I don't think Ethan was capable of killing anyone."

Before I could continue, Lewis put his meaty hand up to stop me. "We'll get there," he said calmly. "Can I get you some coffee or water before we begin?"

"I don't want anything!" I said. The voice that escaped was sharp and shrill.

"I know this is a difficult thing to do," Sheriff Lewis said, his eyes meeting mine. "I appreciate your coming down here."

His steady gaze settled me. "You're welcome, I guess."

"So let's start at the beginning. I'm going to record this, if that's okay." He took out a camcorder that looked like it had been purchased when Michael Jordan was still playing basketball and put it on the table facing me. He also took out a pad of paper and a pen.

"That's fine," I said more tersely than I wanted to. My emotions were so all over the place that I was having trouble modulating my voice. I wanted to reach out and catch the words and stick them back in my mouth so I could try again.

He pressed Record. "When was the last time you saw Ethan?"

"June 5, 2007," I said quickly. The date had been seared into my brain. I saw the sheriff write it down.

"And what happened the last time you saw him?" He looked up at me. His face was open but free of emotion.

"We had a huge fight about money." Even after all this time it still hurt to say it aloud. I wanted to stop making eye contact with the sheriff, because I thought if I kept looking at him, I would cry. But more than that I wanted him to believe what I was saying. I knew from watching years of *Law & Order* that cops are analyzing your body language and behavior when they're talking to you, like shrinks with guns. So I held his gaze.

"I'm sorry about that," the sheriff said. He waited a respectful beat before asking, "Can you tell me about that day a little more specifically?"

I exhaled all the breath inside me. "Yes. I had been going over our finances. After I had paid all our bills for May, I realized that we had about twenty thousand dollars less in our account than I thought we should." I remembered sitting at our kitchen table and looking at the same bank statement over and over, as if the numbers would somehow change. We had three accounts—one joint account, and we each had our own checking accounts, which I thought was a brilliant idea. I had set it up that way when Ethan went to work at Green Wave.

"This gives us both some privacy," I remember explaining to him. All the big expenses, like rent and groceries, came from our joint account. The fun stuff—massages for me, video games for him—was supposed to come from our individual accounts.

"Why hadn't you noticed the discrepancy earlier?" the sheriff asked.

"I didn't keep super-close track of our money. I'm a lawyer and my salary went straight to the joint account. There was always more than enough in there, so I didn't sweat it." I wondered if this would make the sheriff think I was some sort of rich New Yorker, but his face still looked sympathetic. "I assumed there was some kind of mistake, so I started tallying up where all the money had gone. Some of it had been funneled into Ethan's private account. Some of it had gone to a company called Enlightened LLC. I did a public records search of that, and it turned out to be the holding company for the Urban Ashram."

"And what's the Urban Ashram?" The sheriff pronounced *ashram* "ay-shram," which made it sound shabby and silly. I couldn't tell whether he really didn't know what it was or was trying to see if I knew anything more about it. If he had never heard of the Urban Ashram, that meant he really hadn't done any research about Yoni or the Zuni Retreat's past. I didn't believe he hadn't. He seemed too sharp to slack on his homework.

"It's Yoni's old yoga studio in New York. He must have sold it, because I walked past it at some point after Ethan left, probably a year or two later, and it had become a Pret A Manger." I recalled feeling a perverse pang of sadness when I saw that the yoga studio was gone. It seemed like all evidence of Ethan's existence in my life was disappearing. That should have made me happy. But now I saw that I enjoyed clutching the scraps of him.

"Gotcha," Sheriff Lewis said, scribbling again. "So you found out the money was going to this yoga studio. And then what happened?"

"I confronted Ethan about it." It was the worst conversation of my life. I had stayed up all night waiting for him to come home from his shift. I remembered pacing the floors, trying to both exhaust and entertain myself. Our downstairs neighbors must have wanted to kill me. When Ethan finally got home I asked him about the missing $20,000.

"And how did he respond?"

"He fed me some bullshit about how important the ashram had been for his spiritual and physical awakening. I don't remember the specific details, I'm sorry. He was upset..." I trailed off. That night I was so tired, and so furious. After Ethan left and didn't return, I tried replaying the night in my mind a million different ways, but there were huge holes in my recall, like that evening's mental film had been eaten by moths.

I found my voice again. "We had a fight, and I left to stay with my sister, Beth. I came back two nights later, and his Dear John note was there. I never saw him again." I was suddenly exhausted. Resurrecting these memories in this circumstance was really awful.

"What did his note say?" the sheriff asked.

"It said that I didn't understand him anymore, but that Amaya did. He said he was leaving to be with her because she existed on the same 'spiritual plane.' I still have the note, if you want to read it." I could have recited it verbatim, too.

"That won't be necessary, ma'am," the sheriff said. "And that was the last time you had any communication?"

"Yes. Well, I tried to reach out to him after he left so we could get a divorce, but I couldn't find him. It was like he had evaporated. I didn't even know he was in New Mexico until I read about his death."

The sheriff nodded solemnly. "Did Ethan have any enemies?" When I laughed, surprised, he asked, "Why is that funny?"

"It just sounds like something you hear on TV," I said, grateful for anything that brought me out of reliving my last days with Ethan.

"Well, they get some things right on those cop shows," the sheriff said, smiling. He seemed less humorless than I had initially assumed.

"No, he didn't have any enemies, at least not from his life with me." I paused. "But I've been wondering if he had any enemies at the retreat. Or any enemies wherever he was living."

"He wasn't living at the retreat?" the sheriff asked.

"I heard from some friends I made at the retreat that he was living elsewhere—that all the teachers live elsewhere. I don't know where, though."

The sheriff wrinkled his brow just a little. He reached over and turned the camcorder off. "Off the record," he said, "how has your stay at the retreat been?"

"I'm getting the hang of things." I wanted to be helpful to the sheriff. Always the overachiever, I wished I were able to give him even more than I had. "I haven't really been able to learn much about Ethan's life in the days before his death. The women I've asked about it said that Ethan and Amaya were doing something dangerous, but they wouldn't give me any details about what it was." I paused, because it was a struggle for me to say what I had to say next. "It sounds like Ethan and Amaya were both very well-liked there. Amaya especially."

The sheriff nodded. "Is there anything else, let's say, useful, that you learned?"

"I've learned a lot more about what Ethan's life was like at the beginning of his association with Yoni," I said. "In fact, I might have something that will help you with that warrant." I took Ethan's book out of my bag and slid it across the table to the sheriff.

Ethan

DAILY AFFIRMATION: *"Spring is in the air again.
All seeds on the planet are quietly starting to
shine. Ready to stretch, open and grow."*
—Yoko Ono

I thought Dana would notice a change in me immediately. I felt the change in myself, even on the way home from what I learned is called Yoni's Rite of Spring. I left the house on Herkimer after midnight, but instead of being afraid of getting jumped in what I knew to be a dodgy neighborhood, I smiled at every person I passed. They all smiled back, except for the one woman who said, "Back off, faggot." I just bowed to her wordlessly and went on my way.

Before I got on the subway, I had a fantasy that my apartment had transformed into some verdant forest while I was gone, and Dana into some sort of welcoming wood nymph. But my trip on the C snapped me back into my reality, and by the time I got back home, the old plaid Barcalounger and Dana asleep, mouth ajar, in our bed looked shabbier and more dispiriting than ever.

I almost turned and walked back out the door right then. But seeing Dana asleep and vulnerable made me pause. I got undressed and took a shower, and while the water was sluicing down my face, I started to panic. What had just happened?

When I got into bed I tried to meditate to calm down. I was nervous about what Dana would see when she woke up, and the serious conversation we'd have to have. I tried to keep myself awake so that the vibes of the ceremony would still be fresh in my mind, but I must have fallen asleep at some point because I woke up when I heard Dana turning on the shower.

I got up and went to the kitchen, where coffee was already brewing, and made myself some green tea. I sat at the kitchen table and tried to be mindful of my surroundings—the scent of the tea and the silence of the wee hours—until Dana entered the room in her robe, toweling off her shoulder-length hair. "You're up early!" Dana said. "How was work?"

So much for her noticing the difference in me just by looking at my face. I opened my mouth to tell her the truth—that I hadn't been at work, that my entire spiritual being had been altered—but instead I just croaked out, "Pretty good."

"Great," she said. She glanced at the clock. "Shit. I can't believe it's already seven fifteen. The morning goes by so fast! I gotta motor." She came over and kissed me on the cheek and then scurried back out of the kitchen. I could hear her banging around in the closet, taking a suit off a hanger, opening and closing a drawer, then stomping around in her heels. "Bye, hon! I'll try to be home before you go to work tonight!" she said from the living room before closing the door behind her and clacking down the stairs.

She didn't even notice that I'd only said two words to her this morning. That she had no time to share my conscious-ness made the guilt I felt over my participation in the Rite of Spring evaporate. Lama Yoni always had time for me. And so did Amaya.

DAILY AFFIRMATION: *Personal growth*
requires equal parts patience and persistence.

I didn't see Amaya again until almost two weeks after our explosive meeting at the Rite of Spring. Our work schedules had not aligned. I don't know if it was because our supervisor noticed that we were fraternizing or because the heavens or-dained a pause between our first and second unions.

Of course, I still dutifully attended my classes at the Urban Ashram every day. My first time back, Lama Yoni saw me at the end of a meditation class and brought me back into the inner sanctum. My heart was beating fast as I followed him behind the wooden accordion door. The feeling was familiar—it was the same one I had at my first junior high dance, when I was about to slow dance with my crush, Jamie Hines.

Lama Yoni bowed to me, and I bowed back. His white hair flowed down his back, thick and lustrous. Yoni is probably in his sixties, but he has this remarkable deeply tanned yet unlined face. He was wearing a dark-purple robe. It's a regal color, Amaya once explained to me, and so this particular shade is reserved for Lama Yoni. The dedicated yogis wear light-purple robes.

I wanted to blurt out something about how honored I was to be included in the Rite of Spring, but Lama Yoni's presence still left me tongue-tied. I was so awed by his absolute centeredness, I felt hopelessly messy by comparison.

After a few moments of fairly comfortable silence, Lama Yoni said, "Yogi Ethan, I trust you have told no one about the details of our Rite of Spring?"

"Of course not. I would not divulge ceremonial rites to anyone outside the ashram."

Lama Yoni nodded. "I knew we could trust you. Your dedication to the ashram has been noted. I would like you to start coming to our highest-level classes, which are not listed on the website."

"When are they?" I asked. The second the words came out of my mouth I knew they were the wrong ones.

"They are scheduled according to the dictates of the planet," Lama Yoni said. "Someone from the ashram will communicate with you the day before each class and tell you where to go and when to be there. I must attend to some pressing ashram business now. Namaste." Lama Yoni closed his eyes and bowed to me.

"Namaste," I said, closing my eyes and bowing back. But by the time I stood up straight and opened my eyes, Lama Yoni was gone.

I left the studio that day and waited for my call. I went to work at night and spent a nearly wordless weekend with Dana, who finally did notice something was different about me. "You seem nervous. Why do you keep flipping your phone open?" she said while we were eating lunch in Madison Square Park. It was one of the first warm days of the year and she had suggested we go outside for a little sun.

"I just have some excess energy, I guess." I was so excited

about my progress at the ashram, I couldn't focus on anything else. Now that I've seen so many others make this same journey, I know this is a common reaction to making spiritual leaps.

"But you've been going to those yoga classes so much, isn't that enough? Or do you need a higher-intensity workout?" Dana asked. "Maybe we can start running together again."

We used to run together when we first moved to New York, up a path next to the West Side Highway. We'd wake up early in the morning and lace up our sneakers and head out the door. Then we'd have sweaty, athletic sex when we got back home as a reward. But that was before I started working nights, when Dana was still in law school and had more time.

"Maybe," I said, still holding on to the idea that our running together was a possibility.

Dana smiled. "So I'm working on this case with a car company. I can't really talk about the details, they're classified, but I might need to go to Detroit for a week soon."

"That's fine," I said.

"Good, because . . ." then Dana kept talking about work and I stared off into the park shrubbery and hoped that my phone would ring.

DAILY AFFIRMATION: *"Rivers know this:
There is no hurry. We shall get there some day."*
—Winnie-the-Pooh

It turned out all that time playing with my phone was useless, because the call came in person. From Amaya.

We were working the graveyard shift at the office. They only

light half of the space, because there are only a handful of work-
ers there in the middle of the night. I liked to use the handi-
capped bathroom on the dark side of the floor. It allowed me
to have a moment of contemplative meditation while my body
removed its natural toxins.

I didn't think anyone knew about this bathroom besides me
until Amaya knocked on the door.

"Just a second," I said, trying to finish up quickly.

"It's me," Amaya said. "Will you let me in?" I hesitated for just
a second, and then opened the door.

"Um, hi," I said. And before I could say anything else, Amaya
was on me. With one hand she started undoing my jeans
while she kissed me. Before I could say anything we had tumbled to the floor. Her lower body was open to the universe—
unencumbered by the garments that prevent a connection to
the natural world. I didn't think in this moment, because thinking would have ruined what was a true, otherworldly connection of souls and bodies.

We came with equal tsunami-like force, simultaneously.

That's never happened to me with any woman. I only had
sex with one other girl before Dana and I got together in college. It was a freshman-year fling. I lost my virginity to this sort
of homely but sweet Minnesota girl, Melanie, who lived down
the hall. I can't even remember her last name now, but we were
both eighteen-year-olds who were really terrible at sex.

I thought about Melanie for a split second as Amaya rolled
off me. Maybe it was so easy for me to go on this sexual journey
because I'd had so little experience before. But I think it's more

because Amaya offers such a heady combination of spirituality and sensuality. It's something I didn't even know I was craving before I got it.

Amaya sat on the toilet. I watched as she peed. "I'm letting your seed leak out of me like a river," she said dreamily. It was graphic, but it connected our beautiful act to nature, which made it even more meaningful to me.

"I'm not just here for work. I'm here to tell you about the class. We meet in Yoni's inner sanctum Monday at midnight."

"But I have work Monday," I said, knee-jerk, still tied to my responsibilities in the corporate world, though they were increasingly meaningless to me.

Amaya waved it away. "You'll have to figure something out." She wiped herself and flushed the toilet. She put her hands together in prayer pose and bowed to me, wordlessly. She left the bathroom, and it was at least a full minute before I realized I still wasn't wearing any pants.

DAILY AFFIRMATION: *"Love is an infinite commodity."*
        —Lama Yoni

It was a brisk, clear night, so I walked the thirty blocks to the Urban Ashram. I wanted to clear my head before I had another Yoni experience.

The studio space was dark when I got to the ashram. I'd never seen it that way before, and without the peachy lighting it looked much colder. Without bodies and mats and movement filling up the space, those empty hardwood floors looked barren. I shoved these intrusive, unpleasant thoughts away—they were just symptoms of my anxiety.

The wooden accordion door pushed open right before I got to it. I wondered if there were cameras in the studio, since the opening of that door was so perfectly timed to my arrival. Amaya was standing in front of me, resplendent in her light-purple robe. She had freesias scattered throughout her long hair, and she smelled like fresh laundry.

Without speaking she took my hand and led me to a circle where Lama Yoni was lazily strumming a guitar. He did not register my presence when I arrived. The same men who had been part of the Rite of Spring were in the circle, and now that I could get a more prolonged look at their faces, I realized they were guys I'd seen at the ashram classes. One was a meditation leader with a long beard named Abe, who always seemed like a good guy. He had given me shoulder massages because he told me that was where I held my tension.

There were women here, too, and I could only assume that they were the ones inside the tent at the previous ceremony. They looked like they could be Amaya's sisters, or at least her cousins. They were uniformly youthful and taut and their skin was face-wash-commercial clear. They all wore flowers in their hair and formfitting light-purple robes.

Yoni kept strumming his guitar as everyone in the group stared at him. He did not look up once. I'm not sure how long we sat there before Yoni opened his mouth. "The lesson I want to give today is about love," he said. "In our hyperconnected society, we give away so much for free. We can do so much so easily. You can go on the Internet and get information about hiking in the Himalayas without paying for it. You can find any song you hear on the radio. You can read all the sutras with the click of your little mouse."

I looked around the room. Everyone was paying rapt attention to Yoni. I felt immediately guilty for breaking my concentration to see what my peers were doing. The energy in the room was flowing toward our guru and I was trying to push against it. This is normal for early adherents to Yoni's methods. You must push past these distractions to get to what is truly in your soul.

"The one thing we hold on to tightly, with all of our intellectual and spiritual might, is love. We dole it out in parsimonious parcels, only to those we feel are worthy of such a precious emotion. But wouldn't society be so much better, so much stronger, so much deeper, if we gave love away as freely as we give information?" Yoni put down his guitar. "That is a core tenet of what we're doing here at the ashram. Giving our love away to everyone who is part of our humble little society. I want to welcome Ethan to the sanctuary."

Yoni stood and walked over to me. He put his hands on my forehead and used his thumbs to put gentle pressure on my temples. He started rubbing those pressure points in concentric circles, and I closed my eyes and sighed, like a dog getting his tummy patted. His touch allowed me to get rid of the nervous energy and comparison with others that had followed me into this experience. I could become centered into my own essence.

"I also want to give him his new name: the name he will have at the ashram, and in his spiritual life." I opened my eyes. Yoni stood in front of me and looked me in the eyes. "This name is a universal name. It means many different things in many different languages. In Burmese, it means 'unbreakable.' In Urdu, it means 'universe.' The name is Kai.

"A thousand years ago in Tibet, there was a prisoner named Donen," Yoni continued as he reached out and put his warm hand on my forehead. He said this quietly, as if we were in a private conversation, but I could feel the eyes of the rest of the circle on us. "Every day he and the other prisoners were whipped by a guard. This made most of the prisoners very bitter. They looked like they were holding lemons in their cheeks all day. But Donen was different. He did not have a sour expression. He always had a smile on his face, even as he would get his daily lashings.

"On the coldest day of the year, when all the men were getting chilblains through their rags, one of his fellow prisoners asked Donen, 'Why do you keep smiling? Are you a fool or just a madman?' And Donen replied, 'I keep smiling because I have love for every part of nature. I have love for you, and for the guard who whips us every day, and for the frost that accumulates on our bodies.' Donen knew that his fate was fixed, and that the only way to survive spiritually in this life was to give his love away, instead of hoarding it. Love is an infinite commodity."

Yoni stepped away from me then. "I want you to find a partner for tantra. You need to give your love away in this sanctum. We need to feel the thunderous love in this room." I can't reveal the details of our sanctum activities. You must follow Yoni's teachings and reach the appropriate level of enlightenment before you can be privy to our most sacred rituals. But I can tell you the inner work and selfless devotion is worth it. It will change your life.

Right before I left, Yoni put his forehead to my forehead and placed a light-purple robe in my hands. I stepped back and bowed to him. The turmoil I had felt since I started at the ashram had disappeared in that moment. For the first time in my life I felt like my body, mind, and spirit were all one, a pulsing, interconnected system that could not be broken.

It was pitch-black outside when I emerged from the ashram. I was still in that postritual haze, but the cold predawn air woke me up. I felt simultaneously proud and terrified. This was not something I would have done even six months ago. What was I becoming?

The next morning I woke up when Dana closed the door to our apartment. Shamefully, I was glad I didn't have to face her, afraid that she'd immediately read the fear and excitement I was feeling. But the longer I stayed in bed, awake but immobile, the more my mind tumbled over itself. How could I keep going to Lama Yoni's inner sanctum without saying anything about it to Dana? But how could I tell her? She'd either kick me out or try to get me to pull back from the Urban Ashram.

I knew I was violating our vows, but Yoni's message of sharing love is such a real one. I had spent so much of my life until that time withholding love. I just wanted to give it away.

DAILY AFFIRMATION: *Sometimes the families you choose are more powerful than the families you were given.*

I was thinking about Yoni's message about giving love away when I called my dad for his birthday. At that point, we spoke only three times a year: on my birthday, on his birthday, and on Christmas Day.

Dad came to visit me in New York only once. Dana was so

welcoming to him, setting up our guest bed so that it looked beautiful and making a color-coded list of museums and parks he might like to visit. But I could tell he was spooked by all the commotion. He hates being out of his element—he grumbled more than once about New York's restrictive gun laws and how they made him feel unsafe—and there was a palpable relief in his body when I watched him walk away from our apartment to take the subway back to JFK.

It probably didn't help the vibe of that visit that I had held my love away from him since Mom died. You could argue he held his love away from me, too—but Lama Yoni preaches only radical forgiveness, not score-keeping. And I still wanted to try to connect with my father.

My dad was born in the last week of the Aries sun sign—so he's technically an Aries/Taurus cusp. That means he's naturally predisposed to be aggressive, and to be a hardheaded leader. And he has been since I can remember. He's the head of his department at Montana Fish, Wildlife and Parks. He organizes fishing expeditions and takes up collections for his coworkers when they're going through a rough time.

I was trying to remember these things when I heard his phone ringing. He only had a landline. He's resistant to change in general. I've tried to help him move on from this resistance by surreptitiously passing along Yoni's teachings. "A river that does not flow quickly becomes cloudy with silt," I told Dad the last time we spoke on the phone. "Son, what the hell are you talking about?" was all he could say in response.

That day I made sure to call him around six A.M. his time.

I knew he'd be awake but still at home. He lives in the same house he built for our family in 1984. I still urge him to move, to get away from Mom's memories and start fresh, but he has zero interest. He answers every nudge with "I built this house," as if that closes the discussion forever.

He picked up on the fourth ring with a cheerful "Yello?"

"Hey, Dad." He sounded so happy; I was hopeful that this conversation would be a positive one.

"Ethan, good to hear from you."

I thought about telling him my new name straightaway but decided against it. I wanted the conversation to flow naturally into my sharing these new developments with him. "I'm calling to wish you a happy birthday," I said.

"Thank you. Just another year closer to the big corral in the sky."

"Jeez, Dad. That's bleak," I said, though he always said things like that.

"Just God's honest truth."

"How are you?" I asked.

"Can't complain. Spring season just about to start for black bear and turkey hunting, so we just got those licenses out the door. How's things in the Big Apple?"

"They're pretty good. I've been going to a lot of classes lately," I said, testing the waters.

"Classes? Didn't you spend all that scholarship money going to classes at that college?" I could tell from his voice that he was just ribbing me, and I tried not to let it deter me from my goal of connecting.

"They're not academic classes. I guess I'd call them spiritual classes."

"Like church?"

"Kind of," I said.

"Well, that's good. A man needs some of Christ's guidance in his life from time to time."

"It's not really about Jesus, Dad," I said. "It's sort of an alternative religious group. But I think Jesus would approve of the messages. It's sort of about life lessons. Loving your neighbors and being generous, that kind of thing."

There was such a prolonged silence on the other end of the phone that I thought our connection had died. "Dad? You still there?"

"I'm still here," he said. After another long pause he added, "I'm going to try to choose my words carefully here, because I want them to get through your thick skull. You don't know what you're messing with by going outside the church. This shit can be real dangerous, in ways you don't even understand." His voice got more and more emphatic as he spoke.

"What are you talking about? You barely went to church when I was a kid! How can you be so judgmental about something you don't even know anything about?" I could hear teenage angst creeping into my voice. Looking back at this conversation, I wish I had been able to speak to my dad from a place of enlightenment, not from one of destruction. But at that point I was still so new to my practice that I often fell back into old, bad patterns.

"I know a lot about it. You just think I'm some backwoods hick, with your fancy college and your fancy wife. Well, I've been through some shit in my life and you ain't got a goddamn clue about it." I could tell he was really pissed. His voice was so gruff it sounded like he was spitting out each individual word.

"Okay," I said, taking my yogic breaths and remembering that I needed to remain centered. "I don't want to argue with you. I wanted this to be a nice phone call."

"It is a nice phone call. I'm just speaking my mind. You can be naïve, Ethan. You've been like that since you were a kid. You'd befriend any old cur who crossed your path, even if they were dangerous. Like that Miller kid who lived down the street. I always knew there was something wrong with that boy, but you and your mother, you just ignored me."

Dave Miller. Why did my dad always have to bring him up? We were best friends up through junior high. So what if he became an arsonist when we were in high school? He didn't hurt anyone. He just set an abandoned building on fire one time. He's not a bad person.

"I'm sorry, I'm sorry," I said, trying to remove the edge from my voice. "I really didn't mean for this phone call to be like this. I just wanted to wish you a great day, and to catch up."

My dad sighed. I wonder if he felt as bad about our getting trapped in our old, worn-out groove as I did. "Well all right then. You have a good day, son."

"Okay, Dad, you too. I love you."

"I love you, too," he said, and hung up.

I got back into bed and stayed there for a while. I was so upset the only thing I could think of doing was a restorative practice. I put my legs up against the headboard and a pillow under my back and tried some deep, cleansing breaths.

I should have known my dad would be dismissive of any-

thing non-Christian. When I was ten he threw *D'Aulaires'*
Book of Greek Myths into our fireplace after he had a fight with
my mom about it. It had been my favorite book; I read about
Athena popping out of her dad's skull and Zeus turning Io into
a cow with complete reverence. I loved looking at the golden-
hued illustrations and learning about my zodiac sign—Libra,
the scales of balance. My mother would sit with me as I reread
the myths, quizzing me on the difference between Demeter
and Diana.

I couldn't quite remember what the fight was specifically
about; I could only see the look of rage on my dad's face and the
look of resignation on my mom's. The anger was pretty hypo-
critical on his part, since he didn't even go to church on Christmas Eve, and though he'd been raised pretty religious, he never
seemed especially spiritual to me.

When Dana and I were planning our wedding, we didn't think
we would have a pastor marry us. Dana's half-Jewish, and I didn't
feel strongly about it. But when my dad found out, he was apo-
plectic. "You and Dana need to be married the right way under
the eyes of God," he told me. This exchange took place in person
at my family home in Livingston. That was the last time I was
back in Montana, for Christmas a few years ago.

I scoffed at him. This was way before I learned about radical
empathy from Yoni. "What are you talking about?"

"Son, you know I don't ask you for much," my dad said, putting his meaty paw on my shoulder. "But this is important to me.
Your mom and I weren't married the right way. I want you and
Dana to have the best start in life, and I think that comes from a
pastor's guidance."

My dad so rarely opened up even this much that I softened. "Okay. I'll talk to Dana."

"Good," my dad grunted, and then he scooted out of the room, as if staying in the same airspace with his emotions would cause him great physical pain.

Dana, who wasn't even a religious Jew—I always had to tell her when it was Passover—balked at this request. "It would really piss my mom off," she said, not wanting to goad her mother into yet another shouting match over our wedding. Her mother had already given her a hard time about the guest list, the location, and her dress. "You're wearing *that?*" she'd said when Dana sent her a link to the knee-length gown she had bought for the ceremony. I watched Dana fight back tears over the phone as she explained that yes, that was what she was wearing.

Still, Dana and I had a huge fight about the officiant and eventually she agreed to have both a rabbi and a minister officiate. Despite the drama and stress leading up to it, the wedding was wonderful, and my dad was pleased.

I held the image of Montana's mountain backdrop in my head for a while. By the time I came out of my savasana, two hours had passed. I felt better. I had accepted that my dad's deeply held religious fervor is something I'm not meant to fully understand. And in turn, my spirituality isn't something he's meant to understand, either.

Dana

The sheriff told me that the last person outside Zuni to see Ethan was his dad. Apparently Ethan went to Montana by himself for a visit three months before he and Amaya left the retreat and met their deaths in that cave. I asked the sheriff if Ray was helpful to him. "Since this is an ongoing investigation, I can't divulge much from my conversation with Mr. Powell," the sheriff said. Whatever openness had been in his face when I shared the book with him had closed off the second I ventured into unauthorized territory.

I was slightly heartened by the fact that Ethan hadn't cut ties with his dad. They'd always had a complicated relationship, but family was important to the Ethan I knew. That was a big reason I married him. I thought creating a new family with someone supportive and kind would help heal the wounds left by my mother and father—my mother's unending criticism of me, and my father's tacit approval of that criticism. My dad has never once stood up for me or Beth, which is almost worse than my mother's constant disapproval.

But despite my many efforts over the years to get to know

Ray, he gently rebuffed my attempts to get closer to him. I'd always get on the phone when Ethan called, and his responses to my probing questions were kind but brief. When I'd lament our lack of relationship, Ethan would say, "Don't take it personally. It just takes my dad a long time to open up." Ethan told me that it took ten years for Ray to talk to his best friend about Rosemary's death. "Ten years!" Ethan exclaimed, shaking his head. "It takes me ten seconds to tell people about my mom." That Ethan was still in touch with Ray told me that "Kai" hadn't done a total one-eighty. Maybe just a ninety.

I made two copies of Ethan's book at the sheriff's office, one for him and one for me. We agreed that I should put the original back where I found it. It sounded like Sheriff Lewis always felt John Brooks was "hinky," even before the deaths. "Folks around here have always felt a little strange about Mr. Brooks and what's going on over there," he explained. "He bought up damn near about half the county several years back."

"For the Zuni Retreat?" I asked.

"Yep. Folks around here are mostly Christian, so they were concerned that Mr. Brooks was going to get up in their faces with, well, whatever it is that he believes." The sheriff sighed, exasperated. "But then they realized that the people at the retreat mostly kept to themselves. They respect that. Most folks move out here to get a lot of space."

"That makes sense," I said, looking out the window at the empty street. Not a single car had passed the sheriff's office the whole time I was there. "What do they think about the deaths?"

The sheriff shrugged. "They mostly think the deaths don't concern them. They don't trust Mr. Brooks over much, but the retreat has pumped so much tourist money into the economy and has created a lot of cooking and cleaning jobs. So most folks around here are more worried about losing a paycheck than they are about some silly people dying in a cave."

I was thinking about Ray when I approached the turnoff to the retreat. He'd had such a hard life—first Rosemary dies, then Ethan. Knowing what I know about Ray, I'm sure he thought Ethan's new lifestyle was bonkers. He is a meat-and-potatoes kind of guy, not a quinoa one. He must have suspected something off about the retreat, something "hinky," the way Sheriff Lewis did. Ray could certainly understand the desire for an unbothered life—the man lives in a cabin in Montana—but he's got a pretty unflinching moral core. I imagined he'd be disgusted by the inaction of the locals after Ethan's and Amaya's deaths.

I made it back with just enough time to slip the original volume back into the library before dinner with Sylvia and her pals. To my surprise, Mae said, "Everybody, put down your birdseed and lift up your glasses." We held our mugs full of rejuvenation tea aloft as Mae spoke. "This is to Dana. You have made great spiritual progress this week. We've all noticed how far you've come. Here's to your continued progress, and to your youth!"

All the other ladies shouted, "Hear, hear!" as we clinked our misshapen ceramic mugs. Though I smiled, I wondered how they could gauge such a thing as spiritual progress. How could they know what was going on inside me? Maybe in my brain there was an endless cartoon loop of a blank-eyed cow munching grass in a field instead of something deep or "spiritual."

That night, while Sylvia was out at a mystical femininity

workshop, I powered through another chunk of Ethan's book. I still couldn't quite grasp, intellectually, how he had been taken in by Yoni's nonsense. Ethan was an extremely bright guy. I always thought he was smarter than I was, he just didn't have the drive to succeed. But the descriptions of how he fell for both Amaya and Yoni were somehow more upsetting than reading a description of an average affair. It wasn't just that Amaya was meeting physical or emotional needs that Ethan had. I knew Ethan had those needs, I just thought I was meeting them. It was that Amaya and Yoni together were meeting Ethan's meta-physical needs. I didn't even know those existed for him.

We'd never talked about God. It seems like a wild omission, considering Ethan and I had been together for so long. But a higher power just wasn't part of my lexicon in any way. If you had asked me, I guess I would have said that the world works in random and chaotic ways, ungoverned by anything but science. When it came up, which was infrequently, I defined myself as agnostic, because I couldn't absolutely, positively rule out the existence of something greater than all of us. But saying I was agnostic rather than atheist was just a way of refusing to think about it at all.

I had assumed Ethan felt like I did. It was one of the many ways I had mistaken his silence on an issue for an embrace of my own stance. Reading his book, I finally understood that.

I must have fallen asleep at some point, because I sat up with a start when my alarm went off at five A.M. I looked over at Sylvia's bed. She was fast asleep. I left a little note for her, thanking her for taking me under her wing. I really was grateful. I never would have found Ethan's book without her guidance. But more than that, despite learning all that painful shit about the end of my marriage, I felt more at peace than I had in years. I didn't know if it was just getting out of New York, or if it was Lo's weirdly freeing workshop, but I couldn't deny that the old hippies had experienced something substantial during their repeated trips to the retreat—because I'd had a taste of it myself.

The sun was just coming up as I walked up the path toward the main building to check out. I was looking at the horizon instead of in front of me, and I ran smack into a woman in my path. She fell back onto her hands, and when I bent down to help her up, I noticed a dark blue medallion with an asterisk on it hanging off her neck. I stared at it for a moment before I looked at her face and realized it was Lo. "I'm so sorry! I wasn't looking where I was going," I said. "Are you okay?"

Lo dusted some dirt off her long, crinkly skirt. "I'm quite all right, dear. I'm glad to see you before you take off." She gestured to my suitcase.

"Oh, really?" I had really enjoyed her class, but it surprised me that she cared enough to want to say good-bye to a first-time visitor.

"Yes. I couldn't believe the progress you made. I've never seen anything like it, and I've been doing this for forty years." She made deep, direct eye contact as she said this.

Even though the line about progress sounded as bullshitty as when Mae said it, I couldn't deny feeling flattered. Just like when I was in grade school, I loved hearing a teacher's praise. "Thank you," I said, blushing. "You were a great leader."

She waved away my compliment. "I have never, ever done this

for a first-time student. But you have something special," she said, grabbing my hands. "I think you're ready for the next-level retreat."

"Really?" I said, basking in her praise in spite of myself. The "next-level retreat" sounded a little intense to me, but I was still flattered to be asked.

"Yes. Your energy is a color I've only seen a few times in my life. You need to learn how to harness it properly, and I want to be the one to help guide you," Lo said. She bowed to me. "Namaste."

I thought about what Lo had said while I waited for the receptionist to check me out. There was no way I could come back here. I couldn't afford to take more time off work. I was sure I'd already be in the doghouse when I returned. But I did, technically, have more vacation days that I could use.

Then I stopped myself short. I couldn't believe I'd bought into the retreat enough that I was thinking of work logistics. Lo had had me in a class for a couple of hours. How did she know anything about me, or what I was capable of? And my "energy"? Are you fucking kidding me?

"You're all set." It was only when he spoke that I realized the person behind the desk was Janus. Seeing his familiar face snapped me back into the present. "I was just talking to Lo about the progress you've made here," he said. "We are all so proud of you."

"Thank you," I replied as Janus rounded the Ganesha desk and wrapped me in a hug. I had to admit I had never been so earnestly supported by a group of people before. The only person in my entire life who had been such a full-hearted cheerleader for me was Ethan, before our relationship went downhill.

"I hope we see you again soon," Janus said, waving me off.

Ethan

DAILY AFFIRMATION: *When you love yourself, you are wealthy in spirit.*

Making a break from your old self is not without jagged rifts. It's not an easy process, but as you will see from my rupture with who "Ethan" was, the experience was worthwhile. It was the chrysalis I had to wrap myself in so that Kai could emerge into his full spiritual persona.

I got home from work one morning at four A.M. Dana was awake, sitting at the kitchen table. Her shoulders were so tense they were nearly at her ears. As I approached I saw a stack of paper laid out in front of her. I sat down across from her at the table. Her eyes were rimmed with red. The papers were our bank statements, and they were dotted with tears.

"Hi," I said gently. Quietly. "What's wrong?"

"I was going through our finances tonight. I noticed that after I paid our bills last month we had a lot less in the bank than I thought we did," Dana said. Her voice was quavering. "Do you have any idea how much fucking money you have spent?"

Before I had a chance to open my mouth, she went on, "You. Have. Spent. More. Than. Twenty. Thousand. Dollars. In. Six. Months." I could tell she was measuring out each word, trying not to raise her voice.

I didn't realize I had spent that much money at the Urban Ashram. I was just trying to master each level of the courses Yoni offered. Money was merely the worldly metric by which one could judge everything I'd learn from Yoni. In terms of my spiritual progress, those classes were priceless. "That's a lot," I said.

"Duhhh 'that's a lot,'" Dana said, imitating me in a nasal stoner voice.

"Let me explain," I said.

"Explain how you spent twenty thousand dollars in half a year?" Her tears were flowing freely now and her face had contorted into a grimace. Her hands shook as she picked up a bank statement and shoved it in my face.

"Well, some of it has been on yoga classes." I waved the papers away and tried my deep breathing to keep me calm.

"Will they be giving you a degree? Is there a master's in goddamn headstands?" Dana shrieked. I'd never seen her quite like this before. I wanted to calm her down, but obviously I couldn't tell her what was really going on at the ashram. I had been sworn to secrecy.

"Dana, you don't need to be snide." I worked on keeping my voice even, which I had learned to do in one of Yoni's advanced-level breath awareness classes. I would not let this descend into chaos, even if I couldn't be completely forthcoming.

"How dare you. How dare you condescend to me. You have

spent more money on your yoga than we have spent on rent this year. We are supposed to be a team, Ethan."

"You haven't been acting very generous lately. I hardly see you," I said. I wanted her to know that her emotional absence had been wounding to me, just as my spending had been wounding to her.

"You can't turn this around on me. I work ninety-hour weeks, Ethan. I'm trying to provide for our family while you figure your shit out, which, by the way, is taking years longer than you said it would. I'm supporting us and you're pissing our money away on God knows what." She sniffled and wiped her nose with the back of her hand. "I'm not getting any younger," she said quietly. "I thought we were going to start trying for a baby soon."

I didn't respond for what felt like a long time. Dana couldn't look me in the face. I tried to find the right words. I knew she wanted kids soon, and I hadn't been fully honest with her about my reservations. Yoni would not have approved of my concealing such a deep truth. I finally came up with "I don't think it's the right time. I'm not spiritually evolved enough to create another life yet."

"Fuck your spiritual evolution! What does that even mean? Who are you?" Suddenly Dana was yelling again.

I tried to stay calm, but I was getting upset, too. "It's not my fault you haven't been listening to what I've been trying to tell you about my yoga practice for months now. It's important to me. It's changing my life in a positive way, if only you could see that."

Dana sank deeper into the wooden kitchen chair. "I don't

know what to say, Ethan. I love you, but I'm not interested in spending my precious little free time and hard-earned money on self-indulgences."

That annoyed me. "It's not a 'self-indulgence.' It's really helping me be a better person. If only you opened your mind a little bit, you could see that, and maybe start to change yourself."

"I can't even process that right now," Dana said. "This is much more about your spending that money in secret than what you're spending it on." She sounded exhausted. Her eyes fluttered closed for a second and I thought she might fall asleep sitting up. But then she got up abruptly and went to our bedroom. "I can't think here," she shouted. I could hear her rummaging around, and when I went to go stand in the doorway, I realized she was packing a small suitcase.

"I'm going to stay with Beth," she said. "I need to calm down and you need to figure out what you want." She was throwing her fancy work clothes into the case, not even caring if they got wrinkled, which meant that she was really upset. She disappeared into the bathroom and came out with her bag of toiletries. "You cannot keep spending this kind of money."

I kept standing there silently, observing. She needed to process this in her own way, and I had to respect that.

"The money is not even the biggest problem," she said, zipping up her suitcase. "The biggest problem is that we've drifted apart without my even realizing it. The things that are coming out of your mouth tonight sound like they're coming from someone else. They don't sound like they're coming from the Ethan I married."

"I'm still the same person," I said. "Just better."

"I really want to believe that," Dana said. She breezed past me with her suitcase and walked out the door.

DAILY AFFIRMATION: *My lovers should not judge me any more than they would judge themselves.*

After Dana left, I sat in our empty apartment for a while trying to collect my thoughts. I still loved Dana, but my feelings toward her were more like a baby's blanket, an old talisman I kept around for security and comfort. I was starting to wonder if I had outgrown it.

When Dana and I got married, I felt like I was ahead of my peers. I had found my life partner way before the rest of our college friends, and it felt like the relationship part of my life was settled and secure. But now I realized our relationship was just a way for me to avoid grappling with being my own person, developing into my own self. Dana's financial support had become a burden instead of a gift. That's not to blame her. I let it happen.

Part of me felt relieved. I think I knew that this was bound to happen eventually. Did I really think I could absorb Lama Yoni's teachings while still being Ethan Powell, Dana's husband? Dana would never, ever understand.

When the sun rose, I decided to go to the nearest hotel and try to get a room. I couldn't think straight in the apartment, and I didn't want to face Dana if she came home. I needed to separate to clear my head.

The first rays of the morning were warming my back as I walked into a modern Midtown hotel that was usually a bustling scene of Silicon Alley twenty-four-year-olds pounding away on their laptops while drinking overpriced coffee. But all those twenty-four-year-olds were still in bed at six A.M., and the lobby was empty.

I walked up to the front desk, where a sleepy but fresh-looking guy about my age said, "Can I help you?"

"Yes, I'd like a single room, if there are any open."

"I think I can make it work," he said with a big smile. "We have a medium queen open at three hundred and ninety-nine dollars a night."

"Great." I realized how tired I was when he mentioned the queen-size bed. I pictured myself flopping down on it the second I entered the room.

"Can I have a card for incidentals?"

"Sure." I handed over my debit card, which drew from our joint checking account. My account was empty. I'd spent the last of it at the Ashram six weeks prior.

The clerk ran my card, and then his face clouded over. "I'm sorry, sir. Your account has been frozen."

At first I didn't understand. "What?"

He said it more slowly, as if I were foreign, or hard of hearing. "Your account has been frozen."

I couldn't believe Dana had done this without telling me. I muttered something to myself that is too unevolved to repeat here. "Sorry for wasting your time." I took the card and shambled out the revolving door.

I walked down Fifth Avenue, which was still empty but for a bodega owner pacing outside his store and a few white-collar slaves rushing to their offices. I took my phone out of my pocket and looked down at it. A part of me wanted to call Dana and explain, in harsh words, how wounding her actions had been to me, but that didn't cotton with Yoni's nonviolent teachings. And what was I fighting for anyway? I couldn't even answer.

Once I had the phone out, my next step was obvious. I called Amaya. Who picked up on the second ring.

DAILY AFFIRMATION: *A port found in the dark is often the most welcoming one.*

I took the L train to Amaya's, which was in a part of Bushwick I had never seen. She lived in a somewhat dilapidated freestanding house. When I rang the doorbell I heard a harmonic trill instead of the familiar shrill doorbell sound and knew I had come to the right place.

Amaya floated up to the door wearing white linen pants and a white tank top. She looked concerned for me. "Come in, come in. How are you doing?"

"Not so great," I told her.

She opened a door that had an enormous blue glass eye on it. "To ward off the bad spirits," she said, smiling.

Inside Amaya's apartment, the parquet floors were bare but for a few kilim rugs. Every other available surface was covered with various African-looking gourds, bulbous fertility goddesses, and fat golden Buddhas. Her walls were plastered with batiks of sunsets and moonscapes and dream catchers.

Looking around, I felt a sense of peace I hadn't felt for weeks. Now that my life had imploded I felt free. No more pretending that I hadn't radically changed, no more convincing myself that my marriage was anything but a broken shell of its former self.

Amaya motioned for me to sit next to her on a futon covered with a red-and-gold Indian print. Once we were next to each other, she took my hand and smiled. "Yoni will be so pleased you're here. We talked about this happening. We both knew you were ready to get to a higher level in your practice."

I paused for a second to process this. I was flattered that I was important enough to Yoni that he talked about me when I wasn't around. And then I was embarrassed that I was flattered. But I wanted to hear more. "How do I get to a higher level at the ashram?"

"It's not at the ashram," Amaya explained. "An amazing thing has happened recently, something Yoni has wanted for decades but didn't have the resources to see happen before. It was only after he accepted that it was not fate for us to move forward that we received an exceedingly generous donation from the heavens. Yoni was an early investor in a Chinese Internet search company. He only gave a tiny fraction of capital, but when they had their IPO, he made enough money to buy the Zuni Retreat. It's in New Mexico. Yoni bought the land two years ago, and we completed building on the compound last month. It's our heaven. And our haven." She closed her eyes in near ecstasy. "We are leaving tomorrow to live there, and we want you to come with us."

"Wow," I said. "That's a lot to take in." I wanted to refuse, to say that my life was here and I had to honor it, but what life did I really have left? A dead-end job that I hated. No friends who could emotionally support me. A wife who didn't understand me and didn't care to. No money to keep me afloat while I figured out my soul.

"Okay," I said quietly. "I'll come with you."

Amaya smiled. "Fantastic. I will call Yoni's assistant now and make the necessary arrangements. They have your name and driver's license on file at the ashram, so they can get you a plane ticket. Our flight is at five forty-five tomorrow morning. We'll rendezvous at the ashram at midnight to spiritually prepare for our journey."

"What should I bring?" I asked.

"Just bring your robes. You don't need anything else."

Amaya leaned over then and gave me a kiss. "I can't believe you're coming. I sent out positive vibes into the world for months, hoping that we'd be making this journey together."

After we had sex, connecting our minds, bodies, and souls for the second time, I fell asleep. When I woke up it was already ten P.M., which didn't leave me much time to get back to my apartment and get my robe and an extra pair of shoes for our trip. On the subway back I kept rehearsing things to say to Dana if she was there. Did I want to come completely clean? Did I want to go for maximum hurt, since she had so little trust in me? What would Lama Yoni counsel?

When I arrived at our doorstep I was covered in sweat. I trembled at our door, wondering if I would have to have a difficult conversation. I tried to remember Yoni's teachings about radical honesty. He had said that people aren't always ready to hear your truths, but that sharing them is the noblest action in the world. Then I threw open the door, and the apartment was pitch-black, just as I had left it. I flipped on the lights and started furiously pacing the apartment, wondering what to do first.

Yoni always says that a clear mind is an uncluttered mind,

and I didn't want to be clouded when I reached the ashram. He would know. So I decided to write Dana a letter, revealing my journey to her in its fullness. For those of you leaving relationships, you need to learn how to be honest with yourselves and with your former partners, just as I have learned. I know it's not easy. But secrets cheapen our practice, according to the guru.

Since I left my old life and the shell of my old "Ethan" self, I have learned that after honesty, the most important thing is spiritual support. When you have a partner who supports you fully, you can go places—physically and metaphysically—that you did not think were possible. You can walk right up to the edge of darkness, stare into the abyss, and know someone is there to catch you if you fall.

If your partner doesn't love your soul in all its fullness, that is not a partner who you want to take with you on your life's journey. You may regret shedding those negative souls, but remember, they are just hindrances, potholes on the road to enlightenment that need to be paved over with positivity.

I hope that Dana learned to forgive me, in time. I truly believe that if she'd let the honesty of the world in, she could be free.

Dana

I got back to our apartment late at night. On the plane ride back I had tried to make sense of everything that happened at the retreat. I had learned more about who Ethan had become, and a bit more about the woman Amaya had been. This knowledge comforted me, kept me warm in the recycled air. I was already less angry than I had been a few days ago. Still, I had no idea how they died. I wished I had pressed Sylvia more about what she knew, but I liked her and her friends so much. I didn't want to upset them with morbid questions when they'd made it clear they didn't want to talk about the deaths. They were having such a good time together.

I went in to work the next morning extra early so that I wouldn't chance seeing angry Phil in the elevator all hyped up from his morning workout and full of coconut water. I also wanted to get a head start on what I had missed. But I couldn't concentrate. Katie kept coming in and dumping more files on my desk. "Sorry, Dana. Here's another," she'd chirp, ever cheerful. I'd open one and end up reading the same sentence over and over again, not comprehending or absorbing any of it.

What I kept coming back to was this: I needed to find out more about Yoni. Whatever had happened out there in the desert had to be connected to the "enlightenment" Yoni was peddling. I had read about the changes he'd made while we were still married in his book, but after years at the Zuni Retreat, there had to be even more profound shifts that I didn't know about.

I considered calling Beth for a reality check—she'd certainly give me one. I had texted her to tell her I was back in New York, so she wouldn't worry. I saw that I had a missed call from her. But I hesitated. I wasn't sure I wanted to be talked out of my thoughts. Of course Ethan's death was horrible, and it had brought up all the things I had spent so much time and money working through. But these thoughts, and the renewed sense of mission I had about figuring out who Ethan had become, were more vital and exciting to me than anything I had experienced in years.

I finally pushed my work aside. I wasn't getting anywhere with it. I had long feared that I would lose my ambition and my competitive drive. You needed to be unendingly motivated to make partner here, and I'd seen so many people, especially women, lose that push when they hit their thirties. But now that the desire to work was missing, it wasn't scary; it was tremendously freeing.

I took out a legal pad and started listing everything I had learned about Ethan from his book, from the sheriff, and from my time at the retreat. It was like working on any other case. I suppose I'd thought I might do something like this, because I had put my copy of Ethan's book in my briefcase right before I left the apartment.

Sylvia said that Lo had been with Yoni since the seventies, and Lo told me she'd been in the spiritual business for forty years. After that I had a long blank space before Yoni's resurgence in the nineties. I did a little research, cross-referenced with Ethan's book, and found that Enlightened LLC was incorporated in 1996, and that they leased the location of the Urban Ashram in 1998. The Vikalpa commune that Amaya told Ethan about, that he talked about in his book, was purchased through the LLC in 1997, and sold in 2002 for a tidy profit. I tried researching Yoni under his real name, John Brooks, to see if he really had made his money through smart tech investing. But his name was way too common to net me any quick results, and it was possible he traded through some other entity I didn't even know about.

I tried deep Googling Yoni again, as I had right after I found out about Ethan's death. Ethan's and Amaya's demise didn't seem to get much national traction after that big story I saw on the cover of the *New York Post*. There were a few more follow-up articles in the local papers about the investigation, but because there wasn't any new or salacious information, the updates in the New Mexico press were brief.

I pushed past those pages, and then the pages of home birthing and vagina power results, and did find some commentary about Yoni's spiritual leadership. But none that was nearly as revealing as Ethan's book. All I could find were glowing reviews of experiences at the Urban Ashram and one partial PDF of the pamphlet that Sylvia had me read at the retreat. Someone must have scanned it—incompetently—and put it online. You could barely make out the text on many of the pages, and the last half was cut off.

There had to be deeper research I could do. I would have grimaced out loud in frustration, but I didn't want Katie to hear me and come rushing in, ever eager to help. The last time I had done serious historical research on anything was in law school, but back then I had access to an endless array of academic journals and primary sources.

Like Beth still did.

I sighed deeply and picked up my phone. I knew she was going to give me a world of shit for not calling her over the past week.

She picked up immediately. "Goddammit, Dana. Why haven't you been returning my calls?"

"Well, hi, Bethy. How are you?"

"Seriously, Dana. What happened in New Mexico?" The anger in Beth's voice turned to concern.

I hesitated. I couldn't tell her everything, but I didn't need to totally ice her out, either. "It was actually fine. More than fine; positive. I went to see the sheriff investigating Ethan's case, and I think I really helped him. Also, I got a break from New York and took a bunch of yoga classes. That was really nice for me."

Beth hesitated a moment before saying, "I'm glad. So does this mean you got closure? Can you move on from this part of your life that is so, so over?"

"Well, that's part of what I'm calling you about. Could I

borrow your password for JSTOR and the other primary source sites you use? I just need to figure out a few more things about the guy Ethan followed to New Mexico, Yoni. The sheriff's department out in Bumblefuck is woefully underfunded, and they don't even have the resources to do this kind of search. I really want to help them."

"You're using that voice," Beth said, clearly irritated.

"What voice?" I snapped back.

"The same voice you used when we were kids and you were trying to convince me to trade my Malibu Barbie for a piece of 'magic paper.'"

I remembered that. The paper in question had been a piece of purple construction paper with the words MAGIC PAPER! scrawled on it in metallic silver. Beth had happily traded me the Barbie. Ten minutes later she'd realized the error of her ways, sat down, and cried. "This is different, Beth. This is a real thing," I said quietly.

Beth sighed. "I think they're more similar than you realize. But I'll give you the password, because I love you, and because I know you won't leave me alone until you get it. Just please, please remember to take care of yourself."

I logged into Beth's accounts and started going through the databases of newspapers and magazines. At first everything I found was info I already knew about: Yoni's big move to the Zuni Retreat in New Mexico, which was covered in various yoga and meditation journals; old reviews of the Urban Ashram when it had first opened in New York, in *Time Out*. I found an aside about Yoni in an academic article from the *Journal of the*

Oxford Centre for Buddhist Studies, but it didn't give me any-thing to work with.

Buried on the hundredth page of database results, I found a headline from the *Greenwich Rag,* dated 1982: IS LAMA YONI A MONSTER OR A MESSIAH? The subhead read *The most popular yoga guru below 14th Street has a sinister past.* My heart started racing. There was a short description of the *Greenwich Rag* in the database: it was an underground newspaper that published in downtown New York from 1959 to 1987. I clicked on the headline and read on.

Is Lama Yoni a Monster or a Messiah?
The most popular yoga guru below
14th Street has a sinister past.

BY CLARK LINDSAY

Myra Collins was just your typical art history gradu-ate. After matriculating from Barnard last year with no particular plan except a vague desire to eventually find a husband and have kids, she fell into work as a gallery receptionist. "My life had no purpose," Collins, 23, said. "Until my girlfriend took me to one of Lama Yoni's yoga classes at the Jane Street Ashram." By her own description, Lama Yoni changed her life. She quit her job, changed her name to Luna, traded her trousers for a diaphanous robe, and went to live with Yoni and several other acolytes in a dilapidated brownstone on Jane Street.

The Jane Street Ashram is an exercise in complete

communal living. Every morning its residents—except for Lama Yoni—wake up at first light for a sunrise round of sun salutations. They spend their days studying Lama Yoni's texts, listening to his lectures, and running a macrobiotic restaurant on the parlor floor of the building. That's where I met Ms. Collins, who was my server. "I always thought I wanted to be liberated from the kitchen," Collins said as she set down a plate of millet. "I didn't want to turn into my mother. But Lama Yoni has shown me that nourishing people doesn't have to be a gendered task, and that sustaining life is the greatest gift you can give to the world."

Luna is slender and lanky, with flowing dark hair, bright blue eyes and a creamy complexion. When you learn about Yoni's past, her beauty is not surprising. In fact, all of the denizens of the Jane Street Ashram are dewy and fresh-faced young women. They bow to you when they answer the door and sit in submissive silence when the Lama speaks. Yoni's speech—which I have heard at his open yoga classes—is remarkable in its opacity. He talks in riddle-like parables about barnyard animals, but the underlying message of everything he says is the same: only the strong survive.

Yoni, born John Brooks, knows something about surviving. He came from a broken home in Sheboygan, Wisconsin. His father, an out-of-work mechanic and small-time crook, left the family when the boy was two. His mother worked as a waitress until she remarried a local fire-and-brimstone preacher named Elmer Brooks, who legally adopted John. According to locals who knew

Brooks as a child, Elmer was equal parts cruelty and charisma. "He did not spare the rod," one school chum of John Brooks said. "Johnny would come to school with bruises all the time. Once, he came in with a broken arm. He said he fell down the stairs, but it was right after he was caught stealing penny candies from the store, so everyone knew Elmer had given him the whooping of his life."

But Elmer was also an electrifying preacher, and his sermons drew hundreds of followers. He stood out from the other local preachers, who subscribed to a more forgiving theology. Elmer's sermons were about the evils of fornication and drinking, like everyone else's. But, understanding a primal thirst for bloodlust, he preached about the punishments that would be meted out by a righteous God: lakes of fire and screaming penitents. John listened to these sermons in his Sunday best, and bided his time with petty thievery and other victimless criminal mischief until he was 18 and could hitch a ride out of his hometown.

Like many other Americans seeking a new life, John Brooks went west. It was 1965, and San Francisco's counterculture was just starting to bloom. It's unclear what happened to Brooks over the next two years. There is no record of him getting into trouble with the law, and none of his peers from that time could be found. The next time Brooks surfaced was in 1967. He had a new look—long, flowing robes to match his long, flowing hair and beard—a new name, Aries; and a new occupation: street preacher. He was not alone in this occupation; at that time, you could find a bearded man on any corner in the Haight preaching peace, free love, and brotherhood.

But Brooks stood out in this morass. He had been paying attention to his adoptive father's appeal. He had that same charisma, and he was savvy enough to realize he had to distinguish himself. Like Elmer, he knew his audience. But this audience did not want darkness, they wanted light. And Brooks realized that although they claimed to want freedom from capitalism, they were greedy in their hearts. So he combined peace, free love, and brother-hood with the promise of money. He told his followers that if they tithed him 10 percent of their assets, riches—spiritual and worldly—would come back to them tenfold.

That Brooks is also unusually good-looking explains why his first followers were the beautiful young female runaways who littered San Francisco then. They were drawn to the unthreatening matinee idol face beneath that beard, and he offered them a sense of belonging and protection that they deeply needed. These girls, as young as 14 and 15, left conservative towns and their disapprov-ing daddies behind. But they were still unformed as pan-cake batter, and so they were the perfect target for Brooks.

"Aries went after the girls who were bent, but not com-pletely messed up," one ex-follower of Brooks, whom I will call Rumi, told me. "Fully damaged was too crazy, too un-predictable. But bent was easier to control." In just a few short months, Brooks had a pack of young women who sat at his feet and hung on all his words. He convinced them that their major contribution to his community would be to bring more people into his fold. And the best asset they had to offer the universe was their nubile sexuality. Brooks sent them out on "fishing" missions, using the pretty girls as bait to draw in male followers.

Rumi was among the first men caught on the fishing missions. "I went for the girls at first," Rumi said, "but I was really jiving on what Aries was preaching. I was a little lost myself. I just got out of the army and I didn't know what I was going to do. This gave me something to do." The girls kept bringing in more clueless men, fellow lost souls who were bumming around San Francisco doing odd jobs. By 1972, the Aries faithful had swelled to nearly 1,000 people, some more devout than others. Aries called them his children.

Aries' Children would have gone on living in San Francisco indefinitely, but that year one of Brooks's first teen followers ran back to her family in Orange County. She told her parents just the barest details of what happened with Aries, and her father marched up to the San Francisco Police Department and filed statutory rape charges against John Brooks. Instead of facing the charges, Brooks, who by this time had raised nearly $500,000 tithing his followers, bought a parcel of land in Mendocino and took 100 of his most fervent acolytes with him.

After a few years in isolation at the Mendocino compound, Aries began to get paranoid. "By the midseventies he was taking a lot of speed," said Rumi, who was in Brooks's inner circle by then. "And he started to have visions. They were always about us being persecuted for our beliefs. That's when he formed the watch." The watch was a group of the fittest men among Aries' Children. They would patrol the borders of the compound, making sure none of the other young women ran back to their families to report on Aries.

Rumi is ashamed that he participated in the watch. "What can I say?" he said. "I was swept up in the potential of the movement. I was a true believer." Until he wasn't. One night when he was alone on duty, he caught a young female follower trying to leave the compound.

"This girl was always so devoted to Aries. She was one of his favorites. He loved blondes. So I was surprised to see her face when I shined a flashlight on it," Rumi told me. The girl told him that while her sex with Aries and the other men she fished had started out consensually, she didn't want to do it anymore. "She was so young still," Rumi said wistfully. "She realized she didn't feel good giving her body up like that." And that's when Aries turned on her. "She said he raped her, and told her that unless she wanted to become an untouchable in the community, she would keep having sex with him."

The girl was terrified. After hearing her story, Rumi let her go. Though he denied seeing her the next morning, he was nevertheless punished because he was the one on watch when she got away. Aries wouldn't allow anyone to look Rumi in the eye until the new moon appeared—nearly a month's time. He never found out if he would have eventually been forgiven; he slipped out one night himself.

The young woman pressed rape charges in Mendocino

County in October 1978. Because of the nature of the crime against her, we will not use her name in this piece. According to another ex-follower of Yoni's, this woman also carried a secret with her when she left: she was pregnant with Yoni's child. The woman could not be found for comment.

By December of 1978, the Mendocino compound had disbanded, and Aries disappeared. After a lost six months, he resurfaced as Lama Yoni in New York in the summer of 1979.

I called John Brooks several times to comment on this story. Through his lawyer, David Rappaport, he declined to speak to me. Rappaport offered the following statement: "Lama Yoni refuses to dignify the ravings of a disgruntled former friend with any response. The allegations of this 'Rumi' person are risible and borderline libelous. If you print any of this, you will be hearing from my office presently."

Curious things started happening to me after I received that first message from Yoni's lawyer. I started getting mysterious phone calls at home and at the office, in which no one would be at the other end of the line. I found a stack of *American Funeral* magazines on the stoop outside my apartment. Finally, my daughter's kitten, Mr. Whiskers, disappeared from our fire escape. That's when I started to get a little scared. Every time I left my office on reporting business, I felt like someone was following me. My wife was terrified, and for a moment I considered spiking the story.

But I couldn't sit back and let anyone else's daughter

follow John Brooks without knowing the truth. I asked Myra Collins what her parents thought about her life choices. "My parents are no longer a part of my natural universe," Myra said. "They had too many inane questions about my life. And Lama Yoni says inane questions are for inane people who don't understand the importance of the work we do." I tried to ask her what kinds of questions her family had, but she told me she had to attend to another customer. She bowed deeply to me and walked away.

When I finished reading I felt like I was covered in a film of grease. I stood up from my desk and started pacing. How had Yoni been able to start a popular ashram out in the open after something like this had been published? Had he been able to bury the coverage? I supposed it was a lot easier to run away from your past before everything was published on the Internet.

Yoni was also incredibly savvy. He seemed to understand that yoga was a trend that swept the country in the 1990s and 2000s, and he had emphasized the yoga and health food, while keeping the underage women and secret sex games as a clandestine bonus. Lots of people went to his studio and to his retreat and just did yoga, as I did. While some more devoted yoga practitioners, like Sylvia and her friends, also read Yoni's pamphlets, it sounded like they weren't privy to anything like what Ethan had described in his book, or like what was described in the *Greenwich Rag*. But at least what was going on with Ethan and Amaya was basically consensual. What Yoni—or Aries, I guess—did in the '60s and '70s was unconscionable.

I sat back down again. My mind worked methodically, and I needed to finish my timeline before I did anything else. I filled in everything I learned from the *Greenwich Rag* article, which covered the '70s and '80s. Then I jumped back to the '00s—when Ethan left me, and the Zuni Retreat opened. I looked up all of Ethan and Amaya's YouTube videos to see when they had been posted. The last one was from a year ago. I put that date down, then I added the years Ethan had been teaching at Zuni. I thought about the "dangerous things" Sylvia's friend Raina said Ethan and Amaya were allegedly doing at the time, and wished I had been more aggressive in questioning Sylvia and her pals.

The last thing I put down before Ethan's and Amaya's deaths was Ethan's visit to his dad, which the sheriff had said happened just a few months before his death. I looked at the evidence gathered up before me in my neat, even handwriting, and suddenly it became clear to me: I needed to talk to Ray.

"Get me Ray Powell of Livingston, Montana, on the phone," I said to Katie over the intercom about an hour later.

"Can I tell him what this is regarding?"

"No!" I snapped, and then felt guilty. "Sorry, no. You don't need to. He'll know what it's about when you tell him that it's Dana Morrison on the phone."

"Sure thing," she said calmly, putting me on hold. I checked my e-mail six times. I went back and skimmed the *Greenwich Rag* article again. I looked at my phone to see if any messages had popped up from Beth. I tried to occupy the interminable anxious space until I heard Katie's voice. "I've got Mr. Powell for you," she said confidently. She really was a very good assistant.

"Yello?" Ray said. He sounded just like he always did. That he hadn't changed when everything else around me had was a relief.

"Ray? It's Dana. I'm so, so sorry about Ethan."

There was a long silence on the other end. I was about to ask if Ray was still there when he said, "It's a very sad thing."

"It's awful, and I'm sorry it's the reason I'm calling you after all these years." I wanted to stumble directly into everything I had discovered, but I knew I had to hold back. I waited for some signal that Ray was ready to continue the conversation, but when all I heard on the other end was several moments of even breathing, I just started talking. "I went out to New Mexico and talked to Sheriff Lewis."

"Is that right?" Ray sounded surprised.

"Yes. I didn't know where Ethan went after he left me. The sheriff said doing a face-to-face interview was ideal, and I was curious to see where Ethan had spent his time, so I booked a stay at the Zuni Retreat. The sheriff also said, well, he said that he thought it might be a murder-suicide, and I just didn't believe that." I tried to say the second part carefully.

"I don't believe that, either," Ray said firmly.

"You talked to Sheriff Lewis, right?"

"Correct."

"And you told him that Ethan visited you a few months before he died?"

"Correct," Ray repeated, like I was a census taker bothering him with a boring questionnaire.

"What was that like?" I asked.

"It was all right."

Clearly I wasn't going to get anywhere asking open-ended, sensitive questions. "Did he tell you anything about his life there?" I pressed. "About Yoni? About why he left?"

Ray didn't say anything for so long I thought he had hung up. Finally he said, "I told the sheriff everything I know. And honey, it's not any of your business."

I tried to gently cajole Ray into telling me something, anything else about what he knew. But he refused. He couldn't get why I wanted to get involved. "I guess I understand why you went down to New Mexico," he said after we had been chatting for a little while, "but I don't see why you'd want to stay at the retreat."

"Well . . ." I considered lying, because I knew it would sound nuts to him, but I figured we weren't going to get anywhere unless he knew the whole truth. "The sheriff said that he was having trouble getting a warrant to search the Zuni property, and I thought that I could go to the retreat and find something that might be helpful to the case."

"That ain't right, Dana," Ray said sternly. "It's not your job. You shouldn't be getting involved in this."

"Why not?" I said, a little imperious. I had slid into my tough-gal work persona without thinking; he didn't have the right to tell me what to do. Besides, I had spent so many years after Ethan left feeling powerless and clueless about what had happened. I finally had some agency and I wasn't about to give it up.

"You just shouldn't!" Ray snapped.

"Well, I also wanted to find out more about Ethan, what he was like after he left me. Can you tell me anything about that?"

I kept trying to ask the question in different ways, but Ray wouldn't reveal more. Finally, to get me off the phone, he agreed to let me come out to Montana and talk to him in person. I am very, very good at arguing, and I felt eerily confident that I would be able to break Ray's resolve. I could hear a little falter in his tone and just knew he wanted to tell me the truth. I don't know if it was spending too much time in the company of the spiritual and faux-spiritual, but this trip seemed fated.

I was so wrapped up in convincing Ray to talk to me that it wasn't until I got off the phone that I remembered I was still at work, and that I had just come back from a vacation that had been only grudgingly approved. I tallied up all the vacation days I'd saved and thought about the potential excuses I could give Phil that would force him to let me go without censure. Thinking about that conversation made my heart start to race. He was going to be so angry.

I took a deep breath. Maybe there was a way to do this without losing my job or having Phil go nuclear. I took out my employee handbook from the bottom drawer, where it had been languishing since I started at the firm seven years ago. In the back section where they had the information about maternity leave, there was one short sentence tucked under the paternity leave policy (five measly business days) that could be my savior: "Employees that have worked for the firm for five uninterrupted years are entitled to an unpaid sabbatical of six weeks."

Unsurprisingly, no one had ever mentioned this benefit to me. I knew how big law firms like mine worked: they kept

these things on the books to pretend that they catered to work/
life balance but never actually spoke of them. I bet none of my
workaholic peers had ever availed themselves of the sabbatical
even if they knew it existed, because taking a leave meant not
making partner. There was only one woman who was a partner
anyway, and she famously took three weeks of maternity leave,
even though we were supposedly entitled to four paid months.
Word around the office was that she answered her cell phone as
they were wheeling her into the OR for her C-section.

I took out a yellow highlighter, marked the paper, and left
my office to go talk to Phil.

Phil thought I was, quote, "out of my fucking mind" when I an-
nounced that I was taking the six-week sabbatical, which I had
earned. As I suspected, he'd never heard anything about the
sabbatical before, and his mouth hung open as I pointed out
the passage in our employee handbook. He was, for a moment,
at a loss for words, reduced to a very controlled head shake.
When he regained his voice, he sputtered, "You will never make
partner this way, ever. And you were so close." I shrugged. A
month ago, making partner was one of my top-five reasons for
dragging my carcass out of bed every day. But now, it seemed
irrelevant. "I need this time," I told him, "and I'll worry about
making partner later." I knew, as I spoke to Phil, that making
this choice not only ruined my chances for a partnership but
also put my current job in jeopardy. And I was a little surprised
to discover that I didn't care.

I was able to get a flight to Bozeman the next day. As I made
the arrangements, I felt more secure in my hasty plan. I packed

clothing for the massive weather changes that happen in late spring in Montana: rain gear, a big puffy jacket, long underwear, shorts, and T-shirts. I packed Ethan's book, my legal pad outline, a tape recorder, and several pens.

I wasn't just getting physically ready. I was also getting emotionally ready. As much as I had convinced myself that I had moved on from Ethan's departure years ago, I was starting to realize I hadn't. I was still living in the apartment we used to share. I wasn't dating. I hadn't even made any new friends. I simply bludgeoned myself with work and called it a life. Ethan's death, no matter how searing, had woken me up. And my experience at the retreat had nudged something else awake, too. I wasn't yet sure what that was.

Ray was waiting for me at the empty airport. He looked exactly like he had the last time I saw him—he was possibly even wearing the same shirt, though I think all plaid shirts look the same. This was a point of contention between Ethan and me during better times. He maintained that there were many, many different kinds of plaid. "This shirt has a tartan print, and this one is a tattersall," he'd say, faux-serious, picking up two blue shirts that looked identical. I smiled at the memory.

"Hi, Dana, good to see you," Ray said. I searched his face for evidence of grief but found none. Then again, his face was always drawn and slightly dour, with crow's-feet that extended downward. It occurred to me for the first time that perhaps he'd been grieving since Rosemary died.

"Hi, Ray, thanks for letting me come."

Ray took my suitcase wordlessly. I used to be put off by his old-fashioned cowboy chivalry, which I saw as an affront to modern feminism, but now I appreciated it. We drove the seventy-five minutes back to his remote log cabin mostly in silence. I looked out the window at the mountains. The immensity of the landscape was a relief, the opposite of New York's claustrophobic streets and buildings.

Halfway home Ray turned on the radio. I remembered from my last visit to Montana that for large stretches of driving the only stations you can get are Christian radio and NPR, reflecting the divided culture of the state. Ray turned the dial to a Christian station that also played old country music, and filled the silent car with Gene Autry's sweet voice.

It was dinnertime when we drove up the dirt road to Ray's cabin. He brought my suitcase into the living room and went into the kitchen.

"Do you need help with dinner?" I asked as I watched Ray take out a cutting board and a sharp knife.

"No, honey. You've had a long trip. You should take a load off."

"You won't even let me set the table or something?" I asked.

Ray shook his head. "Nope. Get outta here."

I went out onto the back deck wrapped in a blanket I found lying on a couch. The sun was already hidden behind the mountains, and I shivered listening to the rustling leaves that surrounded me. I could smell the savory scent of whatever Ray was cooking. We always stayed with Ethan's aunt Mary when we'd come out to Montana for holidays. She had a big house, and she loved to decorate and cook and fuss over us. She liked fussing over Ray, especially. She didn't know what else to do about Ray's grief, so she stuffed him with food and took him to church.

So I was shocked that Ray knew how to cook something that smelled so good. Ethan always made it sound like he had lived like a feral child after Rosemary died.

"Dinner," Ray called. Inside, the table was set simply but elegantly, with place mats and decent silverware. Ray even had a handmade ceramic vase filled with dried flowers as a centerpiece. There was a plump chicken breast on my plate, with a wild rice salad next to it. I took a bite and was pleasantly surprised. "Wow, Ray, this is delicious! Where did you learn to cook like this?"

"My friend Linda taught me some things," Ray said, shifting awkwardly in his seat.

"Is Linda your girlfriend?" I couldn't stop myself from asking.

"You could say that," Ray said even more uncomfortably.

Seeing how ill at ease Ray was made it hard to figure out what to say next. We ate without speaking for a while. I could hear both of us chewing and swallowing. I drank the water that was set out for me and almost choked on it. I was sputtering and wiping my mouth when Ray finally broke the quiet.

"I know you want to hear more about Ethan, but there's not much to say." He looked so sad, I wanted to break through the discomfort between us, but I didn't know how.

"Can you tell me what little there is to say?" I said. "I'm just trying to figure out how Ethan became . . . whatever this thing is he became."

Ray looked down at his lap. Realizing that my straightforward questioning was putting him off, I tried a softer tactic. It was manipulative to tear at Ray's heartstrings, but I didn't care.

"I haven't been the same since he left, Ray. And getting what-ever scraps of Ethan I can at this point will really help me move on. I know you know what this is like, when a spouse is gone."

Ray pushed his rice around on his plate and didn't say any-thing. But I could tell he was taking me seriously. I tried to concentrate on my dinner to give him time to think, but I could barely get down a few bites.

"Let me sleep on it," he said at last. He got up from the table and dumped the rest of his dinner in the garbage. Then he washed the plate and put it on a pristine dish rack. "The bed's made for you in Ethan's room. I hope it's comfy." With that he walked to the back of the cabin. He was in good shape, but the way he shuffled across the floor made him seem like an old, broken man. A moment later I could hear his bedroom door shutting and locking.

Though it was early evening, I suddenly felt exhausted from the travel. After washing my own plate and adding it to the dish rack next to Ray's, I opened the door to Ethan's room slowly, as if a bogeyman might leap out at me. Instead I saw a cat that had presumably been asleep on Ethan's twin bed and was rustled awake by the door. She looked at me, pissed off, and scurried out of the room as soon as I turned on the light.

Ethan's room was a cultural tomb, permanently fixed in the nineties when he left for college. Posters of the Pixies and Nir-vana were hung on the walls, Kurt Cobain vamping in wom-en's cat's-eye sunglasses. The desk was strewn with ancient totems—bobblehead dolls of Minnesota Vikings and a collage of different photos cut from *Spin* magazine. A dun-colored plaid flannel bedspread that I remembered from previous visits still covered the bed. At first glance, the only evidence that Ethan had been there recently was a small dream catcher tacked above the bed.

I started snooping through Ethan's things. It felt like an intimate privacy violation—a teenager's bedroom is so sacrosanct. I had to keep reminding myself that this teenager didn't exist anymore, and that it was necessary prying. His shelves contained all his old books: guides to the indigenous species of Yellowstone, hiking trails of Glacier, and manly fiction of the Hemingway variety. I searched the titles for anything New Age or yogic, anything he could have left when he was last here, but the closest I came was a decaying paperback of *Linda Goodman's Sun Signs* from 1972. When I opened it up part of the cover came off in my hand. Ethan's mother had written her name on the title page. It was the seventies, after all—everyone, even my straitlaced, skeptical mother, had a copy of *Sun Signs*.

I turned to Ethan's desk. One drawer contained all his high school mementos: writing awards, National Merit Scholarship recognition, and a track and field participation certificate. Another contained his college diploma, still in its puffy frame, and a friendship bracelet I had made for him in a regressive spurt of boredom one summer. I picked up the bracelet and touched its frayed tassels. I felt tears start to collect in the corners of my eyes.

In another drawer I found outtakes of our wedding photos, which I couldn't bear to look at. Underneath those was a slender book with a red and gold illustration of an unfamiliar deity on the cover. The title, in gold lettering, was *Aztec Cosmology: An Exploration of the Ancient Rituals*. I grabbed the book and opened it. It had a LIVINGSTON PUBLIC LIBRARY stamp on the inner flap, and a date that would have corresponded with Ethan's visit. I thumbed through its crisp pages—apparently the denizens of southern Montana did not have much interest in Aztec religion, as the book felt new. I found a bookmark left in a chapter about the butterfly goddess, Itzpapalotl. I skimmed a page and it read like one of Yoni's goofy parables—the goddess with her sharp obsidian wings and her despotic leadership over a mystical world filled with birds. I put it aside and kept pawing around.

Finally I found a drawer with Ethan's childhood relics. I picked up a ceramic plaque with Ethan's handprint, his name, and the date—October 6, 1983—on it. He would have been five then, and I figured his name was written in his mother's fine cursive hand. Ethan had told me that Rosemary was very creative. She was always doing art projects with Ethan and Travis that involved pieces of fabric picked up at the Bozeman Craftacular scrap bin and lots of pipe cleaners.

At the bottom of the drawer I found a familiar-looking dark-blue necklace with an asterisk on it. It had a surprisingly hefty feel, like a paperweight that had been repurposed. I rubbed the asterisk with my thumb, as if feeling the etching would reveal something to me. Had I seen this before when Ethan and I had visited Ray together? Was it one of the trinkets sold at Montana flea markets? Had the Grateful Dead followers in my dorm at college worn it?

Oh, right, I remembered where I had seen it: on Lo, at the retreat. Maybe it was something they gave all the staffers at Zuni, and Ethan had brought it with him when he visited Ray a few months ago. I put everything back in the drawers except the necklace, which I placed on a side table next to the bed.

I lay down on Ethan's narrow bed and pulled his flannel cover up around my ears. There was no top sheet: typical of a house full of motherless men. Encased in warmth and dark, surrounded by the absolute silence of the country, I felt like I was in a sarcophagus. I didn't feel like I was dead, no, not exactly. I felt like I was preparing for my afterlife.

My dream that night took place in an M. C. Escher version of Ethan's room. When I entered his closet, there was a staircase descending down and down and down into a pile of moth-eaten flannels. I was searching for something underneath the flannel, and I threw the plaid this way and that until I pulled out that blue necklace. I brought it up to my face to examine it closely, and it exploded. The explosion woke me up with a start.

I sat up in bed and looked over at the necklace, which was still in one piece. That was when I remembered where else I had seen that blue asterisk. On Rosemary. She was wearing it in that photograph of her with baby Ethan in her tummy that he kept at our apartment, the one I couldn't bear to throw away. I felt dizzy, like I was back in the dream, back on that twisty staircase. I lay back down on the pillows.

I heard Ray banging around in the kitchen. I was light-headed when I got up, and I felt like I was floating down the hallway, like my body was still observing dream logic and any minute the floor might give way. I went to find Ray with the necklace in my hand.

When I entered the kitchen, Ray's back was to me. He was

making coffee, pouring the water into the well. I watched him put the carafe back in its place before turning around to look at me. His eye went to the necklace in my hand, and he sighed. He turned back around and pushed the On button on the coffeemaker. Then he walked over to the kitchen table, pulled out a chair, and said, "Take a seat. We should talk."

Ray

I told the sheriff about all this already. About Rosemary's involvement.

Why didn't I tell you? Because it was none of your goddamn business. You're not solving the crime. You're not putting anyone in jail. I promised Rosemary a long time ago that we'd put her past behind us.

But since you already know what you know, I guess I'll start at San Francisco. That's where I met Rosie. After my second tour in Vietnam was over, I told my CO I would re-up, but only if I could get stationed in California. I grew up in King City, a sleepy, dusty farm town a ways outside San Francisco. My dad had passed while I was in high school, and my mom wasn't in the best health, so I wanted to be closer to her.

I got stationed in the Presidio when the war was winding down, probably '75 or '76. It was like living in a dream. King City was just a few hours south, but I grew up so poor I'd only been to San Francisco once, when I was about eleven. All I remembered was the wind whipping off the Pacific. King City was so stifling in every way—I was trapped by the stink of farm animals and the lack of opportunity for me there. I wanted to live in that clean, eucalyptus-scented air.

I was posted with the Military Intelligence Group, and my office overlooked the Golden Gate Bridge. Sometimes I would just stare at it for hours, watching the fog roll in and out. At night, I'd be lulled to sleep by the repetitive sounds of the foghorns. Those were the first good nights of sleep I'd had since I joined the army right out of high school in 1970.

No, the war wasn't so hard on me. It wasn't a goddamn tea party, but it was my job to serve my country and I did it to the best of my ability. I was not affected in any major way, at least not compared to some of the other guys I came across. I saw some of the worst cases coming into Letterman hospital in the Presidio. Guys so mentally messed up I didn't think they'd ever get back to regular society. They'd pass through the Presidio and then end up on the streets of San Francisco, where they were vulnerable to guys like John Brooks.

What? Hold your horses, I'll come back to him in a minute.

I did love being in San Francisco, but I was a little lonely. A lot of guys on the base were married and starting families. There was one neighborhood nicknamed "Diaper Gulch" because there were so many kiddos running around. I had a few girlfriends here and there, one who worked with me at the base. But nothing serious, even though I was ready to settle down and really start my life.

Most evenings, I would go over to a bar right outside the Presidio gates with some of my buddies. The bar was called Yacht Harbor. It had an old maritime theme and was festooned with rusting anchors and musty circular life buoys. There was even some nasty old netting here and there. Don't get me wrong: despite the nice name, the place was a dump. But we were comfortable there. Most of the gals I met there were employed by the base in some way, usually by the hospital. Which is why when I saw Rosie, it was such a shock.

Rosie was wearing a hippie-kinda dress, a dirty purple thing that nearly dragged on the floor because she was so petite. She had a single long blond braid that snaked around her left shoulder. It sounds silly to say, but she glowed. Her skin just had this freshness and newness. It wasn't like anything I'd ever seen before. And her face was just so beautiful, and she looked so scared.

I wasn't usually very good at talking to women. My buddies had to push me into it, and I'd only let them after a coupla beers. But I was just drawn to Rosie. She sat down at a table near the front of the bar, and I figured some guy was going to sit down with her any minute. But no one did. And the one big thing that being in Vietnam had taught me was to seize opportunity, because you don't know when your time is up. So I took a shot and went over to say hello.

I never believed in it before, but it was love at first sight. From the second Rosie looked up at me and said, "Oh, hello," I was smitten. She was so sweet and gentle. I thought she might want to leave, because she kept looking out the front window of the bar. But she stayed and talked to me for a very long time.

What did we talk about? Oh, a lot of things. She talked about a dog she'd had as a kid, named Chief, and how she missed him.

We talked about Jefferson Starship. I don't know. It wasn't so much what was said as how it was said. We just had a bond from the get-go.

Eventually it was getting late and I had to get up at zero six hundred. So I asked Rosie for her number, and she clammed up. "I don't have a phone right now," she said.

"Well, can I come by your place and take you out sometime?" I asked. This was much bolder than I usually was, but I just couldn't let her vanish into the fog.

She hemmed and hawed in that sweet, high voice of hers, and eventually admitted that she had no place to stay.

I told her she had to stay with me that night. At first she refused, she said she was perfectly happy sleeping in Golden Gate Park. But I was not about to let her spend another night homeless. I snuck her into my room on base, just for the evening. I let her take the bed while I slept on the floor. To this day I can still sleep anywhere, in any situation. Ethan used to make fun of me because I would fall asleep standing up at his orchestra recitals in high school.

C'mon now, you can't get that run-over-puppy look every time I mention the boy's name. That was meant to be funny.

I couldn't keep Rosie hidden in my room, so the next morning I asked a civilian gal working at Letterman if Rosie could stay with her for a little bit, just so she could get on her feet again. She had a sweet little apartment in Cow Hollow and she said sure, she had a Murphy bed that Rosie could sleep on. I went over there every night to take Rosie out. We ate Chinese food in Chinatown and Mexican food in the Mission, and went to North Beach to hear music. I'd try—gently—to get Rosie to tell me what brought her to San Francisco, why she didn't have any place to stay. But whenever I tried to pry, her mouth would crumple like Charlie Brown's. So I backed off. I was happy just to spend time with her. There was a lightness about her, a singular joy. I can be a real grump, and I was the same as a young man. Rosie made me laugh at myself.

After two weeks, my friend in Cow Hollow said Rosie had to find her own place. Her sister was supposed to visit, and I guessed Rosie was cramping her style. Rosie still hadn't been able to find a job, and I didn't have any money to pay for her to get her own place. When I told Rosie we'd have to come up with another option for her, she was trying to fight back tears. "I have no options," she kept repeating, getting more frantic each time she said it.

I couldn't stand to see her feel so trapped, so without really thinking about it, I got down on my knee and said, "You do have options. You could marry me and come live on the base."

She laughed it off at first, but I realized I was dead serious, and told her so. I was head over heels for her. She said she was in love with me, too, but she didn't want to rush into anything. "I spent a lot of time not being my own person," she explained. I asked her what she meant, and she shook her head and went silent.

"How's this," I said. "We'll get married, just so you have a place to stay. We'll get married housing, which is much nicer than the sorry little room I've got now. You don't have to stay any longer than you want. You don't even have to sleep in the same bed with me. I'll sleep on the couch. Hell, I'll sleep on the floor, like the first night."

It took a few hours of pleading, but finally Rosie agreed. We made plans to get married that weekend at the Presidio Post Chapel. I know it sounds hasty, but you have to understand it was a different time. Lots of people got hitched after knowing each other for only a little while. I had a buddy in Vietnam who married a local woman after spending a single night with her.

To celebrate our engagement, I got us a hotel room where Rosie could stay the night, though I had to be back on the base before my morning call. We made love for the first time that night, and when we were lying there after, Rosie started to cry. She finally broke down and told me where she'd been for the past several years. It wasn't at all what I had expected.

Rosie grew up in Sacramento. Her mom and dad were Catholics, but not the fuzzy, gregarious kind. They were conservative in every possible way, especially sexually. When Rosie turned twelve, her mother started measuring her skirts before she left the house. If they were more than a quarter inch above the knee, she was sent upstairs to change. She was not allowed to wear modern bathing suits, even at the beach. Her mother found a 1920s bathing costume at a thrift store and made her wear it for years. Rosie ultimately burned it in a trash can on her way to school.

Rosie graduated from high school in 1970 and left home the next day. She had one friend who had moved to San Francisco, a gal named Sandra, who promised to give Rosie a place to stay if she could just get a bus ride out there. Sandra had written Rosie a letter inviting her to come on down to visit. Said she was living with some guy in the Haight who she said had "blown her

mind." After eighteen years in that household, Rosie was ready
to get her mind blown.

She showed up at 715 Haight Street with her little Samsonite
suitcase that matched the white shift dress she had picked out
for her first day as a grown-up. I remember the address even
now, because Rosie took me by once, to show me her past. It
was an unremarkable Victorian, slightly shabby like the other
buildings in the neighborhood, and painted a dark green. Rosie
remembered the dress she was wearing that day vividly because she had spent so much time fantasizing about leaving
Sacramento, and because she felt so silly when Sandra opened
the door.

Sandra had gone fully counterculture. She had grown her hair
long and stopped shaving her armpits. As Rosie remembered it,
Sandra basically answered the door wearing underwear. Rosie
almost turned around and ran back to Sacramento, but she had
put so much stock in this moment that she pressed on into the
house, determined to adjust to her new surroundings.

That very first night, not wanting to ruffle any feathers,
she smoked pot with Sandra and her man. The guy seemed
really interested in her thoughts and feelings, much more
so than any other guy—or, hell, anyone else at all—had ever
been before. They talked about philosophy and religion, and
how her parents' conservative values were inimical to spiritual progress. He made her feel like the light of the world was
shining on her face. Rosie was nervous that Sandra would
be upset that her boyfriend was paying so much attention to
Rosie, but when she glanced at her friend, Sandra nodded

encouragingly. Sandra's boyfriend even kissed Rosie, and Sandra just watched, smiling, as it happened.

Yes, it does sound creepy. But you have to understand that Rosie was real naive when it happened. She'd barely left her parents' house before. I remember she told me, "I thought this was just how people in the city behaved." She was also a teenager hell-bent on rebelling. So the last thing she wanted to do was embarrass herself in front of her old friend by making a fuss.

A few men and a bunch of women lived at 715 Haight, and Sandra's boyfriend was their leader. Rosie realized this pretty quick. The women all hung on his every word, and the men acted like they were his bodyguards. You know where this is going. The guy's name was Aries at the time. I don't think Rosie knew his real name was John Brooks until after things went sour and she filed those charges.

At first, being part of the communal living experiment at 715 Haight was incredibly freeing for Rosie. She bought into what Aries was selling, hook, line, and sinker. He was big on free love, which wasn't that original back at that time in San Francisco. But Aries was building something bigger than most of the street preachers back then. He claimed he was starting a full-blown utopian society, which he was calling Aries' Children.

But Aries couldn't create his new utopia with the few resources he had. So he convinced all new followers that they needed to sell their worldly possessions and start fresh. Conveniently, he said that the commune needed the funds from their personal yard sales to keep the community going. For the greater good and all.

One of the ways he got those followers was by sending pretty young girls like Rosie and Sandra out on fishing missions for men. They'd seduce guys and bring them back to the commune.

What? I'm not going to tell you what kind of sex! Was it "weird"? Well, I reckon it was. I didn't really want to know the gory details about that one, Dana, as I'm sure you can imagine.

I don't want you to think that Rosie was a total fool, though. She said she loved the fishing at first. It made her feel in control of her body and her life for the first time. Of course, she wasn't really in control. Aries was the one pulling the strings of the whole operation. He even gave her a new name. He gave everyone new names, because he said that being part of the utopia meant shedding not just your possessions but also your old identity.

Rosie embraced the illusion fully. To Aries's credit, he was a very successful community builder. His acolytes were varying degrees of faithful—the ones who lived at the commune, like Rosie, were the most devoted—but a thousand people had given Aries some kind of money, which earned them official status as Aries's children. Their official status was marked by that necklace you found, the blue one with the asterisk.

By this time Rosie had become a true believer. She thought they were building an important new society, a respite from the judgmental world of her parents and Richard Nixon. So Rosie followed Aries without question when he said they had to leave San Francisco in the middle of the night for some land he had purchased in Mendocino County. He said that the San Francisco police were persecuting them because of their unconventional beliefs, and that the only way to continue their beautiful, intentional community was to leave the city.

Even though he had so many other young women, Rosie was always one of Aries's favorites. That's why she helped Aries pack the most faithful hundred or so into a series of vans and trucks one unsettlingly hot evening. She didn't know it then, but that was when things would start to go downhill for her.

Rosie said the land in Mendocino was the most beautiful she'd ever seen. It was surrounded by redwoods, and near enough to the Russian River that in certain spots you could hear a faint rushing sound. Aries had a bunch of locals make huts for his followers to live in. They were basic dwellings, but they suited Rosie just fine.

In the beginning, Aries' Children grew vegetables to eat and weed to smoke and raised their own chickens so they would have as little contact with the outside world as possible. That's how Aries liked it. It was idyllic for a month or two, but after that Rosie started hearing scary rumors about how Aries was treating some of his less favored followers.

So many believers had been left behind in the initial move to Mendocino, and a lot of them wanted back in. But there were whispers that these lesser children were allowed to join the Mendocino group only after they'd proven themselves to be devoted to Aries through a series of increasingly sadistic tests. One of the stories Rosie heard was that Aries made some of his children brand themselves with a special symbol they weren't allowed to show anybody else. She also heard stories about followers walking over burning bricks, and others having to stand alone in a room for a full day. If Aries caught them sitting or, God forbid, lying down, they would be banned from the Mendocino compound for life.

At first Rosie didn't believe that those stories were true. Sandra told her that anyone who would tell a story like that about Aries was probably a narc sent by the San Francisco police to infiltrate the community. I know, it sounds nutty to me, too. You have to understand how sheltered Rosie was. She had gone right from her parents' home to Aries's commune, and she was still in her early twenties then. She didn't have enough experience out in the big world to be skeptical of an explanation like that.

Later, after she left the commune, Rosie reconsidered those stories. Aries's sermons had broadened to include parables about turncoats and deserters. She told me one that had stuck with her because it scared the bejesus out of her. She started getting so upset when she repeated this sermon that it stuck with me, too, all these years.

This parable was about a sacred monkey who lived in the mountains. Both humans and gods revered this particular kind of monkey. The monkey dutifully brought food back to his father for years, until he started getting ideas. "Why am I serving my father when I could strike out on my own?" the monkey wondered. He started hiding extra food at the bottom of a mountain, planning to make his own way when he had built up a big enough store. On his way to hide more fruit one day, a lightning bolt struck that monkey down. It left a burn mark in the side of the mountain, reminding others not to follow in his path.

After Aries told that story, he started up his night patrol. Aries told the rest of the followers that the patrol was there to keep them all safe from disruptive outside forces, but really what the patrol did was make sure no one ever left the compound. The few people who managed to get away and into nearby towns were always discovered and brought back. They seemed resigned when they returned, as if they'd assumed this would happen.

Despite the night patrol, Aries was also getting really paranoid about people leaving the fold, becoming "unfaithfuls," as he called them. Rosie suspected he was taking a lot of speed, because she'd seen a few speed freak-outs at the commune before and Aries was displaying all the signs: he wasn't sleeping, he was alternately grandiose and depressed, and his pupils had receded to little pinpricks of black in his cloudy eyes. But she never fully believed the stories about Aries's violent side until she saw it for herself.

Why? Well, I think Rosie didn't want to believe them. She had given all of her adult life to Aries, and it was humiliating to admit she had made a mistake. Rosie also didn't know what she would do if she left Aries. She wasn't about to go back home to Sacramento, and that seemed like the only option, in her blindered view.

But one night Aries called her into his personal cabin, which was much grander than the humble cabins everyone else in the commune shared. It had electricity, for starters, but it also had a real king-size bed, while everyone else slept in cots or hammocks.

Yes, Dana, Rosie was still having sex with Aries. Jesus. Like I said, free love was a major part of the commune's foundational ethos. When Rosie started to think about it, she realized the love was freely flowing only in one direction: toward Aries. Because she was one of his favorites, when Aries started getting more paranoid, he barred Rosie from sleeping with other followers. He told her that her energy was getting too depleted from all that connection, and that saving herself for him was for her own good.

That night, though, Rosie just wasn't in the mood. She was tired and had pulled a muscle in her back in the vegetable garden that day. She had never turned Aries down for sex before, but that night she looked around and saw Aries's amenities, and she thought about how he was going to sleep on a nice, comfortable mattress while her back injury worsened in her lumpy cot, and she just wasn't in the mood to give him anything else.

When she said no to him, Rosie said he got a look on his face that was unlike anything she'd ever seen. She sensed a pressure drop in the room, and got up to try to bolt to the door. But Aries grabbed her by her braid and yanked her to him. She tried to resist, but he smashed her head against the floor until she lay still. She thought she might not survive if she tried to fight back.

No, no. Jesus, Dana. I don't need a hug. Just give me a second to collect myself. It still makes me so angry I could spit.

The only upside to the assault was that Aries's spell on Rosie was broken. She knew she had to get out of there, and she spent a few weeks plotting her escape. She observed the night patrol schedule and figured out which nights a certain guy was working. She calculated that he could be persuaded to let her go, and she was right. Once she was past the borders of the commune, she ran through the woods all night until she reached a highway. She hitchhiked back to San Francisco the next day and set up camp in Golden Gate Park. I met her a few weeks after her return.

I guess Rosie's escape wasn't the only upside to the assault. There was one more blessing: Ethan.

Rosie suspected she was pregnant when she left Mendocino. The pregnancy kept her from returning. Leaving was so hard— she had only a high school education and she had no way to support herself. Those first nights when she was shivering in Golden Gate Park, she had moments when she thought things would be easier if she just went back to the life she'd known with Aries. But she couldn't bear the thought of raising a child there.

Aries made mothers separate from their children forty-eight hours after birth, because he said parental attachments were damaging to spiritual development. You couldn't become your own being if you were overly influenced by your biological fore-bears. New mothers would come in and nurse a different baby every day in the nursery, because Aries thought that was a way to break individual bonds. Rosie was assigned to nursery duty sometimes, and the kids seemed happy enough.

But after Aries assaulted her, Rosie was able to see his dictums for what they were—just a way to control his female followers. The paternity of the children was often in question, so fathers weren't attached to individual children as a rule. But Aries knew that devoted mothers would be more concerned with their chil-dren's well-being than with his wants, and he couldn't allow that to happen.

Yes, you can ask a rude question.

No, she never considered getting an abortion. It was legal then, but Rosie felt the life growing inside her had given her a strength that she otherwise would not have had. Even though she knew that the origins of the child were less than ideal, she was not going to let Aries take something else away from her.

It didn't bother me that she was carrying someone else's child. I loved her with all my heart, and I wanted kids myself. By the time Ethan was born, Rosie had fallen fully in love with me, too, and she wanted to settle down and start our family. And the first time I saw Ethan's face, I knew he was my son. He barely cried when he came out; he was such a peaceful little man, even from the first moment.

We got moved to housing in Diaper Gulch just after Ethan was born. I loved living there, surrounded by California poppies and happy young couples. Rosie liked it for a week or two, but then she started to get angry. She loved Ethan with all her body and soul, and she started thinking about the other women and children stuck back in Mendocino, separated from their newborns. It drove her mad. I'd come home after a day of work and see her pacing the kitchen floor, wild with rage, with Ethan strapped to her chest in a Snugli.

I encouraged her to report the rape and file charges against Aries as a way to get closure. Rosie was wary; she still had Aries's distrust of the police. And she was scared. She didn't want to have to see Aries ever again, and she knew she'd have to face him in court. But I convinced her that filing charges was the only way to help the children who were still up at the compound without their mothers caring for them.

The prosecutor was all set to take Rosie's case. She was a great victim, he said: a young, beautiful mother who was married to an army man. These guru-grifter types were so common in the Bay Area in the sixties and seventies, and the D.A.'s office was desperate to nab at least one of them and make an example out of him. Because of an earlier statutory rape charge against John Brooks, the prosecutor could make it look like all the sex Rosie had was coerced, even though Rosie told him it wasn't.

But then, no one could find Aries. Rosie got word from another female follower who fled to San Francisco that the compound had disbanded and John Brooks had disappeared into thin air. That's when she stopped being angry and started being terrified. Aries—John Brooks—could do the math and realize that Ethan was his son, and Rosie was convinced he'd try to take Ethan away from her.

Months went by and Aries did not reappear. My commitment to the army was over, and Rosie and I decided together that I would not re-up this time. She wanted to get the hell out of California, and she wanted us to have more control over our lives. So we decided to move to Montana, which has long been a place where people go when they don't want to be found. Right, like the Unabomber.

Once we were settled in here, Rosie made me swear that we would never, ever speak about the past. It wasn't as hard as you might think. Aries had no bearing on our daily lives—the changing of diapers, the commute to work, the clearing of dinner plates. It really is possible to start over.

That doesn't mean that Rosie didn't carry some baggage with her to Montana. Sometimes we'd be at a store, and Rosie

would just hightail it outside without even saying anything
to me because she thought she caught a glimpse of someone
from Aries' Children and wasn't about to stick around to make
sure. She still woke up in the middle of the night sometimes,
screaming Aries's name. Rosie had the same nightmare over
and over, about a monkey chasing her through the California
woods with Aries's face.

What? No, no *Greenwich Rag* reporter ever contacted us.
What is the *Greenwich Rag?*

Christ. I didn't realize parts of her story were told in a newspaper. Did they have her name? No? That's good.

No reporters and no one from Rosie's past ever found us, as
far as I know. You're the first one to put it together. It was much
more difficult to find people and information before the Internet, obviously. Rosie took my last name when we got married,
and none of the commune people knew who I was. Besides,
Aries—Yoni—John Brooks, whatever you want to call him, was
on the run from those California charges.

Yes, I get that he harassed that reporter from the *Rag,* but
there was no incentive for him to find and then harass her.
Rosie knew all his old secrets, so why would he disturb that
hornets' nest? When she died, I swore to myself that the secret
would die with her. I just didn't think that it was relevant to any
of our lives.

Jesus, Mary, and Joseph, Dana! Of course I don't think Rosie's
death had anything to do with John Brooks. She was in a car
accident during the middle of the winter. She was driving back
from visiting a friend who had moved to Missoula, and she hit a
patch of black ice. Her car spun out of control and flipped over.

The cops said she must have been driving pretty fast because of the skid marks her car left.

No! No one was following her that day. C'mon. It had been more than a decade since she saw anyone from Aries' Children, and as we both know now, John Brooks had reestablished himself in New York. Why would he bother tracking Rosie down? It just doesn't make any sense.

I didn't know anything about the Zuni Retreat or John Brooks's involvement with it until after Ethan's death. When he came up here a few months back, all I knew was that he was living in New Mexico with Amaya, teaching at a yoga spa.

I mean, I was wary of his talk of spirituality. It sounded like some of the stuff Rosie had encountered, and obviously that put me on edge. I tried to speak to Ethan about it when he first moved to New Mexico, but he waved me off and stopped mentioning it in our phone calls. I told myself that that New Age stuff is lots of places now. There's yoga in even the most one-horse town in Montana, and one of the guys I go hunting with meditates. It's not as fringe as it used to be.

Ethan did seem a little disturbed when I saw him. I asked him if anything was wrong, and he said no. I hadn't seen him in the flesh since you two split up, but he did call me once a month or so to see how I was and catch up. He told me he was visiting because he wanted to reconnect with his old self a bit. I wasn't quite sure what that meant, but he did seem like he was working through something big. I would look at his face over dinner and see his eyes cloud over.

We did get along when he was here, though, and for that I'm grateful. You know, Ethan and I didn't always see eye to eye on things, but I loved him with all my heart. I didn't think of it this way until after he died, but in some ways, he was my last piece of Rosie in the flesh. Of course, I have Travis, but Travis has always been more like me. Ethan took after his mother. In more ways than I appreciated at the time.

Dana

At the end of his story, Ray seemed wrung out. I didn't really know what to do. I had never seen him look as happy as he did when he was talking about his and Rosemary's first days together, or as crushed as when he described how Ethan took after his mother.

I waited for him to say something, and when he didn't, I asked gently, "How did the sheriff react when you told him all this?"

Ray shrugged. "He didn't seem to react much one way or t'other. He asked me if I had any documents that proved what happened in California really happened, and I said no. Rosie and I tried to leave all that stuff behind."

"Did he seem to know any of it before you told him?" I asked.

"Couldn't say."

"Did he know about the *Greenwich Rag* article? About Yoni's past?" What sounded like mild questions in my head came out of my mouth like aggressive interrogations, but I couldn't help myself.

Ray shrugged again. "Couldn't say. I didn't know about that article until you just told me. Gurus, communes, and speed freaks were a dime a dozen in the Bay Area in the seventies. It wasn't necessarily newsworthy."

"Okay, okay," I said, putting my hands up. "I'm sorry to be so intense."

"Let me make us some breakfast," Ray said, standing up. He looked over at the clock, "Jesus, it's almost nine A.M. We've been talking for two hours straight."

"You really don't have to go to all that trouble," I said. "I don't usually eat much breakfast."

Ray waved me away. "Nonsense. It's important to have a square meal to start the day." I thought back to the solo dinners I made for myself after Ethan left. There was certainly something soothing about routine; about going through the same motions every day.

I got a glass of water and sat back down while I watched Ray crack eggs into a ceramic bowl. "Can I just ask you one more question about everything?" I asked.

"Shoot."

"Why did Rosie keep that necklace? I thought she never wanted to speak or hear or think about her past again."

Ray turned to face me. "Just because Rosie didn't want to talk about her past doesn't mean she didn't want to take some lessons from it. She couldn't erase her memory bank even if she wanted to. She kept the necklace as a reminder, like a rubber band on her wrist. Every time she looked at it, she'd remember to keep her own counsel. She was determined that no one else would ever tell her how to live her life."

I opened my mouth to say something else, but then closed it. I couldn't formulate a coherent thought. Exhaustion washed over me. "Do you mind if I go rest before breakfast is ready? That was a lot to take in."

"Suit yourself," Ray said, taking out a green pepper and a cutting board and not looking up. "I'll knock on your door when it's on the table."

"Thank you." I walked back to Ethan's room and flopped down on the plaid comforter. I looked at my phone to distract myself from the thoughts and emotions churning in my head. I had two bars of service—the first reception I'd gotten since arriving at Ray's—and seventeen missed calls and twelve voice mails.

The first voice mail was from Katie. She was managing my desk while I was away, and she left a detailed message about all the tasks that awaited me on my return. I could hear an edge to her voice. She thought that climbing the ladder at the firm was the apotheosis of making it in New York. She couldn't understand why I would take a leave and potentially jeopardize my progress (and hers—she knew that her ascent at the firm was tied to mine). I texted her to say thank-you and that I'd be back soon enough, raring to go.

The next ten messages were from Beth. She sounded increasingly hysterical with each one. "Dana, it's me," she said in the first message. "Please call me back. I just want to talk. I promise I won't yell at you." An hour after that, she called back, the pretense of niceness already gone. "What the fuck, Dana? I called your work, and Katie said you took a leave of absence? Call me *now*. I am really scared for you." I didn't even bother listening to the next eight messages from her. I just deleted them.

The final message was from a 575 number, I assumed Sheriff Lewis. I touched Play, but before I could listen to the message, Ray knocked at the door. "Dana, soup's on."

"Just a minute!" I paused the 575 message, then thought about the two voice mails Beth had left that I actually listened to. It was unfair to leave her upset. I hastily texted *In Montana visiting Ethan's dad. Everything is OK. Will call you soon.*

When I came back to the kitchen, I found that Ray had set the table just as he had the evening before, cleanly and elegantly. A vegetable-and-sausage scramble was already portioned onto two plates. Looking at the meal, I realized how rare it was for someone to do me such a simple but meaningful kindness.

After breakfast, I retreated to Ethan's room. I'm not sure whether it was colder in that part of the house or it was a kind of existential chill, but I was very cold. The light wool sweaters I had packed felt too scratchy and harsh against my skin.

I went over to Ethan's closet to see if there was anything in there I could wear. I found a fuzzy bright-blue poncho that looked like it was part of a Cookie Monster Halloween costume folded on a shelf at the top of the closet, and some dress shirts with Sears labels that also looked like artifacts of Ethan's high school days. Then there was a tie rack with a few polyester novelty ties that I hoped Ethan hadn't worn after the age of eighteen: one had Bart Simpson's face on it; another was purple and printed with tiny yellow Minnesota Vikings.

And then I found a long-sleeved waffle-knit shirt that looked like it had been purchased in this century. I rubbed the fabric between my fingers. It was soft, bordering on luxurious. I took the shirt off its hanger, pressed it to my face, and breathed into it. It had a particular spicy musk that pricked my nose and lit up years of sense memories. It smelled like Ethan.

I put on the shirt, turned off the overhead light, closed the blinds to keep the sun from streaming in, and crawled under Ethan's flannel comforter. I just wanted to shut off for a little while—to get a respite from everything I had learned. I squeezed my eyes closed and tried to sleep, but I couldn't even stay in one position for more than a few seconds. I kept turning from side to side and kicking the blanket up with my restless legs.

Finally I stopped pretending that I was going to get to sleep, and sat up and looked around. My eyes fell on the only light in the room, coming from my phone. I picked it up and saw a text back from Beth: *xoxoxox*.

I planned to call her back, but I wanted to listen to the rest of my messages first while I still had two bars. I went right to the 575 message. Maybe Sheriff Lewis had found some remarkable break in the case and was calling to tell me about it. More likely he just wanted some elaboration on something I had told him.

But Sheriff Lewis hadn't left the message. Instead, an unfamiliar woman said, "This message is for Dana Morrison. We're calling to invite you to an exclusive event at the Zuni Retreat's homestead. This invitation is for superlative students only. You were recommended by your instructor Lo. If you're interested in attending, please call 575-555-1982 for further information."

This must be the "next-level retreat" Lo had told me about. I put the phone down and got back under the covers, pulling the long sleeves of Ethan's shirt down over my cold hands to warm them. The warmth traveled through my body quickly and ended up in my chest, and even though I knew it was crazy, I felt Ethan's presence with me, like I was goddamn Demi Moore throwing a pot in *Ghost*.

It was suddenly very clear what I had to do. I had to go to the next level. If I could get some more alone time with Lo, I could get information from her about Yoni's past that might be helpful to the investigation. And I could also ask her more about Ethan, and find some kind of answer for myself.

I called the 575 number that had been left by that unfamiliar female voice. On the third ring, someone picked up. "Hello," said the voice that had left the message. Hearing it the second time, I noticed it had a lazy, drawn-out Southern California quality.

"Hi, this is Dana Morrison. You called me about a special retreat?"

"Oh yeah. We've been waiting on your call."

"I'm interested in coming," I said.

"My name is Aspen. I want to tell you a little bit more about the experience. You've been specially chosen for the Homestead, Dana. This is an advanced-level retreat that we only offer to students who have been recommended to us by our teachers. We advise that you come for the length of an entire moon cycle in order to create new spiritual habits that will stay with you when you leave."

I was a little hesitant to agree—a whole month? That would be pretty much my entire leave of absence. Did I want to waste my one moment away from work dwelling on my fucked-up life? Also, knowing how much a week cost, a month must be astronomical. And why were they offering me an advanced-placement class when I'd only been at Zuni for a few days? Wasn't

I a beginner in their spiritual terms? Did I trust someone named after a tony ski resort and/or tree to give me the full story?

"I was wondering. Will I get personal instruction from Lo at this 'Homestead'?" Aspen didn't respond right away, so I added, "We just had such an intense spiritual connection during my time at Zuni."

"Oh, yes," Aspen said brightly. "Lo is the one who recommended you for the Homestead, so she'll be your main guide once you're here."

"And how much is this going to cost?" Since I knew Lo and I would have quality time together, I hoped the cost wasn't so insane that I wouldn't be able to go.

"You've been given a special scholarship for emerging students. Only three people in the history of the Zuni Retreat have been given this honor of intensive study." Aspen's otherwise relaxed voice became tense, emphasizing the importance of this gift.

"Wow," I said, feeling a surge of pleasure in the honor before realizing she hadn't actually answered my question. "Sorry, how much would I need to pay?"

"You'd only be responsible for fifty percent of the fee," Aspen said, her voice stretching out again. "So it would cost just ten thousand dollars for the month, but that includes all of your individualized instruction and meals, as well as the comfortable, low-key luxury our retreats provide."

I swallowed, hard. That's a ton of money. But I had so much saved up that I was just sitting on. I lived so frugally by New York standards and earned so much. Was this really the time to cheap out? I couldn't help Ethan or Rosemary unless I pushed forward.

"Okay. I'm in."

"Wonderful news," Aspen said. "Let me check the availability for you at the Homestead to see when you might be able to start your spiritual journey." I heard the clacking of her keyboard. "We actually just had a cancellation, so we have room for you this week. As early as tomorrow, if you can come then."

"Great," I said. I figured it was more convenient this way. If I had to return to New York and wait, I might fall back into work and lose my momentum.

"Where will you be coming from?" she asked.

"I'm near Bozeman, Montana."

"Excellent, that shouldn't be a difficult journey," Aspen said.

"My cell service is a little spotty here, so it might take a while for me to book my trip," I explained.

"I can look up flights for you now, if that would be easiest." She was sounding more competent and less dippy with every sentence.

"Sure," I said.

I heard her typing in the background. "There's a Delta flight that leaves around eight A.M. tomorrow that has you transferring in Salt Lake City. Would that work for you?"

"Yes."

"Wonderful. If you book that, your connecting flight will get into Albuquerque around noon. Call me as soon as you've booked it, so that I can arrange to have the courtesy van pick you up."

I hung up and booked the flight right away through an app on my phone, then called Aspen back to confirm. After I hung up, I put the phone down next to the bed and felt my body go boneless. Now that I had a plan, the unanswerables stopped spinning in my brain. I fell into a sweaty, dreamless sleep.

That evening over dinner I told Ray, "I have to head back to New Mexico. I have to bring the sheriff my research." Ray nodded in understanding or acceptance, I couldn't tell which. Then I added, "And I'm going to go back to the retreat."

That broke Ray's silence. He shook his head, his ears turning red. "No, no. Absolutely not. Do not go back down there. Haven't you heard anything I told you? Yoni is dangerous and unpredictable, especially when he feels threatened by the law."

I felt my face go red, too. "I heard everything you told me. And what I took away from it is that only someone with proof of what goes on in Yoni's inner circle is going to figure out what really happened down there." What I didn't say was that I felt a true connection to Lo, and that I needed to see that through. Being out in New Mexico felt like a necessary pause from the real world, and I wasn't exactly eager to go back to New York or to my job.

"You're a grown woman. Do what you like," Ray said. "But I don't like it."

I asked him to drive me back to the Bozeman airport at five the next morning. It's a testament to his core decency that he agreed.

On the drive to Bozeman, we didn't talk much. Ray turned on a CD he had—his car was so ancient it still had one of those five-disc changers all my friends had in high school. I didn't recognize the singer, but he had a low, plaintive wail. I glanced over at Ray's face from time to time, but it was just a solemn mass. There was no evidence of what had passed between us the day before.

"I'm so sorry about everything that's happened," I said after we stopped in front of the airport. It was around six A.M., and Ray's was the only car idling.

Ray sighed and ran his hand over his mouth, like he was wiping something away. "I'll manage," he said. "I always do."

I leaned over and gave him a sideways hug. He patted my arm gently. I pulled back and grabbed my bag from the floor, got out of the car, closed the passenger door, and stood on the sidewalk. Ray's car sat there for a moment, so I waved at him. He looked over at me, and I detected a little bit of tenderness around his eyes. He gave me a salute with two fingers of his left hand and drove off.

The second I saw his car pull away, I went into the airport, got my ticket, and settled in at the gate. Unlike at JFK or LaGuardia, there were only a handful of people around me. I knew from flying into Bozeman that most of the flights out of this airport were on small, rickety shuttle planes, so there weren't that many seats to fill.

As I sat in the Scotchgarded airport bucket chair, I started to sweat. It seemed to be coming disproportionately from my left armpit. My face flushed, too. What the fuck was I doing? This was potentially dangerous and definitely weird.

On instinct I called Beth. "Dana! I'm so happy you finally called," she said, sounding truly elated. "Are you still in Montana?"

"Yes, I'm at the airport." This was true, if incomplete information.

"Oh, great. I can pick you up if you need me to. When does your flight get in?"

"Uh. Well." I took a deep breath. "Beth, I'm not coming back to New York right now."

"Where are you going?" Beth's voice became small and tight. I recognized that tenor from when our parents would fight and she'd crawl into bed with me.

"I'm going back to New Mexico," I said, trying to sound confident.

"Why would you do that?" Beth sounded earnest and confused.

"I need to talk to the sheriff more," I said, and I thought I heard her sigh with relief. I briefly considered not telling her the whole story, but that felt unfair. So I added, "And I need to go back to the retreat for myself."

"Dana!" Beth cried. "That's a fucking terrible idea. Why would you go back there?"

"It's a long story. I'll tell you when I get back," I said. Beth's warning had the perverse effect of making me more confident about my trip. *She doesn't understand what's going on.* My sane self said: *Of course she doesn't understand, because I'm not telling her any of the details.* But I pushed that voice down.

And I wasn't lying to her. I was going back to New Mexico, and not just to figure out what happened in Ethan's final days. I was going back because I thought I could do good work with Lo. Underneath the New Age jargon, something real had happened for me at Zuni. Maybe with more work, I could find out what happened to the real Dana, too.

Beth took a deep breath. "Dana, I'm really scared for you. I don't think you should go back there. You've been evasive and weird since you heard about Ethan's death. You're not acting like yourself at all. We haven't even talked about your taking leave from your job."

"Bethy, it'll be fine," I said, not even sure if that was true. But I had to tell myself that to go forward. "Don't you trust my judgment?"

"Yes?" Beth said totally unconvincingly.

In my most soothing, fearless big-sister voice, I said, "Good. I love you. I'll call you when I'm heading back to New York."

"I love you, too, Dana." Beth sounded resigned. "Just promise me you'll be careful."

"I'm always careful."

When I arrived at the Albuquerque airport, I saw a woman in a loose lavender shirt and matching trousers holding up a piece of paper with my name on it in bubble letters. When I saw her, I remembered that Yoni had a thing for young blondes. This woman had luminous skin, too, and even though she wasn't conventionally beautiful, she had striking emerald eyes. She reminded me of Amaya. At this thought my brisk walk slowed down a little. How was I coming back to this? But I was already here in New Mexico; I needed to keep going.

When I approached the woman, she shook my hand. Her handshake was as flaky as she appeared to be—she just placed her hand limply in mine. "I'm Juniper. I'll be driving you."

I pumped her hand vigorously. "Nice to meet you."

She removed her hand from my grip and smiled a warm but empty grin at me. "Follow me. The car's parked nearby."

I followed her outside to a gleaming white van, which looked like a stereotypical pedophile's getaway car, except that it was clean and new instead of rusted out and decades old. I opened the passenger door and saw a clear crystal dangling from the rearview mirror, but other than that, the inside was entirely uncluttered. It smelled a little odd, like a combination of lavender and body odor. Or maybe that was Juniper.

As we turned out of the airport Juniper beamed at me. "I'm so excited for you," she said. "That you get to experience this for the first time!"

"I've actually been to the retreat before," I said. "But I'm looking forward to being back and studying even harder."

"Oh, this is really, really different from the regular retreat. I don't want to spoil it. You'll see!" She got onto the highway still beaming, this time as she checked the rearview mirror. I think the only time I've ever looked so happy was on my wedding day. I briefly wondered if she was high, and felt the strap of my seat belt to make sure it was untwisted and ready to engage.

The drive to the retreat wended through a lush national forest: verdant mountains, rushing rivers, natural dams, scenic overlooks—the whole nine yards. It reminded me of the better moments in my childhood. There are so many lakes in Minnesota, and Beth and I loved it when our dad would take us on fishing and hiking trips. Managing our mother's mood swings felt like a full-time job, and so when we were away from her and in nature, we really felt we could blossom.

I was still musing about the distant past when we went from the verdant forest to a more arid climate, cacti and sage lining the dusty road. "There's the regular retreat," Juniper chirped as we drove past the turnoff. "The upper-level retreat is thirty minutes from here."

Sure enough, about half an hour farther down the two-lane highway, we took a turnoff that was almost imperceptible from the main road. It was shrouded in high shrubbery and cacti and there was no signage or any other kind of indication that there was a residence nearby. The road was narrow and deeply rutted, so even if you had mistakenly turned off on it, you'd probably turn right back around. I tried to swallow a nervous ball that rose in my throat.

It took twenty more minutes of slow, careful driving before we reached a circular yurt squatting out in a sparsely covered, pebble-filled field. As we pulled up to the yurt, a man walked out of the structure and waved at us. Juniper jumped out of the car like a sprightly woodland creature, and I galumphed out, hoisting my bag along with me.

As the man got closer I recognized his unusual, handsome face: Janus, my yoga teacher from my first visit. He enveloped me in a hug. "I'm so glad to see you, Dana," he said. "I'll take you to the main house. Junie's going to take the car back."

"Have a wonderful time," Juniper said, also giving me a hug. They were bigger on hugging here than they were at Zuni Regular, I noticed.

I followed Janus along the rutted road, which after a few turns became a cobblestone walkway. After five minutes on the walkway, the main building, a modern pueblo revival, rose up from the ground all of a sudden, like a mirage that a starving wanderer would see in the Sahara in old-fashioned cartoons.

The pueblo was an off-white color, almost a pale yellow, and it was just one sprawling story. Like some of the buildings at the Zuni Retreat, it was oriented around a courtyard, and through the open front door I could see a few residents doing yoga there. The reception area had what looked to be hand-painted lapis tiled floors, like the kind you see in Morocco or Turkey. *Lama Yoni's cash reserves must be huge,* I thought, feeling another twinge of nerves.

Another young woman—clad in that same lavender color—was manning the front desk. "Coral, can you tell us who is reading Dana's energy today?" Janus asked. Coral looked down at her computer screen. I tried to angle myself so I could see what was on it, but I couldn't bend toward it without seeming obvious. "I have her down for a reading with Gaia," Coral said.

"Ah. The first thing we have for you is to get your energy read by one of our experts. This will help us learn where to place you in our residential buildings. It will also help us come up with a set of appropriate classes for you."

I nodded and said nothing. If I was going to learn anything about Ethan, I had to accept that I would be buffeted along from charlatan to charlatan. Someone had to have taught him all that numerology he spouted in his self-help book. Hopefully Janus wasn't going to lead me down a narrow hallway into a room full of nude men.

"I'm sensing a bit of resistance from you, Dana," Janus said. "You were so gung ho at Zuni. Remember, your admission to this next level is a privilege." He looked me right in the eye, and I felt like he was trying to bore into my thoughts. I squirmed a little under the scrutiny.

"Oh, no. I'm really excited about this," I assured him, trying to soften the intensity of his gaze. "It's just a lot to take in."

"Good. Because if you're coming to our process with any negative energy, it will really hurt your progress. We want you to get the most out of this experience. It's a very special thing."

"I know. That's why I wanted to come." I summoned every ounce of sweetness within me to respond. I had to remember why I was here—it wasn't for the spiritual jargon about energy. It was for Lo's guidance. I couldn't wait to get into her class again.

"Wonderful," Janus said, breaking out that blinding grin of his. "I know just how special it is myself. I'm actually a little jealous of you, getting to experience everything for the first time!" It was like he and Juniper were reading from the same internal script. "Follow me," he added.

We walked down a long tiled corridor. The walls flanking me were painted a terra-cotta color, and they had pictures of Hindu or Buddhist deities in expensive-looking gold frames. I didn't see or hear a single soul. "It's so quiet," I whispered, taking smaller steps than I usually did so that I would slow down to Janus's languid pace.

"You arrived during one of our midday silences," Janus said.

"Oh," I whispered. "I thought the silence was in the morning?"

"That's just at the Zuni Retreat. The rules here are different, but you will learn them in time."

We arrived at a door with a wheel the size of my hand painted on it. I counted six spokes on the wheel, and Janus knocked six times in a particular pattern before a woman opened the door.

She was probably in her forties, but it was hard to tell because she was in magnificent shape. She had the slender yet muscular frame of yoga and Pilates instructors, and was wearing light purple, like the others. She looked into my eyes and then bowed. Feeling a little silly, I bowed back. Janus also bowed, and stayed in that bent position as he walked backward several steps. Once he saw me move toward the woman, he turned and walked away. I put my bag on the ground near the door.

Everything in the room was low to the ground. There were no chairs, just large cushions and throw pillows on the floor. The place obviously had the same lysergic-acid-addled decorator who did the Zuni Retreat décor. The woman gestured for me to sit on one of the cushions. I tried to plop down on a purple-fringed pillow but I missed the center, so I teetered off to the side before righting myself. The woman sat down gracefully in the center of her personal cushion. "Namaste," she said, putting her hands together and pointing them toward me.

"Namaste," I parroted back.

"My name is Gaia. I know you are Dana. As you take your journey with us, you may find that you are given a new name by our wonderful spiritual leader. But that's all in good time." She smiled.

I didn't know how to respond to that, so I said nothing and waited for her to continue. But she didn't. She sat staring at me with a completely serene expression on her face for what felt like minutes. I thought about Ethan's first connection with Yoni, when he was made to stand alone in a room and look deeply into the guru's eyes until he felt like he was going to crack up. This seemed like one of the group's standard tests of devotion, a test I was not about to fail. So I remained silent until Gaia said, "We're here to do an energy reading, so that we can figure out the best individualized program for you."

"Yes, Janus told me," I said.

She closed her eyes and let out a sigh with a *hmmm* sound. "I'm already feeling significant blockage from you. But a lot of people have big blockages when they first arrive at the retreat. I'm glad you're here. You need these practices in your life." She opened her eyes and reached for a red lacquered tray that contained a bunch of stones and crystals of various sizes and colors. "I'd like you to choose a crystal. Close your eyes and move your hands over the tray. When you feel a tingling or a burning sensation, pick up that crystal."

I had to try my hardest not to laugh. When Beth and I played Ouija board when we were children, I always tricked her into thinking our dead grandmother was behind the board, answering her questions and planning on haunting her forever. This felt like it had as much credence as the Ouija board.

My mouth was twitching with the effort of suppressing a smile when my hand quivered from nerves. I lowered my hand, scooped up a crystal, and opened my eyes.

"Just as I suspected," Gaia said. "Orange kyanite."

"What does orange kyanite mean?" I asked, looking at the splintered crystal in my hand.

"Your sacral chakra is severely blocked. I could feel it as soon as you walked in the door. This just confirms it for me."

"My what?" In spite of myself, I was sort of angry. How dare this woman judge my sacral chakra! Lo hadn't said anything about that.

"Your sacral chakra," Gaia explained, "is located in your lower abdomen. Right here." She pointed below her belly button. "The sacral chakra is what allows us to be open to new experiences and new relationships, and I am feeling that yours is almost completely blocked." She shook her head.

I felt like I had just failed a final exam. I knew she was talking nonsense, but I really, really hated not succeeding. "Is there anything I can do to fix it?" I asked, not quite believing I was engaging in this.

"Of course," Gaia said in a sweet voice. "We'll start with doing some initial energy work here, and then I will confer with Lama Yoni about the best coursework to help you unblock. Please lie down."

She spoke with such calm authority that I lay down immediately and instinctively closed my eyes. My heart beat a little faster knowing that she was going to mention me to Yoni. My interactions with him so far at Zuni had been distant—I was just one of hundreds of students there. This felt more intimate and even invasive. I tried calming my increasing anxiety by clenching and releasing my fists, which was a movement so small, I hoped Gaia wouldn't notice.

Gaia knelt by my hips and placed her hands over them. She rotated her hands to the right, and then put them back over the center of my hips, then repeated this action five or six times. I heard her take something out of her pocket and suddenly smelled a strong citrus scent right below my nose. "This is bergamot essential oil," Gaia explained. "It will help with your unblocking process."

I felt her hands rubbing my temples. The citrus smell still

hung in the air. I knew that I should be skeptical, but I couldn't help but relax. Gaia's presence was that soothing.

Gaia finished her temple massage with a bit of a head scratch. "Take your time getting up," she told me. "When you feel ready, you may leave. Someone will meet you to lead you to your lodgings. Namaste." I opened my eyes in time to see her put her hands together and bow to me, then slip out a door, partially camouflaged by a wall hanging in the back of the room, that I hadn't even noticed was there.

I didn't want to get in trouble for leaving too quickly. Maybe they would think I wasn't reflecting sufficiently on my energy levels if I left the room too soon. So I waited there with my eyes closed for an indeterminate amount of time until I heard the door open. I turned my head to the noise and saw Janus entering the room, so I sat up. "Let's go to your room," he said.

I felt unsteady on my legs, like I had just stepped off a boat, and I appreciated Janus's slow pace this time. We walked along a corridor. I couldn't tell whether it was the same corridor we came up; they all looked the same to me, with the terra-cotta walls and the unfamiliar gods and goddesses. There were doors every few feet, all closed. Finally, after about a ten-minute walk, we stopped at an orange door.

"This is where you will be staying. You have been paired with the roommate who we believe will aid your spiritual development most completely," Janus said. I started to roll my eyes internally, but then I realized the spiritual jargon here was no stranger than the way we spoke to each other at my office, with terms like *circle back* and *bandwidth* and *run it up the flagpole*.

Janus carefully opened the door. It was a lovely, if spartan, room. There were two full beds, each with a bright white bedspread patterned with gold and orange throw pillows. The wall art—two more deities, sitting on opposite white walls—was also tinged with orange. The room was about 50 percent more upscale than my room at the Zuni Retreat.

A woman was sitting on one of the beds, concentrating deeply on a book. She looked up at us. She did not seem particularly happy to see me. "Willow, this is Dana. I trust you will make her feel at home?" Janus said.

Willow nodded tersely and plastered a fake smile on her face. She had tiny blue eyes that turned into narrow slits with this insincere grin. She wasn't quite as fit as the other people I'd met so far, though she was still young and still pretty. She wore standard-issue black yoga pants and a form-fitting top, and she surveyed me from head to toe like she was sizing up her competition. I was not getting Sylvia vibes from her at all.

"Sorry to have interrupted your reading," I said.

"I will leave you now to get settled," Janus said. "Please note that we're still in our midday silence, which means that only fully realized residents can speak. It's something you have to earn."

I nodded back in assent.

"Namaste," Janus said, then bowed and left me alone with Willow. Willow turned back to her book as if I weren't there. I started unpacking my bag to occupy my hands and unquiet mind.

When I brought my toiletries into the bathroom I decided to take a shower. The shower was beautiful, maybe the most beautiful I'd ever seen. It was an open stall made of wood, with a rainforest showerhead, and it was stocked with half-empty bottles of Dr. Bronner's products. I assumed these were provided by the retreat; for $20,000 a month the least they could do was provide us with toiletries. I used them liberally on my hair and body. There were two clean but slightly frayed towels folded neatly next to the shower. I took the top one and used it to dry off.

I came out of the bathroom in my towel and Willow shot me a look of death. I didn't want to get off on the wrong foot with her, so I smiled back at her scowl, grabbed my clothes, and tiptoed back into the bathroom to change. When I came out again, Willow was gone.

Since I had no one to talk to and had no idea how to get anywhere anyway, I lay down and fell asleep as soon as I was supine.

I was startled awake by a knock on the door, and Janus walked in before I could say anything or get up. "Good evening. I'm here to take you to dinner."

I rubbed my eyes and sat up. I wiped the drool from my mouth, embarrassed to be seen in this state. "Can I have a minute to freshen up?"

"I'm sorry, no." Janus's voice was firm but kind. "It's time for dinner and we always eat as a community."

I got up and went to put my shoes on, but Janus shook his head. "You won't need those while you're here." I put them down and sidled up to him. He turned and started walking away, clearly meaning for me to follow him. "It's important for you to learn the rules here," he said crisply. "That's a big part of our intentional community: everyone must put the 'we' before the 'I.'"

"Of course," I said. "I'm committed to the community whole-heartedly." Wasn't that what he wanted me to say?

Janus stopped walking and turned toward me. "I heard about your energy blockage, and I want to make sure you're doing everything possible to overcome it."

Shouldn't energy practitioners be like doctors and keep their mouths shut about their clients' personal information? Where was my guru-patient confidentiality? I swallowed a flare of rage and plastered a thin-lipped smile on my face. Why had I wanted to come back here, again? "I understand. I'm so, so sorry. It means everything to me that I am part of this thriving community."

"Good," Janus said, turning back around. I followed him wordlessly through the terra-cotta corridors until they opened up into a huge, airy room with four long tables in it. There must have been a hundred people there, all sitting with their hands in prayer position and their heads bowed. About a fifth of them were in lavender, and the rest were in upscale yoga clothes like the ones Willow wore. The vast majority of them were under thirty-five, and there were more women than men, but not by a huge margin.

I could see there was just one open spot, on the end of one of the long tables, right next to Willow. Janus gestured for me to sit there, and so I did. Like everyone else, I put my hands in prayer position and bowed my head.

We sat without speaking for several minutes. My mind raced with memories of Ethan and snippets of what had happened to me since I arrived at the Homestead. I could almost hear the gears of my brain whirring, trying to figure out the subtext to my energy reading and to the mannered language Janus spoke. But it couldn't be jammed together in any way that told a coherent story. It was like trying to put together Ikea furniture: frustrating, and there was always a missing piece.

The thoughts were so agitating, I was about to jump out of my skin when I was saved by a booming voice. "It is now time for our evening sermon." I could hear the people at my table moving, so I figured it was okay to lift my head. The voice came from a man in his forties who was wearing lavender and standing at the head of one of the center tables. From a door on the left side of the room, Yoni emerged. He was wearing dark purple instead of lavender, and his white hair was gathered into a shiny bun atop his head. He walked slowly and deliberately until he reached a slightly raised platform at the front of the room. He was still attractive. A silver fox with burnished skin. Even before he opened his mouth, the charisma wafted off of him. You wanted to watch this man—or at least I did. I felt some combination of lust and shame. I was supposed to suspect him, not want him.

Yoni just stood there for a minute, taking us all in. I swore he made eye contact with me, but I blushed and looked down at my plate. "Namaste, children," he said at last. His voice was unremarkable. It sounded like the voice of every middle-aged male colleague I had at the law firm.

"Tonight I want to tell you the story of a mischievous llama." Yoni paused, put his hands behind his back, and started pacing around the platform. "This llama was the smartest animal in the barnyard. Now, llamas are very clever animals to begin with, and that's why they are easy to train." Another pause. "But this llama outshone her kin. While her brothers and sisters would follow the commands of their master, this llama would only pretend to follow the commands. She'd secretly go her own way. She would sneak scraps out of the food bin, and extra sips from the trough." His voice became more powerful as he got going with his parable. The entire room was rapt. I realized that Yoni had many oratorical tricks I hadn't picked up on the first time I met him. His use of pauses in particular made you want to hang on every word.

"One day, the farmer left the gate open for a few minutes, because he had to bring medicine to one of the other llamas. The clever llama saw her opportunity and ran for the hills." Yoni stopped pacing and smiled. "She ran up into the mountains, where she relished her new freedom. But then the sun set, and the llama got very cold without her brothers and sisters to keep her warm. She had never been on her own before, so she did not know how to forage for food. She wasn't used to the ragged terrain in the mountains, so she slipped and broke a leg. She could not be saved because she was all alone." That final sentence hung in the air for a long moment before Yoni said, "Namaste." He bowed to the crowd and exited through the same door he'd entered from.

I couldn't help wondering if that parable was really about Ethan and Amaya—a veiled warning not to stray? I didn't have time to parse it before communal bowls of food started going around. I spooned a helping of the mystery dish onto my plate. It was brown and lumpy, and when I looked closely, it appeared to be a mélange of lentils, carrots, and tofu in some kind of sauce. It seemed just like the food at Zuni.

"Ooh, red lentils!" Willow exclaimed, sounding like a totally different person than the sour woman who had glared at me earlier. "These are supposed to be great for my solar plexus chakra. Gaia was telling me all about it." This sounded like a brag—like she'd had a private audience with Gaia and wanted everyone to know.

The other members of the table immediately chimed in. "Well, Gaia told me that brown foods were not that good for clearing blockages," one man in his thirties said.

"Sage said that carrots are excellent for balancing your energy," another woman added, as if this won the discussion. I made a mental note about carrots.

I scanned the room to see if I could find Lo. She must be here, I figured, since she was responsible for my return. I found her with two other women roughly her age, and was surprised by the wave of relief that rolled over me at seeing her familiar face. Lo and her friends seemed to be the only elderly people at the Homestead. They were all wearing lavender, but their outfits were a shade darker than everyone else's, except for Yoni's, of course. They seemed set apart from the crowd, and very focused on one another. I could hear laughter from their corner above the din. I tried to catch Lo's eye so I could send her a little wave, but she was completely caught up in her conversation.

I turned back to my table and tried to make eye contact there. None of the people at my table introduced themselves or even bothered to look in my direction. They continued to prattle on about their chakras and their ins with various community members. Finally, after ignoring me the entire meal, Willow threw me a bone. "I'm sorry about being a little unfriendly before," she said. "I am just starting to have some breakthroughs on my spiritual journey, and I can't afford any setbacks."

"That's okay. I have so much to learn from you," I told her. I figured flattery was a good option. Though I wasn't really clear how being friendly to me would set her back on her "spiritual journey."

"You'll pick things up," Willow said.

"I hope so," I said, nodding vigorously.

Willow finished her meal and moved to get up from the bench. "There are several after-dinner activities you can partake in. Ordained members all teach classes or workshops—each one of them has something different to teach us. There's meditation on the south patio, and Sarai leads an evening lecture on orgasmic nutrition in the Pima yurt."

God help me, even if I did want to listen to a lecture on orgasmic nutrition, I knew I would never find the Pima yurt on my own. "Is there a map of the grounds or something that I can look at?"

Willow shook her head. "No, I'm sorry. You need to follow your inner compass. Once you are more open to your surroundings, you will be able to access that compass." She said this as if I were so painfully misguided, it hurt her to explain it to me.

"What are you going to do?" I asked.

She wrinkled her nose. "I am going to walk the grounds to open my airways."

She didn't invite me, but she didn't explicitly tell me not to come with her, so I trotted along after her like a pesky kid sister. We walked in silence for fifteen minutes. It was getting dark, so I focused on my feet and the path in front of me. The air was clear and crisp, and I could feel the temperature drop as the sun slid farther and farther behind the mountains.

Finally, Willow turned to me and asked, "What brought you here?"

"I, uh, I was feeling really empty," I said, caught off guard. "I needed something big to change. Then I got a call out of the blue that I had been recommended for this next-level retreat, and it seemed like everything was falling into place." As soon as I finished speaking, I felt exposed. Because it was true.

Willow nodded, looking vaguely sympathetic for the first time. "I relate to that completely," she said. "I, too, am a refugee from the outside world. I wanted to go someplace where I would not be monitored by our Big Brother government." She gestured up to the sky.

I thought she sounded bonkers, but I smiled anyway. "I'm really looking forward to disconnecting from negative energy."

She smiled and nodded. "We have a lot in common, sister. I feel as if it is fate that we have been joined. When we get back to the room, I will do our charts and we can figure out how we can best compliment each other on our respective spiritual journeys."

"That sounds lovely," I said. Willow led me back to our room, and I tried to take in my surroundings so that I would be able to find my way on my own. I'm not sure it sank in, though; each bush looked like every other bush, and there weren't many man-made landmarks to help me along.

Back in the room, Willow pulled out a complex chart that looked like a wheel with many, many spokes. I gave her my birth date and year and found I was genuinely curious about what she would say. She examined the chart for several minutes, making light grunting noises as if this was a major intellectual effort, then started flipping between the chart and a book she had with her. I couldn't see the title when she opened it, but it had a huge, groovy sun on the cover.

At last she murmured, "You are a Taurus with a moon in Cancer, and I am a Gemini with a moon in Virgo." She said this with a little hesitation, like she was a doctor telling me I had a slightly suspicious-looking mole.

"Is that bad?"

"It's complex. You are good at accepting different viewpoints, but you sometimes lack conviction and can be negative. Also, your chart says you will have a rough time transitioning to new experiences, because your major source of stability is your family."

At first I was mildly offended. But then I remembered that it was total mumbo jumbo. Me, lack conviction? What nonsense. I masked my negativity, though, because I didn't want to conform to the stereotypical Taurus. "How fascinating. What are the qualities of a Gemini with a Virgo moon?"

"I can be extremely bossy, and I have trouble listening to other people." Normally, this would be a nightmare in a roommate, but in this case, I thought, it could be a blessing. She'd get off on being the knowledgeable one, and would be excited to teach me things about the Homestead. I could pretend to be far meeker than I actually am.

"That seems like something you could work on here," I said, trying to sound supportive.

"But what's good about this combination is that as long as we call on Mercury to help us communicate, we can learn a lot from each other." She smiled, looking more secure now that she had me figured out. Then she closed the book and folded up her chart. "I'm going to do some solo energy work before I get ready for bed. I am going to need the bathroom for forty-five minutes, because that's where the energy is most positive in this room." She got up and walked briskly to the bathroom before I could ask to brush my teeth first.

I took out my phone to see if I had any messages. There weren't any, and for a second I was hurt. Where were Beth's creative insults? Why hadn't she told me she was going to "cooter stomp" me if I didn't text her back? Why hadn't Katie left another nervous voice mail? Didn't anyone in the real world care about me?

But then I looked at my phone more closely and realized I didn't have any bars. I went to the settings and tried to see if my phone could pick up a Wi-Fi network, but there weren't any. I only had 10 percent charge left, so I looked around the room in case there was a place to plug it in. But there wasn't an outlet anywhere.

I started feeling hot all over, and my trusty left armpit sprang a leak. If I needed to reach Ray or Beth, I simply couldn't. If I wanted to talk to Sheriff Lewis, my best bet would probably be finding my way back to the main road and hitching a ride into Ranchero with some potentially methed-out local loner.

I lay down on my bed and started to take deep breaths to calm myself. "You're okay," I said quietly, over and over again. "It's only a month. People survive torture in third-world prisons for years. I can survive a creepy guru and essential oils for a few weeks." I breathed in and out, in and out, in and out, until my pulse stopped racing and my armpit dried.

Once I was calm, I realized the other downside to having no phone. I had no distractions. There was no Internet or prattling of local newscasters or bitching of the Real Housewives. I had to sit with my thoughts.

It was painful at first. I couldn't stop my mind from racing. How was I going to find out more about Ethan and Amaya? I'd have to learn how to speak these people's language a little better before broaching the subject. I also had to reconnect with Lo as soon as possible. She saw something special in me, or else she wouldn't have invited me to this place.

What I tried not to think about was how I was trapped here, miles away from anything or anyone I knew, with a bunch of gullible, stunted freaks. And I really couldn't think about what the fuck I was going to do with my life after all this was over. Was I really going to go back to my old job? Working ninety-hour weeks with zero balance, in an emotionally bereft atmosphere? It didn't really seem possible.

But I didn't think I was done with law entirely. I had worked so hard to get my degree and build a career. Maybe I would go into family law and save children from situations like the one Ethan would have been trapped in had Rosemary not fled the commune decades ago.

I took one more deep breath. For the time being, I just had to stay positive and in the moment, put on some mask of warm energy like everyone else here. And who knew, I might as well try to benefit from some of these woo-woo classes. It couldn't be all bad—the people here seemed happy, and they certainly looked great. Maybe if I just circumvented Yoni's evil and took the parts that were positive, I could emerge from this experience not just having cleared Ethan's name, but in a better place and with super-toned shoulders.

The whole place woke with the sun. I wondered if someone looked at the almanac to see when the sun was supposed to rise, because it seemed like the minute it peeked above the horizon, I opened my eyes to a whirring sound and saw the bamboo shades gathering and the light streaming in. The shades must have been set with a timer.

Willow got out of bed. I knew by this point not to speak first, and to follow her lead. So I got out of bed, too. She got dressed, so I did, too. Then she pulled out a yoga mat from under her bed. I looked under my bed and found an identical mat. She positioned her mat facing the window and sat with her legs crossed, her mouth open, her eyes closed, and her hands resting palm up on her knees. I placed my mat right behind her and did the same.

For a while—what felt like fifteen minutes, but who knows—I hated sitting there. I kept opening one eye to see if Willow was stirring, but she remained still. So I tried to lean into the silence.

Though I didn't want to be thinking about Ethan, it was impossible not to do so here, surrounded by all the stuff he had believed in when he left me. It occurred to me as I sat there that I still loved him. Reading his book and going on this journey had helped me make sense of that residual love. I'd numbed myself out when he left, but now that he was back in the forefront of my mind, I realized that I didn't love him like a man anymore. I loved him like a relic, an immovable piece of the past that was still dear to me, that still mattered in a historical sense.

My mind flitted to one particular moment, shortly after we'd graduated from college. We had no money, but we wanted to take a vacation. So we took a camping trip out to Glacier National Park in Montana. Ethan knew it well because he'd hiked there so much as a kid, and because he spent so much of his childhood poring over nature books. He knew that there were sixty different kinds of ferns in Glacier, and could tell me which ones were moonworts and which ones were horsetails.

One morning we went on a very early hike. We didn't see a single soul while we were walking, and we found a little waterfall with a small pool below it. We stripped off our clothes and jumped in. I remembered the chill of the water on my skin—so cold that we shrieked and gasped. After we swam, we found a flat rock near the pool and lay down on it. The smooth rock caught the July sun. We held hands and touched feet and giggled. I remembered thinking, *This is just the beginning of our beautiful life together.*

Before Ethan died, I thought of that moment as a tragic memory, because our marriage ended the way it did. But as I sat there I began to realize the memory was actually beautiful in its own way. It could stand alone as a perfect moment, because we really felt that happy at that time. What came afterward didn't have to mar what was real and true.

I was so deeply inside the memory that Willow had to tap me on the shoulder to snap me out of it. She beckoned for me to follow her to breakfast. She sat in the same place she had the previous evening, so I did, too. A vat of porridge went around and was slopped into our bowls. It seemed to be made of quinoa and tasted like sawdust.

We were finishing up our gruel when rough brown pieces of recycled paper were handed to each of us. I looked down at mine and saw that it was a class schedule. My morning class was called Inner Child Workshop, it was in the Owl Lodge, and the instructor was Lo.

I wandered around the grounds looking for the classroom. Every time I saw someone new, I would follow them, in hopes that they'd bring me to the Owl Lodge. After several fruitless follows, I arrived at a building with a giant golden-winged owl statue out front—I figured this was the place. I worried I'd be late, but since there were no clocks anywhere, I also wondered what *late* meant.

When I walked by other classrooms en route to Lo's, I saw rooms filled with five or ten students and a teacher. But when I arrived at the classroom I'd been assigned, I saw Lo there alone. I couldn't tell whether it was good or bad that I seemed to be getting individual attention, but before I could complete the thought, Lo embraced me. She was wearing a Peruvian woven poncho over her purple robe. The poncho was red with purple stripes and fraying fringe, and it smelled grandmotherly, a particular nose-twitching combination of decay and perfume. It was the first time I'd thought of Lo as old.

"I'm so happy you came back," Lo said. "Inner child work is such an essential building block to making spiritual progress. I'm not surprised that this is what they've assigned you to do.

Not that I had a hand in that decision." She winked at me, and I smiled back. Her earnestness was contagious.

"I am in serious need of some progress," I said confidently.

"Good. Normally inner child work goes better in a group setting, but since it's just us we will have to muddle through. The upside is you will get one-on-one counseling."

I shifted and felt the warm wooden floor with the balls of my feet. There must have been some heating system under the floorboards. Lo took off the poncho and folded it before placing it gently next to her. She offered me a fringed pillow to sit on and put another pillow on the floor a few feet away from it. "We're going to start off by facing each other and connecting through eye contact and matching breaths. I want you to follow my lead as we take deep, soothing breaths together. I don't want shallow breaths, I want these to come from here." She reached over and grabbed my diaphragm. I giggled like the Pillsbury Doughboy.

"That's good!" Lo said. "That sounds like your inner child is ready to come out to play. Now breathe in . . . out . . . in . . . out." We breathed together. I settled into the pillow. By the time she told me we were finished with our breathing exercises, I did feel really calm.

"I think of this as an ongoing process," Lo explained. "There's always a lot to unpack, even if you had a happy childhood. I want to tell you a story from my past. I think this process only works when spiritual communication is a two-way street. Even though I have been here a long time, I have so much to learn from you." She smiled at me warmly.

"I like to begin with our first memory, which says a lot about how much work needs to be done. My first memory is of ringing a stranger's doorbell." The ease with which she launched into this narrative suggested that she'd told the story many times before. "I grew up as a Jehovah's Witness, and I went door-to-door with my family starting when I was six weeks old.

"When I was seven, my mother sent me out on my own to proselytize. I had six brothers and sisters, and it was too hard to bring all of us with her when she went door-to-door, so she sent us off on our own as soon as she thought we'd be able to find our way home. I don't remember who answered the door at the first house I approached. It must have been a housewife. I just remember the feeling of abandonment. For me, the first step in my healing process was to live in that feeling of abandonment for a fortnight, and then let it go with a special ceremony in which I released a dove into the heavens. It is pretty difficult to get doves around here—believe me, I tried—but we can find other ceremonies to help you shed unwanted baggage during your journey."

"Wow. That must have been hard for you, growing up like that." I was genuinely moved by Lo's story. How coddled I was as a child by comparison! My mother didn't even let me walk to a friend's house alone until I was in high school.

Lo shook her head. "It was just how I was raised. I have made my peace with it through years of energy work. Now, you go. What is your earliest memory? Take your time, dear. We have all the time in the world." Lo reached out and patted my hand.

I closed my eyes and tried to go back. Something I had never thought about before flashed into my head. "I was sitting in the backseat of the family station wagon," I said, the words tumbling out of my mouth uncontrollably. "It was the way, way back, so I was looking out at the road. I must have been in the first grade. I had been fighting with my sister, and my mom had had it. So she said I had to sit back there, even though I hated it. It didn't have any seat belts, and when my mom would make a turn, I'd go flying. I remember she said she didn't want to look at my face." Tears welled up in my eyes. What was happening to me?

"How did that make you feel?" Lo asked, not breaking eye contact.

"Scared. Alone," I said, really starting to blubber. Where was this even coming from? It felt like this story was being excavated from underneath layers and layers of detritus. But I couldn't stop. "Uh, ugly. Because she didn't want to see my face."

"There, there," Lo said, reaching forward to pull me into a hug. We were still sitting down, so the position was awkward. I cried into her shoulder anyway. She smelled like clay and clean skin when the poncho was off.

When I pulled away, a string of drool trailed from my mouth. I had left three distinct wet spots on Lo's purple robe where my mouth and face had rested. "I'm so sorry," I said, wiping my nose with my sleeve and trying to collect myself. "I have no idea where that came from!"

"There is no need to apologize. You should actually feel very proud. It is rare to have a breakthrough during your first session of inner child work," Lo said warmly. "Usually these things are not so close to the surface, and we must dig to get at them." She paused and examined my face. I could feel red blotches appearing on my cheeks and my eyes getting puffy. "I'm sensing that you're still processing the trauma of your husband's abandoning you."

I sniffed the tears up and nodded pitifully.

"When you were at Zuni, I understood you were hurt by your husband, but I couldn't fathom the depths of it until just now. When you arrived this morning, the energy field fractured around me. That only happens when someone has suffered a profound trauma," Lo told me.

"I'm really fine," I said.

Lo gave me a sympathetic look. "It's quite all right, dear. You shouldn't unburden yourself all at once. That's a way to overwhelm the work we do. It's better to go through it piecemeal. The idea is that every time you visit me, you will mature. Today, I think your emotional and spiritual age is around six. That is when your first memory took place, and that is where you have to grow from."

I nodded. I was still catching my breath. I was angry at myself for losing control. I would never get to the bottom of what happened to Ethan if I let my emotions get the better of me. But all the same, Lo had tugged at something that I didn't even know existed, and that was terrifying. How could I let myself be so affected by what I knew was babble?

"I'll see you tomorrow morning," Lo said, bowing a little to me. When she leaned down, I saw a flash of her blue asterisk necklace again, and it sobered me. Lo *must* have known Rosemary. How could I get her to talk about it, let her know I knew Yoni's past?

For now, I just chirped, "Great!" I'd figure out a way in by my next session with her.

"Good. The next time you're here I want to try something a little different. We will spend part of the time working through our memories, but I also want to do some aromatherapy work, because I think that will help unlock a little of what's closed off here." She pointed to my sacral chakra—just where Gaia had done her energy work.

"How can you tell I'm blocked there?" I asked.

"Honey, it's written all over your face. Any experienced practitioner could tell within minutes that was what ailed you. And then your inner child confirmed it."

"Oh." Again I had that sinking feeling that I had failed a test. I wanted to get good marks, even in a class I'd call bullshit spiritual theory. I hated when things didn't come easily to me. This was something that had bothered Ethan a lot. I would refuse to try any new activity if I thought I wasn't going to be good at it right off the bat. This kept us from cross-country skiing, beach volleyball, and salsa dancing. In the grand scheme of things, these weren't great losses. But I was starting to see how my bad attitude had worn him down over the years. Maybe that was part of what drew him to Amaya. She was game.

"Don't worry. You're here for a reason," Lo said.

"You're right," I agreed. "I will be here tomorrow. Same place?"

"Always," Lo said. "I never leave."

Everyone seemed to have yoga classes in the afternoon. Mine was a beginners' class, and I got a lot of personal instruction from a man in his fifties named Karma, who had a pleasantly ruined face. After, when Willow and I were back in our room preparing for dinner, I told Willow that Lo was my morning teacher. She smirked, then sighed with false sympathy.

"What?" I asked, insulted. I felt protective and fond of Lo.

Willow stopped braiding her hair and looked at me. "Lo isn't really considered to be one of the premier teachers here. Her methods are seen as . . . How should I put this? Outmoded. I don't understand why she even bothers anymore. I think the other women her age here just sleep and gossip all day. I heard Yoni only keeps them around out of loyalty, because they've been with him for so long."

"Do you know how long Lo's been here?" I asked.

Willow shook her head. "Not exactly. But it seems like she's furniture here, a real fixture."

"Have you ever been assigned to her workshops?"

Willow smirked. "No way."

"Then how do you know her methods are outmoded?" In addition to hating being belittled by Willow, I hated older women being dismissed because of their age.

"Word of mouth is very powerful at the Homestead," Willow said. "You'll learn that once you've been here a little longer." She smiled condescendingly.

She had no idea what she was talking about. Hearing her disparage Lo and talk down to me had a perverse effect—it loosened my tongue. I wanted to wipe that arrogant grin off her face, and I knew just how to do it. "Speaking of word of mouth, I keep meaning to ask you about this thing I heard about before I got here. I don't really read the newspaper, but I saw something about some death or something that happened near here? I can't really remember the details."

Willow's face darkened. Her eyes narrowed to slits and her mouth puckered. "I haven't the faintest idea what you're talking about," she said. She got up from her bed. "Excuse me. I feel

I really need to do some energy work right now." She disappeared into the bathroom.

Message received, I thought as I sat on my bed.

On my fourth day at the Homestead I arrived at my assigned afternoon yoga class and saw that Yoni was sitting at the front of the room in lotus pose with his eyes shut. I stopped short, rooted in the doorway, as one of Willow's friends, Bodhi, and some other non-ordained residents streamed past me. I forced myself to go forward and set up my mat toward the back of the room. The front of the room was reserved for the ordained.

Bodhi was next to me, and he leaned over to whisper, "I'm a little starstruck, too! We never know which classes the great master will attend ahead of time."

I smiled wanly. At least he'd read my fear as excitement.

Word around the Homestead was that Yoni had studied with the notable hatha guru Tirumalai Krishnamacharya in India in the early seventies, which was why that kind of yoga was practiced at Zuni. I had no idea whether that was true. People said a lot of things about the guru—that the Dalai Lama went to him for advice; that he had once cured a woman's scoliosis through the power of touch; that he and Steven Seagal were best friends. But whether or not he studied with Krishnamacharya, the poses we did were heavy on headstands and shoulder stands, which I was getting better at every day. I liked the lightness in my mind that I felt when I was inverted.

I managed to relax a little while Yoni was leading the class. Once my initial pang of fear subsided, I could see that he was an excellent teacher. I had been too clouded with rage when I attended his class with Ethan years ago to notice. He spoke slowly and clearly, and he seemed genuinely pleased when people were making progress. "This is good work, Clover," he said to one woman, who adjusted one of her poses after a correction from Yoni.

I was in the middle of a headstand, a brand-new skill of mine, when Yoni came up behind me. His footsteps were so light and I was concentrating so deeply that I didn't realize he was there until I felt his hands on my hips. "I want you to come out of this pose and try again," he murmured.

I brought my legs down to the floor and tried to listen to his words as if I were any other student. Above all, I didn't want him to see how scared I was.

But Yoni didn't seem to notice. "You need a strong foundation with your neck and shoulders, like this." He adjusted me so that my hands were cradling my head and my elbows were a little farther away from my head than they had been previously. "Good, good. Now try going back into the headstand from this position." I went into my headstand from this base. He was right—I wobbled much less this way. My back was less arched, and the whole structure felt firm.

Yoni stood back and examined his work. "Very good," he said. Then he knelt down next to me and whispered, "You've come a long way." He stood up and said to the class, "Slowly and gently come down from your headstand. When your knees are on the mat, leave your forehead down and shift into child's pose."

I tucked into child's pose, the good feeling I'd gotten from the adjustment to my headstand totally gone. How did Yoni know I'd come a long way? Did he recognize me from the class

I had attended with Ethan years ago? That seemed impossible. Thousands of people had come through his classes since then. Did he murmur words of encouragement to all his new acolytes, as a way to get them to stick around? Or had he been talking to Lo, who might have told him my inner child work was going so well?

Whatever was going on, I did not want to draw attention to myself. When Yoni said, "It's time for savasana," I rolled onto my back like everyone else. I closed my eyes and heard Yoni bang a gong three times.

"I would like to tell you a story about a wild donkey," Yoni said. "The donkey was a few years old, and just starting to come into his own. He told his mother that he had to go and seek his destiny on the road to the Yarlung. She tried to stop him. 'You are such a young donkey,' she said. 'And you have never left our village. How will you find your way?' The young donkey reassured her. He had received a prophecy in a dream that told him to seek a waterfall."

Yoni took a long pause, so long that I wondered if the story was over. But at last he continued, "At first, the donkey was afraid. He encountered many pitfalls on his journey. He got a nettle stuck in his hoof. He was bitten by a serpent. His coat became drab and itchy. But he was not deterred, because he believed in the destiny set out for him. And his persistence was rewarded. The donkey arrived at the Yarlung Valley after a season of travel. He found the hidden waterfall that had appeared to him in his dream. It was shrouded in shadows and tucked behind a hairpin turn, but a kindly fox showed him the way."

Thinking that the story was over, I opened my eyes. Yoni

looked right at me. His face was stern and disapproving, and I squeezed my eyes shut. "Though his mother did not hear from him again, she was at peace. The same waterfall appeared to her in a dream, and she trusted that her little donkey's destiny was fixed."

When Yoni stopped speaking we all lay in silence for several more minutes. I didn't dare open my eyes again. I tried to figure out whether Yoni's story was specifically meant for me—had he discovered that I was Ethan's wife?—but I couldn't fathom how it applied.

Finally Yoni said, "Namaste," and left the room before students could approach him.

I sat up, dazed. I was just being paranoid, I told myself. There was no way Yoni could know who I really was. He was just being a good teacher, giving a new student a bit of positive reinforcement.

A few nights later, Willow finally invited me to hang out with her friends. "We're having a drum circle, and then a rap session," she said. "We've decided you should be included." I had all the rhythm of a wind-up toy and I was already in a baggy T-shirt and leggings, ready for bed, but I knew I had to go. I put on a pair of flip-flops and left our room with Willow. I figured it was okay to wear shoes, since we weren't doing an official activity, and Willow didn't say anything to me, though she went barefoot.

Willow led me down a series of paths to a clearing in the brush. I tried to orient myself as I followed behind—left at the yurt, right at the cluster of three cacti—but dusk had fallen and I doubted I could find my way back without a guide. The temperature had dropped about twenty degrees with the disappearance of the sun, and I hugged myself to keep warm, squeezing the goose-pimpled flesh of my upper arms.

Willow's friends Bodhi and Maria were already there when we arrived, and we sat in a small circle. Bodhi had a drum the size of a four-year-old strapped to his chest. Maria had a set of dainty bongos. Willow pulled two tambourines out of her bag and handed one to me.

"Namaste," Bodhi said. "We're here tonight to honor the Egyptian goddess Nephthys. She is the goddess of night, but also the goddess of death." He began to softly thump on his drum. "I want us to chant for her. As night falls, we want to let our bad feelings and negativity die. When we wake every day, we should think of it as another opportunity for rebirth." Maria syncopated Bodhi's thumps with a jaunty beat on her bongos. Willow started shaking her tambourine and nodded to me to do the same.

Then Bodhi started chanting, "*Nam myoho renge kyoooooooo.*" He said it three times before Maria and Willow began to chant it along with him. I was busy trying to keep time with my tambourine and didn't say anything until Willow shot me that death glare. I started mouthing the words, pretty sure I was messing them up. But my effort must have been enough for Willow because her glare was replaced with a satisfied smile.

We continued chanting for several minutes. At last, Bodhi held the last note of *kyooooo* for a long time and slapped his drum three times with great force. Then he took his shirt off. A dark forest of kinky hair covered his lanky torso from shoulder to hipbone. His drawstring pants rode so low that I saw where the stomach hair trailed into his pubis, and I tried not to stare. As I averted my eyes from his form I noticed that Willow and Maria had both taken off their shirts. Neither wore a bra, and though it was almost completely dark I was close enough to see that their nipples were hard pink points in the cold desert air. They were both looking at me expectantly.

I shook my head no. I was happy to bang a tambourine in the middle of the desert, but getting naked in front of virtual strangers was not part of my agenda. My face burned—how dare they assume that I would just go along with this? As I stood there, wordless, Willow grabbed my hand and pulled me twenty feet away from Maria and Bodhi. "What are you doing?" she spat.

"I just don't feel comfortable taking my shirt off," I whispered back.

She squeezed my hand so tightly it started to hurt. "Dana," she said, "I invited you here because I wanted us to connect spiritually. I thought you were ready for it. Don't embarrass me."

I really did not want to do any weird sex stuff. But we were alone out there, and I felt like I had no other choice. I didn't want to stand out as someone who wasn't spiritually evolving, or have my reticence gossiped about over lentils. I scowled but took my shirt and bra off. I was so worked up I didn't feel the cold.

Willow led me back to the circle, where Bodhi was patting his drum dreamily and Maria was lying down on the ground, looking up at the sky.

"So glad you are joining us," Bodhi said. I sat down and didn't say anything, still annoyed. Maria came up behind me and started petting my hair. Then she started to braid a section of it. I have always hated the feeling of strange hands on me, but I sat there and took it, while rage and fear beat inside my chest in tempo with Bodhi's drum.

I don't know how long we sat this way before they started talking. I expected another chant, another ritual of some kind. But they just began to gossip. It was all about people at the Homestead whom I hadn't met yet, so I couldn't really follow the thread. But I did gather that Maria's favorite thing in the world was to rat out another guest to Janus for breaking a rule. "I caught Coyote and Genesis whispering to each other during the afternoon silence," she boasted. "Janus was extremely pleased to hear that."

Though Maria seemed to take special delight in narcing on her fellow non-ordained, Bodhi and Willow appeared to enjoy a little light squealing, too. Bodhi said, "Did you hear about River? He's been leaving his assigned yoga classes if Yoni's not the teacher. He either goes back to his room and hides out there, or goes looking for the class Yoni *is* teaching."

Willow scoffed. "Ugh. It's so against everything we stand for."

"What do you mean?" I asked, the first thing out of my mouth since she had snapped at me.

She turned to me with a simpering expression on her face. "The guru has carefully planned each of our schedules in con-sultation with the dictates of the universe. Thinking you know better than the guru is the height of hubris." She shook her head like she couldn't believe she even had to explain this to me. "Yoni wants everyone to experience him equally, except, of course, for his 'nymphets.'"

"Willow, that's not kind." Maria *tsk*ed. "Yoni's assistants are very sweet and they're just doing their job. Everyone wants a piece of Yoni, and he must guard his time very carefully."

"Fine," Willow said. "But no one knows how those particular girls got *that* particular job. I just think it's a little convenient." It sounded to me like she wanted the job for herself.

Maria looked uncomfortable and changed the subject, so the conversation moved on to their origin stories. That's what they called their lives before they got involved with Yoni, as if they were *X-Men* characters. I found out that though they all had different superficial reasons for being at the Homestead those reasons boiled down to the same core: they were running away from something.

Willow was running from the government. She didn't seem to be accused of any crime—in fact, it sounded like when she was at home in Marin County, she didn't leave the house very much. But she was upset about potential government surveillance. She was obsessed with Edward Snowden, whom she called "Eddie." She did not seem to grasp the irony that she was watched much more closely inside the Homestead than she probably ever was outside it. But perhaps because the surveillance was low-tech—you were being watched by other people, not by drones or video cameras—she was less perturbed by it.

Maria was a college dropout who was trying to cure her eating disorder through spiritual awakening. She was still painfully skinny after trying several normal rehab programs without success, Maria's parents were willing to foot the bill for this spiritual retreat so she could possibly find a little peace.

Bodhi made a lot of money in Silicon Valley and went to Burning Man every year. He came to Zuni to get some space from his ex-girlfriend (though he still called her his "love star"). "And what brings you here, Dana?" Bodhi said. Everyone turned their eyes on me.

"Oh," I said. "Well, it's sort of like what happened to you. I had a relationship that didn't work out, and it was hard for me to move on. I'm trying to evolve here, um, spiritually, and make something of my life." Just like in my first class with Lo, I had begun my story thinking I had to make up something that sounded realistic, and once it was out of my mouth, I realized it was 100 percent true.

Everyone seemed to accept my origin story. And I felt lighter after I told them why I was there. I wasn't so worked up about taking my shirt off anymore. It didn't seem like that big a deal, and it didn't seem like anyone was going to make me do anything weird or sexual, or both. Not much later, Bodhi licked his finger and put it up in the air. "I think the wind is telling us it's time to retire for the evening." He chanted *Nam myoho renge kyoooooooo*" one more time and then put his shirt back on. Willow and Maria did the same, and so did I. Then we walked in a single-file line back to our rooms.

My sessions with Lo were the only places I felt any sense of calm. My concept of time continued to blur. I didn't know what day or date it was, since every day melted into the next. It was both destabilizing and soothing. I was so used to being on a workday schedule and responding to my bosses' needs, it was nice to float around in a timeless netherspace. As the days went by, it threw me off-kilter because I was so disconnected from everything I'd ever known.

Lo was my stability. She was full of praise for my work with her, which helped me feel supported in her presence. We were establishing a true bond, and I hoped that I'd soon feel comfortable asking her about Ethan and Amaya, as well as whether she had known Rosemary. But I was also learning more about myself, and how I'd let my life end up this way.

The second time we met we discussed our elementary school years. Lo's family of Witnesses had settled in Sacramento, which she called "Sactown." She made it sound like a barren hellscape where the sun shined unremittingly and her unfeeling parents either ignored her (she was the second youngest of seven) or beat her for her dirty thoughts.

"There was a lot of shame in my household," Lo explained. "That's why I was drawn to this work in the first place, to process that shame."

"My household wasn't filled with shame, exactly," I said, and then didn't say: *It was filled with land mines set by my mercurial mother.* "But your mention of shame brings up one particular memory."

"Please tell me about it," Lo pleaded.

"I'm not sure. I'm afraid it's going to bring back up a lot of bitterness. I'm trying to move on from that kind of feeling."

"If you're afraid to discuss it, the emotions need deeper processing. Remember, this is the safest space in the world." I looked at her kind, open face and believed her.

I took a deep breath. "Okay." I sighed. "My mother had planned a big fourth of July party in our yard for the whole neighborhood. She rented a bounce house. She spent the week before preparing all her signature dishes: rhubarb pies and deviled eggs and burgers with her own proprietary blend of spices. She picked out the dress I was going to wear. It was a white sleeveless sundress with big red bows on the shoulders. I remember her staying up almost all night before the day of the party, just to make sure everything would be to her liking." Lo maintained eye contact while I took a breath and then continued.

"The morning of the party, I could feel she was on edge. Whenever she gets anxious, she starts cracking her knuckles, and I could hear the *crack crack crack* from ten feet away. As people started arriving, I kept looking over at my mom, and she had this scary smile plastered on her face. But everyone seemed to be having a good time, so I relaxed a little. The kids were bouncing on the bounce house and drinking juice boxes. The moms and dads were drinking their spiked lemonades, waiting for their burgers to be ready." I paused for a second. I could feel the weight of what I was about to tell Lo, like a barbell perched on my chest.

"Everything was fine until the food was ready. I bounded over to get my burger, and I could feel my mother watching my every move. I sat down to eat, careful to put a napkin on my lap because my mother hated it when I made a mess. But when I took my first bite, a dollop of ketchup fell onto the front of my white, white sundress." I couldn't help it; I started to cry. Sharing the memory made it feel new and raw again. "The second the ketchup made contact, my mother started to scream at me in front of everyone. I can't even remember what she said. But I remember I spent the rest of the party locked in my room, sobbing."

"And how did that make you feel?" Lo asked, sidling up to me and putting a comforting hand on my back.

"Fucking terrible!" I shouted.

"There, there," Lo said, pulling my head into her chest and stroking my hair. For a moment I recoiled at the intimacy. Lo's touch was so maternal, it felt too close. But it also felt nice, so I relaxed into her.

After a few breaths I sat up and wiped my face with my sleeve. "I feel like I spent my whole life on tenterhooks, worrying that any misstep would set her off."

"That must have been a very hard way to live," Lo said.

"It was awful. And it's why I stopped talking to her. I needed her support when Ethan left me, but all she offered was judgment. About eighteen months after he left, she was nagging me about getting back on the dating scene and finding a man before my eggs dried up. I told her again that I still wasn't ready. That I was still working through our breakup. And you know what she said? She said it was no wonder he left. That I emasculated him with my big career and all my money. I made him feel small."

I started crying hard again. Reading Ethan's book, I'd worried that my mother was partially right, even if she'd said it as cruelly as possible. "And then she said I was too good for him anyway, so what was I still so down about? Good riddance to mountain trash." Ethan was a lot of things, but he wasn't trash. My mother's casual malice shocked me, now that I was saying it aloud to someone else. Lo patted my head until I was finished. I sat up and told her the rest of it.

"I stopped answering the phone when she called and blocked

her e-mail. My sister still speaks to her sporadically, so she told Mom why I cut ties. Mom very quickly stopped trying to reach me, and the last I heard, she'd cut me out of her will."

Lo pulled a handkerchief out of her poncho and handed it to me. "I'm glad you told me that story. That was very brave of you, and it was brave of you to distance yourself from your mother's negative energy. You've done very good work today. Don't you feel lighter? Less blocked up?"

I dabbed my face and nodded back. "Yes, I do."

One night after dinner, Willow and I were both reading on our beds. Each of the rooms had a shelf filled with Yoni's writings— some were professionally published books, some were graying pamphlets. They had titles like *You Can't Spell Empower With-out* M *and* E and *The Dharma of Business: Using Ancient Virtues to Win in the Modern World.* I kept trying to find useful information in these books, but the woo-woo jargon in them was so thick, I couldn't parse it.

I kept thinking I felt Willow's eyes on me, but when I looked over at her, she was buried in her book. I got up to pee, and when I came out of the bathroom, Willow was gone. I hadn't heard a thing, so she must have crept out as quietly as possible, purposely waiting until I went to the bathroom to leave. Since she'd included me in her drum circle, if she purposely ditched me, she must be doing something secret. I ran to the front door and saw her at the end of the hallway, about to round the corner. I scurried on tiptoe down the hall after her.

Willow looked like she was heading for the building where we had our classes. I crouched behind a big cactus twenty feet away and watched. A few other people trickled into the building behind her. I saw Bodhi among them, but he was the only one I knew by name.

I waited until it seemed like no one else was coming, and then I counted to one hundred and snuck into the building. All the lights inside were off. I groped along the wall, feeling the outlines of sconces and Buddhas and doorknobs. *This is crazy*, I told myself. But I pushed forward. I hadn't found out anything about Ethan during my stay so far, and I wasn't going to change that by wussing out the second things got really weird.

Finally I saw a tiny flicker of light coming from a small window in the door of one of the classrooms. Cautiously, I looked into the room, hoping no one would be able to see my face in the blackness of the hallway. The room was lit by candles, so it was still dim inside, but I could see a row of decorative samurai swords stacked neatly on the wall. Then, as my eyes adjusted further, I made out twelve men standing naked in a circle. After staring for a few moments I realized they had symbols painted on their torsos. For a second I thought the symbols were marked in blood—maybe carved out with the swords? But then I realized the paint was purple, not red. Bodhi, who was close to the door, had a crab on his stomach, its pincers caught in his ample body hair.

I looked around for Willow, and it took me a while to locate her, because she was on the ground, with eleven other women. Why were they crawling around like penitents on the floor? They looked like they were in a choreographed formation, and I wondered where they were getting instructions. Then I heard a voice from the back of the room. It took me a moment to recognize the voice as Yoni's because he was speaking too quietly for me to make out his words. I recognized it only from the cadence—he had all those pauses. His quiet was an ominous hum.

As I watched, Willow grabbed Bodhi's penis and started furiously jerking it. All the other women did the same with their male partners.

Yoni increased his volume. I could finally understand him: *"Spill the seed, sow the seed. Spill the seed, sow the seed."* The other men in the room began to chant with him. Their voices were almost screaming when Yoni interrupted the mantra to yell *"FINISH!"* At that moment, every single man in the room ejaculated. Their come went everywhere, all over the women, all over the floor. I looked at Willow's face, and she was ecstatic.

I saw Yoni emerge from the shadows to stand in the middle of the circle. He was naked, too. His penis pointed directly out, at a ninety-degree angle from his body. "Your seed is now sown," he said. "Let the earth reap your spirit." He walked over to one of the girls in the room, someone I'd never seen before. She sat still on the ground as he approached her. Faster than I'd ever seen in any porn, as if propelled by an inner force, Yoni was inside her.

I couldn't watch any more. I turned around and broke into a run. The sweat dripped down my back as I took wrong turns in the darkness. Finally I found my way back to the outside door and burst into the desert night. I kept running until I was back in my bed with the covers drawn over me. My heart continued to race and the scene I had just witnessed looped through my mind. I started touching myself to release the pent-up energy and fear. I came hard and felt my entire body unclench. I fell asleep immediately after.

"What's with you?" said Willow at lunch a few nights later. "You've barely said a word to me for two days. Are you okay?" She seemed genuinely concerned.

I glanced around the table. Maria and Bodhi were looking at me expectantly. I could barely make eye contact with Bodhi. "Nothing's with me. I'm just processing a lot of my experiences here. It's a lot of spiritual work. It feels heavy."

Willow seemed satisfied with my bullshit explanation. She nodded. "That happened to me when I first started my work here, too." She started telling a story about how all her instructors were blown away by the quality of her efforts, and I zoned out again.

For the past two days I had been having a very slow panic attack. I was equal parts turned on and creeped out by what I'd seen. I was seduced by my work with Lo. Two months ago, I would have found everything here either deeply silly or intellectually bankrupt. I kept wrestling with the same question: Who was I anymore?

And I still wondered about Ethan and Amaya, who rolled into my consciousness like a rogue wave at odd times. I tried to game out my stay here. I had about two weeks left before my month was up. I had basically given up on finding out anything from Willow and her pals, because they didn't care about anyone or anything but themselves and how they could get ahead here. I could still talk to Lo, but I had no guarantee that would get me any closer to the answers I needed. She had been with Yoni so long, who knows how she'd react to questions about their shared past?

And when I left, then what? Would I just go back to New York? Stay in that old apartment and go back to my old job? Would I even have a job to go back to? Phil couldn't fire me for taking a sabbatical that was listed in the company handbook, but he could definitely come up with some other reason. And if I did get fired, he wouldn't recommend me for dogcatcher. He was an asshole—not someone interested in human frailty or growth.

I started to truly panic as the what-ifs started screaming in my head. What if I had blown up my life for nothing? What if I left this place with nothing more than a few orange crystals and a depleted bank account? And then, the most disturbing— *what if Yoni continues to destroy lives and there's nothing I can do to stop him?* The thought turned my stomach, and I pushed my plate away.

When I walked into Lo's classroom after that unsettling lunch, my head spinning, I saw that it had been transformed. Instead of sitting pillows, yoga mats overlaid with Navajo blankets were strewn around the floor. Around the perimeter of the small room, candles were lit.

"Because we're processing our adolescence today," Lo said, "I wanted to re-create a kind of teenage slumber party. I want your inner teen to feel at home."

I was genuinely touched. "Thank you," I said, and sprawled out on one of the mats.

"Though this work is always called 'inner child' work, it

shouldn't be taken literally," Lo said. She lay down on her side and propped her head up on one hand. "The point is to go back to any time in your past when you were innocent and suffered emotional trauma." She hesitated. "I would like to tell you the story of my early days with Yoni. But I want to remind you that what we share in here is between us. If it goes beyond this room, it will violate the work we've done here. It will cause our inner children to feel great shame, because no child likes a tattletale."

"I understand," I said, feeling a pang of guilt because I didn't mean it. I had grown so loyal to Lo in our days together, I didn't want to betray her. But I had to remember that Lo might have valuable information about Rosemary, and even about Ethan and Amaya.

Lo nodded and began her story.

Lo

I started running away when I was fifteen. Our community of Witnesses had eyes everywhere in Sacramento, so someone always brought me home. Each time I got a bigger and bigger whooping. One morning, after the worst beating I'd had, I vowed that the next time I wouldn't be caught. Some friend of my older sister's had run away to San Francisco. I'd never been—I'd barely left the neighborhood—but my dad called it Sodom on the Bay and said my sister's friend was going to meet a terrible end there. It sounded like a place where no one would come looking for me.

The day after my eighteenth birthday I waited until the house was asleep. It must have been three in the morning when I crept out and walked to the bus station. I took the five A.M. bus to San Fran. I remember what I was wearing: a knee-length A-line dress with a floral pattern that I had made myself. It had a big floppy bow at the neck. I had a matching purse that I made sure to carry with me. I was small for my age and must have looked all of twelve years old.

Another girl around my age got on the bus with me. She was

wearing a micromini skirt and beads. Her hair was long and wavy and she wore it loose and unstyled. I was so scared to be alone, I sat down next to her and started talking. I have let go of my anger about my upbringing, so I can appreciate the good things about it. The best part of going door-to-door was that I learned early to be able to talk to anybody.

The girl said she was going to San Francisco, too, and that she was going to stay in the Haight. "What's that?" I asked her.

"It's heaven," she said. "I'll take you there."

Those first days went by real fast. I think I burned that outfit I was so proud of. I had my first taste of grass. I started meditating. The girl—her name was Veena, by the way—taught me how. She's one of the women I eat my meals with here at the Homestead. We go back a long, long time. Veena and I were living with friends of her friend. We slept on the floor in their tiny apartment, which was filled with vermin. I got a rat bite the first week I was there, and I just let it fester because I didn't know what else to do. When it started looking real infected, someone told me to go to the free clinic.

I was waiting in line there, with my arm in a makeshift sling made out of an old dish towel, when I first met Yoni. He had a different name back then, but he was the same man he is today. He came up to me, out of all the girls in the line that day, because he said he could feel my aura from down the block.

"You glow purple," he said. "And purple is a regal color. I feel like you were my queen in a past life." It was love at first sight. He asked me where I was staying, and I told him what had happened to my arm. He said that he had a big, clean house where I would get warm meals and a good night's sleep. He said

someone there would fix my arm—they had all the supplies—
and that I should just come with him. I took one last look at the
line and thought, *Sure, why not.*

Those first few days with Yoni were probably the best of my
life. I had a warm bed to sleep in and wholesome meals. There
were other girls like me in the house, and they were just as
sweet as could be. They reminded me of my sisters back home,
and I wasn't lonely or scared anymore. It seemed natural when
Yoni came to my bedroom one night and we made love. He was
so gentle, and he explained that this was how we could be celes-
tially bonded. The other girls in the house were already bonded
to him, and I wanted to be just like them. I even got Veena to
join me at Yoni's. She was smitten with him, just like I was.

What? Oh, no. I wasn't jealous of the other girls. Not at all.
We were all sisters, you see. We were part of this new commu-
nity where no one owned anyone else, especially not sexually.
In fact, we started getting more men to join the commune, and
Yoni encouraged us to sleep with them, too. "No one owns your
essence," he would say.

Well, maybe I was jealous of one girl. She was actually a close
friend of mine from high school. I wrote her a letter from San
Francisco when I moved in with Yoni and told her to join me
there, too. A year later, she did. She was so beautiful, and she
was clearly Yoni's favorite. He called her Safflower, and she had
just the whitest blond hair you've ever seen. She looked like an
angel. It was hard to hate her, though, because she was so sweet
and kind. Never had a harsh word for anyone or anything.

Things were copacetic for a while in San Francisco, but then
Yoni decided that the energy had gone sour. It's true there was

a lot more violence around, and a lot of people were leaving. So he found this beautiful place up in Mendocino County, and we all shipped out there.

It was heaven on earth, at first. I'd never seen such beautiful trees, and I would spend hours napping in the shade. It felt like we were really seeing the potential of our community fully realized. Veena had a child, a little girl she named Sierra. We both worked in the nursery part-time, where the children were cared for communally. I loved caring for those babies. We studied midwifery from one of the other members, and so we birthed those babies, too.

Everything was perfect until Safflower ran off. She left in the middle of the night. Yoni was crushed. I think he really loved her, in a different way than he loved the rest of us. It turned out she was the first of many. Once people saw someone anointed leave, they started losing their faith in Yoni, which really seemed tremendously unfair to me. Like they were kicking him when he was down. He and I got closer then. I was there to salve his heart wounds. We'd spend hours together meditating, and that's when he made me his new spiritual wife. He said that we had a special bond that transcended our bodies and this world.

I'm okay. I just got a little emotional there for a second, remembering how wonderful that closeness felt. Yoni and I have a different kind of bond now. He's had other spiritual wives since me. I understand, of course. To really develop along our own paths, we must follow what the fates have laid out for us.

Ultimately Yoni decided that it was our mission to spread the word about our community, and that it was best done on the road. A lot of the community had turned out to be dirty traitors.

We left 'em behind, never looked back. It was just me, Veena, Dew—that's the other woman I eat my meals with here—and Yoni, then.

What happened to Sierra? We had to leave her behind. Veena realized that her spiritual development could not proceed if she was yoked to a child. Sierra's daddy took her away when he left. Anyway, Veena and Dew had become lovers themselves, and we traveled around as a foursome before landing in New York, ultimately. I celebrated my twenty-eighth birthday in a ceremony at our new home in the Village. Twenty-eight seems so young to me now, but I felt like I had lived three or four different lifetimes by then.

Woo! That felt good. It can be good to retell your story. In the act of retelling, our bitterness becomes smaller and smaller, until it is the size of a flea, and we can flick it away.

Dana

"Now you go," Lo said. My mouth opened but no sound came out. Lo was Sandra—Rosemary's high school friend. The one Ray told me about, the one who had encouraged her to join Yoni decades ago. I hoped that even though she was upset about Rosemary leaving the fold, she retained some residual tenderness for a friend she'd had since she was a girl.

I felt I had been given an opening to tell her the truth. And though it made me wonder if I had lost my mind, I perceived a beneficent force field surrounding the room. I closed my eyes and took deep, soothing breaths so that I could better witness the vibes. I felt like Rosemary was there watching us, and her positive energy would protect me from censure.

"Can I be radically honest with you?" I asked.

"Of course. That is what we are here for," Lo said, her eyes twinkling even more than usual.

I took a deep breath. "I'm not the person you think I am."

"None of us show our true selves to the world. We are all just showing a version," Lo said. "I know you feel unlike yourself, dear, but that's normal when you do as much inner child work as you have been doing. I'm very proud of you." Lo looked so kind that I almost couldn't bear to go on, but I had to.

"I used to be Dana Powell." Even I could hear how shaky my voice was. "My husband. Ex-husband. Ethan. Kai." I took a deep breath. Lo's expression remained blank, uncomprehending. "The man you knew as Kai. I used to be married to him. I came here to find out what really happened to him."

"What do you mean?" Lo said. "He and Amaya just left. They had been experimenting with some questionable ancient rituals that were bringing negative energy to the environment, so Yoni asked them to go. They could be anywhere. A lot of people who leave the retreat go on to India or Bali to do additional spiritual work. And of course it would be very difficult to contact him if he's taken a vow of silence somewhere remote."

I couldn't believe it. Was Lo really that isolated from the outside world? "Don't you know what happened? Ethan and Amaya are dead." It came out more harshly than I wanted it to.

Lo's face fell. "That's not possible. I would have heard something." She paused, thinking, and then said, almost to herself, "But Yoni did say after they left we were never to speak of them again."

"It *is* possible. It was all over the news right after it happened. They were found dead in a cave near here. The police say it was a murder-suicide. But I don't believe that Ethan would ever murder anybody. And that's why I'm here." I reached out and took Lo's hand.

Lo said nothing. I couldn't read the look on her face. "I've been trying to figure out what happened to Ethan, and in my research I discovered that his mom was a follower of Yoni's years ago. Her name was Rosemary. Safflower's name was Rosemary before she met Yoni, wasn't it?"

I saw a flare of shock cross Lo's face. She didn't respond, so I continued. "And that Aries—Yoni—whatever you called him then, was Ethan's dad."

Lo said, "But . . ." She trailed off. I waited for her to continue, but she didn't. I pushed forward, because if I didn't, I wouldn't finish what I had to say. "She married another man—the guy who raised Ethan—right after she left the commune. Did you know she charged Yoni with rape? I don't know how that's related to Ethan's death, but it just has to be."

I could almost see Lo going back in time in her head, trying to rebuild her life's chronology when the story she had told herself for so long had shattered, realizing they didn't leave Mendocino so they could spread the good word about their new spiritual practices. They left the West Coast entirely because Yoni was running from the law.

"I didn't know any of that," Lo said. "Ethan was such a gentle soul."

"How could you know about it? Yoni's been keeping you in the dark about the entire world for forty years." I was starting to get worked up now, and my voice rose.

"Keep it down," Lo said tersely. She sat in silence for several moments before slowly removing her hand from mine. She closed her eyes, and I could hear her taking deep, soothing breaths, like she was physically processing what I had just said.

At last she opened her eyes and looked at me. "I think our session for today is over. I need to work through what has just happened, and I can't do that with you here watching me."

"But I really think we should talk this through," I pleaded, grabbing her hand again and holding it to my chest. "I need to know more about Ethan's last days here. It's so important for me to be able to put the pieces together so I can get the real story. So I can move on with my life!"

Lo yanked her hand away. Her voice became a hiss. "Please. Leave. Now."

I was desperate to tell her more, to make sure she believed me, but I obeyed her. As I walked out of the room, I turned back to look at her. Her eyes were closed again, and she was shaking her head back and forth and chanting quietly.

I thought about leaving then. Just marching up to the front desk and asking for a ride back to Albuquerque. I wouldn't even ask for a refund—I'd just hightail it back to civilization as fast as I could. But I knew that if I left now, I would never find out what happened to Ethan. My money and time would be lost. I had no proof that Lo would use what I said for malicious purposes. I had to believe that the connection we had was real.

I decided the only course of action was to continue at the retreat as I had been. I went to breakfast with Willow. I attended my usual afternoon yoga classes. There were no more Yoni appearances—I saw him only at occasional mealtimes like everyone else. I went to dinner with Willow. After dinner, I listened to Willow, Bodhi, and Maria gossip.

The day after my run-in with Lo, I arrived at her workshop at the appointed time. I thought we could work through things together, but she wasn't there. When she didn't show up I went over to Coral at the front desk to see where she was.

"Lo didn't show up for our morning workshop," I said. "Is she okay?"

"Let me check on that for you," Coral said, plinking something into her keyboard. "Hmm, I have no record of a cancellation from Lo this morning. I'll look into it and get back to you."

I went back to my room and tried to occupy myself with showering and paging through Yoni's "books" until lunchtime. I looked for Lo at mealtimes, but she wasn't there. I thought about asking Veena or Dew if they had seen her, but I didn't want to call any additional attention to myself, especially not from the ordained.

The next day at breakfast, I was assigned to a new morning class. The new class was called Brush Meditation, which involved using paintbrushes as a "contemplative tool." That meant sitting in front of a blank piece of paper and making random brush-strokes, like elephants or gorillas do when their keepers are making them "paint."

I tried to sleep at night, without much success. I was so afraid that Lo would turn me in to Yoni. After the bad press he got with Ethan's and Amaya's deaths, he wouldn't be brazen enough to harm me, too, would he? If he tried to get me alone and attack me, how would I get out of it? If I tried blaming the guru for anything, no one at the Homestead would believe me. I started fantasizing about escaping into the desert brush. I had no food or water. My cell phone was dead. I had money, but what good would that do me in this forbidding landscape? I had a disastrous sense of direction. I could picture myself wandering through the brush, totally lost, and ultimately slumping over from dehydration, dying out there like Ethan and Amaya did. I obsessed over these visions until the sun rose and the shades disappeared into the ceiling.

The days went by like this. I wandered through my schedule, not fully paying attention to anything because I was so exhausted. I barely spoke, but no one seemed to notice. Willow loved hearing the sound of her own voice, so she was sated with random *mm-hmm*s that I exhaled in the middle of her monologues.

I started seeing Lo at meals again, but she would avoid eye contact. Her eyes would dart down to her plate the second I looked over at her. Every time she looked away from me, it was like a stab in the gut. I thought our connection had been something profound—something that stood apart, unsullied, from whatever else was going on at the Homestead. But I was wrong. It was like getting rejected by my mother all over again.

Except for her refusal to look at me, from outward appearances, nothing seemed to be amiss with Lo. She seemed to be plugging along as she ever did, gabbing with Veena and Dew. I wasn't particularly worried that she'd inform on me; she seemed to want to pretend that our talk had never happened at all.

I was at the end of my third week at the Homestead when my stupor was interrupted by the juiciest gossip Willow and her pals had ever chewed over. We were at lunch one day, passing around a bowl of coconut chia pudding, which tasted like coconuts mixed with dirt. I was choking it down when Maria started flapping her hands in excitement. "Oh oh oh! I almost forgot to tell you the most exciting thing!"

Willow looked up from her pudding. "What?" she said, sort of harshly.

Maria ignored Willow's tone. "I heard from Songbird that someone is going to be ordained soon." She smiled proudly, like a dog that had just killed a backyard gopher and dropped it at his owner's feet.

Willow put down her spoon. "Wow! Are you sure?"

"I'm pretty sure. Songbird wouldn't say where she heard it. But I know she's had at least one special session with Janus, and we all know Janus has Yoni's ear."

"I don't know," Bodhi said. "I've been here six months—longer than almost any of the other non-ordained residents. And I haven't seen anyone ordained in that time. I'm not sure anyone has really stood out." The wrinkles between his eyebrows deepened and he started stress-eating his pudding.

"Well, I think a lot of people have been doing really important soul and body work, and that it's high time Yoni noticed," Willow said. "Don't you think, Dana?"

Everyone turned to me for a response. I didn't care about who got ordained, and I didn't want to get in the middle of their bitchfest. But I had to say something, so I said, "Mm-hmm," in what I hoped was a noncommittal way.

"See? Dana has also observed that *some* people are making a lot of progress." Willow sat back, satisfied.

"I think you're a lock for getting ordained," Maria said to Willow.

Bodhi blanched. "I actually think that Tarot has made the most progress," he said quickly. "His dedication to his spiritual awakening is leaps and bounds beyond anyone else's. Did you see the way he came up with that mantra on the spot the other day during our Co-creation class?"

Willow looked like she was going to stab Bodhi with her spoon. "I haven't been impressed with Tarot at all," she said. "In fact—"

I couldn't listen to this any longer. "I'm going to go to the bathroom. I'll be right back," I said. No one responded; they weren't paying any attention to me.

I went into the cool, tiled restroom and washed my face. I looked in the mirror, which I didn't do much anymore. Who was I trying to impress? My dirty-blond hair had brightened a little in the New Mexico sun, but the ends were ragged without my expensive shampoo to smooth them. I had huge bags under my eyes from getting so little sleep. But otherwise I looked surprisingly good: my skin was clearer than it had ever been (probably from all that hippie food) and my eyes seemed brighter. I searched my expression to see if this experience had changed me in some fundamental way. If I looked older, or warier, or sadder. But I looked as much like myself as I ever had.

I dried my face with a hemp washcloth and walked back to my table. I was almost at my seat when I saw Janus standing there, talking to Willow. He had a concerned expression on his face, which lifted as soon as he saw me. "Oh, there you are," he said, grabbing my upper arm. "We need you. Come with me."

Willow looked up at me, confused and maybe a little jealous. I tried not to look terrified, but it took everything in me not to start crying. I scanned the room. People were starting to look at me, and I wanted to find Lo in the crowd. But she wasn't there. An empty space sat across from Dew and Veena. My stomach dropped. I said nothing and followed Janus out of the room.

Janus led me down a series of corridors that at first looked like everything else here: terra-cotta walls and deity pictures. But then we passed through a glass door I'd never seen before. He needed a punch code to open it, and it made a great sucking sound when he pulled at it, like the following corridor was hermetically sealed. After that, the décor changed. The walls were a rich purple and hung with the kinds of samurai swords I'd seen displayed during the sex ritual. The floor was laid with pristine blond wood. I could tell that the floors were heated because the boards beneath me felt almost the same as my body temperature.

We had been walking for several minutes when we reached a room without windows. The walls were covered with Indian throws and twinkled with little mirrors, reflecting the candles lit in the four corners of the room. Big pillows lined the floor, and next to each pillow was an empty trough. It looked like a hookah lounge for horses.

Janus led me to one of these pillows. He sat down on another one. We waited in silence for several beats, and I started to tremble. He noticed and patted my arm reassuringly. Then, through a door that had been covered by Indian fabric, Yoni emerged.

He bowed and sat down on a pillow facing us. "We've been aware of your actions here," Yoni said, looking right into my eyes.

I wanted to defend myself but said nothing. What could I say? I looked over at Janus. But, confusingly, Janus did not look angry.

"You have made great progress, Dana," Yoni said. "I've seen the work you have done. You do not gossip like the other magpies. Gossip hinders our self-work, because it is other-focused. You quietly go about your studies and seek to get rid of all the negative energy in your life. You're a true penitent." His eyes lit up as he spoke. He took out a tiny set of hand cymbals that were tied together with an orange ribbon and clanged them together three times.

One of the nymphets, holding a golden lacquered tray with two mugs on it, appeared in the hidden doorway Yoni had come through. She knelt between Janus and me. Janus took a mug, and I followed suit. I peered inside mine. Whatever was in there looked dark and murky. The nymphet bowed at us, her tray never moving, and left the room again.

"Congratulations, Dana. This is your ordination ceremony. This does not mean that your work here is done. On the contrary. The real work of your journey is just beginning." Yoni's eyes sparkled, but his mouth was set in a serious line. I could see the wrinkles in his brow tighten. He nodded at Janus, who drank from his mug. I took a small sip from mine. And instead of fear, I felt pride.

Some part of me knew it was completely fucked. That everything I had experienced over the past few weeks was potentially dangerous mumbo jumbo based on a foundational lie. That the *real* work I was supposed to be doing wasn't even going well: I was only half a step closer to finding out what had happened to Ethan than I had been when I arrived at Zuni.

But another part of me knew I *had* done real work here. The things I told Lo were completely true. For the first time in memory, I didn't feel angry. I wasn't cursing fate and the hand I'd been dealt. I wasn't blaming my mother—or Ethan—for everything that had gone wrong in my life. And I was grateful for that.

Janus took another big gulp from his mug, so I did the same. It was only after this second gulp that I really tasted the brew, which was like baker's chocolate infused with twigs and snot. The aftertaste lingered in my mouth for a moment and I almost threw up. I wondered if it was poisoned.

But when I looked over at Janus, he continued to take shots of the brew, making faces like he'd just had a jigger of cheap tequila. Aside from those faces, he looked fine. This didn't seem like some Jonestown scenario with cyanide-laced Kool-Aid. I took a few more little sips of my drink: big enough that I could get the liquid down, small enough to keep me from gagging.

After Janus and I finished our drinks, Yoni said, "Lie down," and we did. We used the pillows to prop our heads up. "Close your eyes."

I felt Yoni's hands gently combing my hair. His nails were surprisingly long, and his touch maternal. After a while, my limbs felt heavy, and my stomach began to roil. Fuck, what if this *was* a Jonestown scenario? It would be too late. The fear was so intense that it short-circuited my brain; the thoughts kept bumping into one another like a roomful of toddlers learning to walk. My heart beat a fast, syncopated track. The pain got worse and I turned over to my side and curled up in the fetal position.

"You may need to use the troughs for your eruptions," Yoni said. "Vomiting is a common side effect of the ayahuasca journey you are on."

I looked over at Janus, who was doubled over his trough, retching his life out. Just watching him caused me to start heaving, and as my lunch came back up the same mantra kept repeating over and over again in my head, erected in big neon letters that flashed on and off: *Pride goeth before a fall.*

When I was empty I lay down again, and the mantra disappeared. I started to see vibrant colors burst across my brain. Pink and then green, blue and then black. Black black black. I imagined myself groping around in the dark, feeling for some sort of exit, but my hands were slippery. I found a hatch in the ceiling and I opened it. My mother fell out. "I'm in pain, I'm in pain," she kept wailing. "Can't you see? I'm in pain."

I picked her up and comforted her. She was the size of a baby. It was suddenly so clear to me that she was nasty because she was hurting. I felt revolutionary empathy for her, unlike anything I'd ever experienced. I cuddled her until she stopped wailing and fell asleep.

I started groping around in the dark for another entry. I found ornate French doors, and when I opened them I fell into a garden. Birds chirped in my ears, and gargantuan butterflies flapped their huge wings so that I felt a fresh breeze on my face. I wandered through the garden until I found an open field. I sat down and started picking cornflowers, then wove them into a daisy chain and put them on my head. Beth appeared next to me. She was wearing a white nightgown, like the ones we wore as children. I wove a daisy chain for her, too. She thanked me. "I'm so proud of you," she said, before she floated away. I waved good-bye to her as she disappeared into the sky.

I got up and kept walking until I came to a pond. I looked down and saw my reflection, but I also saw Ethan's face. "Dana," Ethan said, "you don't need to worry about me. You've done enough for me in the earthly world. You were a good wife. I couldn't live up to our sacred vows. I'm sorry." The water in the lake rippled in the butterfly wind, but Ethan's face remained clear. "My spirit is at rest," he said. "Please don't disturb my spirit. I've found perfect peace."

I turned around to see if Ethan was behind me, but there was no one there. I looked back at the water. Ethan's reflection was gone. In his place were two otters. They floated on their backs while holding hands. I knew that these otters were Ethan and Amaya, and in that moment I released all my jealousy toward them. I was so happy their spirits were at peace that I started to cry.

I saw Janus drifting above me on a cloud. "Do you understand what you are seeing?" he asked, reclining on his white puffy chaise. "Kai and Amaya brought each other to the physical brink. They were worshiping an Aztec goddess of death, the obsidian butterfly. She told them to prove their love to her by spilling their blood on sacred soil. That's why they fled the Homestead. The butterfly has claimed them. But their spirits are free as the breeze." With that, he floated off into the distance. He got smaller and smaller and smaller until he was one with the sky.

And then I heard Yoni's voice in the background. He kept saying my name: Dana, Dana, Dana. Like a chant. Was this only happening in my mind? I felt him putting his hands on my forehead. They were cool to the touch. My face was hot. Yoni started speaking.

"I want to tell you a story about a pair of coyotes, a male and a female. They lived blissfully together in the Mezquital Valley, feasting on the abundant crops and sleeping in the cool highland air with the rest of their pack. The male was the alpha of the group, a natural leader. And the female had the glossiest, healthiest coat of any coyote in the valley." As Yoni spoke, I saw those coyotes saunter in front of me and lie down together, nuzzled into each other. "One day, those coyotes were blessed with a single pup." A sweet baby coyote appeared on the scene, walked over to his parents, and snuggled into his mother.

"Coyotes are unusual in the animal kingdom: the raising of children isn't just the mother's job. While the mother nurses her young, the father protects them both and brings food from the outside world. But this mother coyote got spooked; she heard strange noises at night in the valley, noises she never heard before. Instead of looking to her mate for safety, she fled with the pup." The mother and child ran off, leaving a lone coyote wailing at the moon.

"The mother and child were never the same. They wandered in the wilderness for twenty-seven years. The mother died, and her son had no one. His journey was meandering and without purpose. His father finally sent an envoy to look for him, a young female coyote who would bring him home. After a long journey, she found him crying alone by a stream that was almost dry. The young coyote returned him to his pack, where he belonged." I pictured the group of coyotes trotting happily into the distance and smiled.

"Dana, do you understand what I am telling you?" Yoni said, his cool hands shifting off my forehead to my temples. He was so close I could smell his breath, a pure peppermint waft. "Kai—your Ethan—he had to come home to his pack.

He was not being nourished by a world he didn't belong in. I sent Amaya, my most precious companion, to find him. She brought him home."

I opened my mouth to speak. I hadn't said a word since I began my ayahuasca journey, and my voice was a deep, unfamiliar croak. "But what about me? Hadn't he made a new home with me?" Tears leaked from the corners of my eyes.

"My child. Your streambed was dry. Don't you see that now? You weren't being nourished by your surroundings, were you?" Yoni started to stroke my hair again.

As he lulled me, I had to admit I wasn't. I hadn't been happy with Ethan even before he left with Amaya. I had to acknowledge that now. We had been connected once, but that connection had frayed and frayed. And I certainly hadn't been nourished by anything or anyone in the years since our break. "No. I wasn't fulfilled."

"And you weren't your true self. I can see that now. I can see that true self shining through after all the work you've done here." He kneaded my temples gingerly as he said this. "Amaya had a darkness within her. She hid it so successfully that I didn't see it until it was too late. I should have sent another envoy to embrace Ethan. Their bond became tainted just before they left the Homestead. I should never have sent them off into the hills. But I thought they would work themselves out and return to the fold." Now he was crying. I felt his teardrops sprinkle my forehead. They dripped down my face like a pleasant rain. "This was all fated. Don't you understand? Nothing happens for no reason. The cycle of events that began forty years ago with Saffie has culminated in your arrival. You are the true gift to the Homestead."

In my mind I saw a red door open, a golden light glowing behind it.

Yoni lay down next to me and whispered in my ear: "You are meant to be." He kissed me on the mouth. It was the most tender kiss I'd ever received. I could see his lips as a cloud in the sky: pillowy and pure white. He touched my breasts and I felt his power burrowing into my heart. I saw a giant snake, which turned into a slide, which turned into a rope, which coiled around an anchor, which led into a boat that floated out to sea. I floated with the boat until I felt something touch my shoulder.

I opened my eyes. The troughs had disappeared, as had Lama Yoni. In place of my trough was a tray that held a tea set and an envelope.

Janus poured us two cups of tea. He handed me a cup. "Do you know why Yoni named me Janus?" he asked. I shook my head no. "In Greek mythology, Janus is the doorway. He is the patron saint of beginnings and of changes. That's my job here. I welcome guests to stay at the retreat, but I also welcome the ordained by taking an ayahuasca journey with each of them. You learn so much on each journey, it is the greatest gift any member of our tribe could ever receive."

"I do feel transformed," I told him. "I never thought I would take a journey like this. I have never felt so free, so empty, in my entire life."

"That is the power of ayahuasca. We use it as an ordination rite because it is truly transformative. In observing your journey,

Yoni has been given your new spirit name. It will reflect what he saw when you were experiencing your deep soul change."

Janus slid the envelope toward me. I picked it up. It was soft and pliable, unlike any paper product I had felt. I opened it. Printed in ornate calligraphy was the name Devi.

"Ah, Devi," said Janus approvingly. "This is an extremely special name. Maya Devi is the mother of the Buddha. This means that Yoni sees you as an awesome creative force. Mothers birthed the whole world." Janus looked a little awestruck. It all made sense now. This was how I was meant to be a mother: not by having Ethan's children, but by becoming a more nurturing soul.

Ethan's spirit was at rest. I knew this much. It all made sense now. He and Amaya had been playing some kind of dangerous game that she had initiated, and they couldn't survive it. Her negative energy had severed the deep connection they had to the spiritual world, and nothing could bring that back. Whatever happened to him—and everyone else—was fated. I had come here to revivify my life. Not his. All my petty grievances, once so important to me, had now dissipated into the ether. That was why I reacted so strongly to Lama Yoni that first time I saw him, years ago in New York: he was showing me my soul, but I wasn't ready to accept the true me. But now I was finally reborn.

"It's time for you to go to your new quarters," Janus said. "Your things have been removed from your old room. You will find your robes—the robes of the ordained—waiting for you."

A pretty young woman appeared again. I followed her back down the rich purple halls, and into my new life.

One Year Later

The Buddhist Predator of the New Mexico Desert
Did a guru's actions lead to a young couple's death?

BY LUCINDA CROSLEY

The guru's voice on the police recording is matter-of-fact.
"Two of the teachers at my retreat have gone missing," he
says. "Their names are Kai Powell and Amaya Walters.
They didn't show up for their class this morning, and
someone saw them go off into the mountains." The call
alone was notable. The Sagebrush County Sheriff's Office
had never heard from the guru directly before, even
though he owned two upscale yoga retreats in the middle
of the county's empty, arid land.

The charismatic guru's real name is John Brooks,
though he's known to his followers as Yoni. His main retreat is called Zuni. It's popular among wealthy New Age
types, particularly in Silicon Valley. Yoni's ancillary retreat is called the Homestead, and is more expensive and
exclusive—it's invite-only, and its residents are teachers
at the Zuni Retreat and obsessive acolytes of the guru. The

Homestead's guests stay for months at a time, draining their fortunes in a never-ending quest for spiritual salvation.

The authorities, led by Sagebrush County sheriff Matt Lewis, started looking for Powell and Walters immediately after they got the call. Camping in the mountains is illegal because the landscape is so barren. Locals say it's filled with bad spirits and scorpions.

It took searchers a month to find Powell and Walters, and it was too late. Their desiccated bodies were found on the hard ground in a remote cave, a sharpened piece of obsidian between them. Autopsies revealed stab wounds deep enough to nick bone. The placement and depth of those wounds led the county coroner to suspect that what went on between Powell and Walters was a murder-suicide. But the corpses had deteriorated so much that it was impossible to make a definitive judgment based on the forensic autopsy alone.

From all accounts, Ethan Powell was a gentle soul who was so devoted to Buddhism (or at least Lama Yoni's fractured interpretation of it) that he would not kill a mosquito even as it was sucking his blood. According to a former follower of Yoni's, Powell was also deeply devoted to Walters. He left his wife to follow her to the Zuni Retreat, and the pair made popular yoga videos together under the name When Two Become One. Now that they're dead, watching these videos is a macabre and intimate experience. Powell and Walters do not break eye contact, no matter what yogic contortions their bodies are making.

The journey that ended in Powell's and Walters's deaths began forty years ago and a thousand miles away from New Mexico in San Francisco. It's a winding road filled with alleged sexual assault, secrecy, spiritual malpractice, hidden family ties, and a body count. For the first time, an ex-follower who had been with Yoni since the late sixties will go on record with everything she's seen. We also have the exclusive first interview with Ethan Powell's ex-wife, a former attorney named Dana Morrison.

Lo has warm brown eyes and hair that goes down to her shoulders. I'm meeting her in an undisclosed location in New Mexico. She doesn't want to reveal her specific whereabouts because she fears Yoni might try to suck her back in. "This is the shortest my hair has been since 1968," she says. "Yoni didn't like women with short hair. He said that it removed us from Mother Nature. But really, I think it just turned him off." Lo joined Yoni as a teenager. Despite the gray hairs and the smattering of wrinkles, at 62, Lo still has the giddy air of an adolescent. Back when she first met him, Yoni was known as Aries, and he led a band of young followers from San Francisco to a commune in Mendocino County, California.

"All the young girls, we worshiped him," Lo said. "He was so handsome, and he had all the answers. You have to understand, most of us were runaways who landed in San Francisco. We were desperate for some guidance, wherever we could find it. And here was this sexy guy telling us we could throw off all the shackles of our uptight upbringings and live in this perfect world. It was very appealing."

San Francisco was a hotbed for this kind of spiritual leader. According to NYU professor Darius Smithstein, there were at least 1,000 popular alternative spiritual leaders in Northern California between 1966 and 1975. "The most successful of these hucksters had thousands of followers. Your Jim Joneses, for example," Smithstein explains. "John Brooks was somewhere in the middle. He had about 100 hard-core adherents, give or take."

Lo said she was so blinded by her love for Aries that she didn't see the dark side of the Mendocino commune. "I now believe he was sexually abusing some of the other women. I never refused his advances, so I didn't experience it myself." Lo couldn't understand how anyone could refuse the guru's advances. "He was basically a god to me," she says, shaking her head.

So much so that Lo, along with two other women, fled that Mendocino commune with him on his say-so. He told them he wanted to spread the word about his teachings, but in truth he was running from the law. A former follower of Aries's had accused him of rape.

Lo says that immediately after they left Mendocino, she and Yoni got married—but only in the spiritual sense. "I think he married me to keep me under his thumb. Sexual faithfulness was never part of our union, but I stayed because I knew that being married to the guru gave me a kind of power that his other partners didn't have."

They ultimately landed in New York, where John Brooks

adopted the name Yoni and found a place in the downtown counterculture of the late 1970s. He ran a macrobiotic restaurant out of his Jane Street residence, and used
that base—called the Jane Street Ashram—to befriend the
leading lights of the New York Buddhist community. "At
first he seemed very devoted to teaching Tibetan Buddhism," says Columbia University professor Daniel Bauer,
who is one of the world's leading experts on Eastern reli-
gions and is an integral part of New York's Buddhist community. "He said he had studied under a guru in one of
the most revered monasteries in India. At first we had no
reason not to believe him. His followers really seemed to
love him."

But Yoni's fellow Buddhists soon grew suspicious.
"There were an inordinate number of beautiful young
women falling at Yoni's feet," Bauer says. "We started worrying that Yoni was exploiting the power differential in
ways that were not appropriate for a leader. We were concerned about the doctrine he was teaching, which seemed
to have no relation to true Buddhism. Then we started to
hear stories about what was going on behind the scenes at
Jane Street."

Those stories included mandatory orgies, sexual mind
games, and sacred rituals involving the guru's semen.
Lo confirms these stories, but will not give me any additional details. "It's too painful," she says, shaking her
head. Yoni's popularity really began to explode beyond
the tight-knit local Buddhist community when he started
combining his teachings with yoga classes for the public.

His public front was different from his private, sexual self. "I will say those rituals were kept among a handful of trustworthy followers," Lo says. "Yoni knew that our practices would not be acceptable to outsiders."

Yoni was smart enough to get the best yoga teachers around, which lent his studio an air of legitimacy. By that point, Yoni had moved out of the Jane Street Ashram into a bigger studio in Tribeca. He started preaching a kind of Eastern prosperity gospel, telling followers that if they developed good karma, all manner of earthly riches would come their way. Part of developing good karma involved giving their guru a tenth of their yearly income. In the early aughts, he took on a new spiritual wife. Her name? Ruth "Amaya" Walters.

"I knew we were entering a different phase in our relationship when Amaya started coming around," Lo says. By then she was in her late forties, and Yoni was no longer interested in her sexually. "He said that I had become too holy for sexual contact," she says, tearing up a little. "But obviously he just didn't want to touch me anymore."

Walters was in her early twenties then, a recent college graduate and obsessive follower of Yoni's. She became his assistant and gatekeeper. In 2006, she started working at Green Wave, an advertising agency, as a nighttime copy editor, at Yoni's behest. He asked Amaya to work there because that's where Ethan Powell was employed, and Amaya had explicit instructions to seduce Ethan and bring him into the fold.

"I knew that Yoni was going after Ethan, but I didn't

know why," Lo says. "He'd fixate on certain people, so it wasn't that out of character. I assumed, at the time, that he'd seen Ethan at one of the regular yoga classes at the ashram and had taken a liking to him." It was only much later that she realized Yoni had tracked Ethan down because he had been conceived through the alleged rape back in Mendocino. His mother, Rosemary Powell—who was called Safflower in her Mendocino days—had died in a car accident in Montana in 1993. As of this writing, there's no evidence of foul play in her death.

Even though Amaya and Ethan initially got together because of Yoni's machinations, "Amaya genuinely fell in love with Kai, that much I know," Lo says. "They were very sweet with each other." When they fell in love, Amaya began to move away from Yoni emotionally. She had no way to know that her behavior would ultimately seal her fate.

Yoni was a savvy investor, and had used his followers' tithings wisely. He invested in a tech company that went public, and by 2005 he had enough money to buy the land in New Mexico that would become the Zuni Retreat and the secret Homestead. Two years later, Kai, Amaya, and Lo went with him to New Mexico. "I had nowhere else to go," Lo says. "I'd been with him the whole of my adult life."

Lo says that while Yoni superficially accepted Kai and Amaya's relationship, he never really forgave Kai for stealing his bride—or Amaya for influencing his son. "Not that he was ever faithful to Amaya," Lo says bitterly, "but he resented their love." He couldn't really do anything about it, though: Kai and Amaya were the most popular teachers at the retreat, and he needed them to keep the high-paying visitors coming. It can cost over $10,000 a month to stay at the Zuni Retreat, and a reported $20,000 a month to stay at the Homestead, though the latter's fees are not publicly listed. "Yoni needed to keep getting those good reviews," Lo says.

But Kai and Amaya were getting increasingly sick of paying homage to Yoni, which began to isolate them from the rest of Yoni's followers. Their isolation led to paranoia—a kind of folie à deux. "Kai became obsessed with some Aztec death goddess he read about. He and Amaya declared themselves her followers and started performing their own bloodletting rituals," Lo says. "They'd come to dinner with bandages on their forearms. I pulled Amaya aside and asked her what was going on, because I was worried. But she said all of their activities were consensual—they were cutting themselves, not each other—and they were just exploring the limits of their connection."

They were already deep into this isolated experimentation when Kai discovered the truth about his origins. "We were hanging around one evening after dinner," Lo says. "Kai asked to look through a photo album I had kept from the early days with Yoni. I said sure, no problem. I was touched that he cared. He saw a photo in there that deeply disturbed him, and asked me about a woman in the image. I said, 'Oh, that's Safflower. She ran away from the compound.' He asked me what happened to her, and I said something like 'Who cares?'" Lo shakes her head when she tells me this, embarrassed by the memory. "I had no idea Safflower was Kai's mother. I didn't find out until I met Dana."

Dana Morrison Powell was a high-powered litigator at a white-shoe law firm when she found out that her ex-husband was dead. "It destroyed her," says Beth Morrison, Dana's younger sister. "She never really got over it when Ethan left her in the first place, and finding out he was dead just scrambled her fucking brain." Dana didn't believe that Ethan had killed Amaya and then himself, as law enforcement personnel seemed to think. This led her to the Zuni Retreat, and ultimately to the Homestead.

"It made no fucking sense," Beth says, wiping away tears as I interview her over a latte at a Hungarian café in Manhattan. "I tried to talk her out of it. The only part of it I understood was that Dana is a tenacious person. When she gets an idea in her head, there's no convincing her to drop it."

Lo first met Dana when she was staying at the Zuni Retreat, hoping to learn more about who her husband was in the years before he died. "We really bonded," says Lo. Dana stood out to her, and she mentioned her to Yoni. Yoni, to Lo's surprise, suggested that Lo invite Dana to the Homestead, which was a respite for only the most devoted visitors to the Zuni Retreat. "He hadn't let me invite any students to the Homestead thus far," Lo says, "and he'd never let anyone invite someone so new to our process."

Lo looks down in shame. "I realize now that he told me to invite her because he knew she was Ethan's ex."

When Dana got to the Homestead, Yoni enrolled her in Lo's Inner Child Workshop to keep a close eye on her. "She was the hardest-working student I have ever had, and we really made progress," Lo says. They made so much progress that Dana felt she could tell Lo the truth about her identity. "She said that Safflower was Kai's mother, and Yoni was his real father, and that she believed that Kai had figured it out." Lo laughs. "I was so clueless, I didn't even know Amaya and Kai were dead. I thought they had just gone on a spiritual journey somewhere. Yoni said we were never to speak of them or it might hurt their silent journey, and I believed him."

Lo was so shaken by Dana's admission, she felt she needed to work through it. So she went to her two oldest friends, the only two women who were still around from the Mendocino days—they go by the names Veena and Dew—to tell them about it. They surprised her by informing her about everything that Yoni had shielded from her for all those years. "Veena said, 'You old fool. How did you not know who Kai really was?' I guess I kept my head in the sand for a lot of years as a way of coping." Lo starts crying at this point in our interview, and asks for a few minutes alone to collect herself.

When she returns she has a woven handkerchief in her right hand that she will clutch tightly for the rest of the interview. She tells me what she knows about Ethan's and Amaya's deaths. "According to Veena, Yoni knew that

Ethan had discovered the truth about his origins, and he decided the best course of action was to freeze Ethan and Amaya out completely. Yoni knew that having two people who no longer believed in his hype could poison his entire following. So he started taking their classes away from them one by one, moving them to the worst room at the Homestead, and ignoring them when he would pass them in the hallway."

This only compounded the pair's paranoia. Ultimately, they felt their sole option was to flee into the hills. Only Ethan and Amaya will ever know exactly what went on in that cave, but based on the evidence and their behavior before leaving, Lo believes it was a self-inflicted accident for both of them. "Because of the stab wounds, I bet they were doing one of their cutting rituals. It just went too far, and because they were all alone in the desert, they couldn't get help."

After putting all of this together, Lo confronted Yoni about what she knew. "He denied the whole thing, of course," Lo says. "He said he never froze them out, but that they left to do their own spiritual work. He said their deaths were a very sad thing, but it was fated because they had bad karma. He claimed that he had no idea about Safflower's connection to Kai."

At that point, Lo decided it was time to leave. She found another ex-follower of Yoni's here in New Mexico who helped her get back on her feet. "He knew I had been isolated from the real world for so long. I never had a bank account of my own. I never paid a bill or found an apartment." This follower helped her with all the quotidian details of life in the twenty-first century. Lo fell in love with him, to boot. "He's probably the only person who could understand everything I've been through." She will not allow me to print his name for fear of retribution from Yoni's camp.

"I assumed Dana would be okay, so I left without saying good-bye to her," Lo says. "She was only supposed to be staying for a month and I thought she had a good head on her shoulders. Leaving her was the worst decision of my life."

There is still a photograph of Dana Morrison Powell on her LinkedIn profile. She's wearing a suit that leaches the color out of her already pale face. The photograph looks nothing like the Dana I see before me on-screen. She has agreed to a Skype conversation from the Zuni Retreat. Numerous requests to visit the retreat and the Homestead have been denied, and I was escorted off the land when I tried to approach without explicit permission.

This interview has been granted through Lama Yoni's publicist, though the Lama himself will not speak on the record. Yoni's lawyer has denied all of Lo's assertions about Ethan Powell's and Amaya Walters's deaths. "Lo is a bitter ex-lover of my client's," says David Rappaport, who has represented John Brooks and his business interests for decades. "There's no proof of any of her assertions, and I would think a publication like yours would not be interested in exaggerations and outright defamatory falsehoods peddled by such a person."

Dana—who tells me to call her Devi because "Dana is my past; Devi is my now"—has a much more relaxed expression than her earlier photo depicts. Her hair falls around her face in long, gentle waves. She has a deep tan and is wearing a light-purple robe. I ask her what she thinks happened to Ethan and she gives me a condescending, tight-lipped smile. "Ethan's journey led him to that cave, where his spirit came to rest. He had incredibly bad karma, in part because he left me the way he did." What about the connection between Ethan's mother and Yoni? Doesn't that seem like a strange coincidence? "It's all written in the stars," she says. "It was the necessary step to bring me to Yoni."

I ask her about Yoni. "Yoni has completely changed my life," Dana says. "I used to be a sad, angry little person. I had no peace. I am actualized. I am living in my now." I try to get her to explain what she means by that and she tells me that I couldn't possibly understand, because I'm not on the same spiritual plane that she and Yoni are. She says the same thing about her sister, Beth, and about experts like Daniel Bauer who question Yoni's teachings. "I actually feel sorry for you," she says. "You would be so much happier if you were here with us. You would not be concerned about having an answer for every little thing."

Sagebrush County sheriff Matt Lewis will not comment on Lo's assertions. But someone from the sheriff's office, who spoke on the condition of anonymity because he is not authorized to speak about Ethan Powell's or Amaya

Walters's cases, said that the police believe what Lo says to be close to the truth. "We find her very credible. We just can't prove any of it."

I ask Lewis about Dana Powell. "It's strange," he admits. "At the request of her family, we went over to the Homestead to ask her a few questions. She swears that she is there of her own volition, that she was not coerced, and that she is free to leave at any time. She's a grown woman who is legally of sound mind. Unless her family wants to try to get a court order to commit her, there's nothing we can do." Beth Morrison says her family is still considering their legal options.

Lo says she will never forgive herself for what happened to Dana. But she has found some happiness away from Yoni. She lives with the ex-follower who helped her adjust to twenty-first-century life. "I feel like I've been given a second chance at this mortal coil. I'm not going to mess this one up. I'm not sure how much time I have left."

Dana has also found love. At the end of our conversation, I notice a simple gold band around her left ring finger. I ask her about it and she blushes. "If you must know, I've entered a spiritual marriage with Yoni. It's the closest bond I've ever known. Our souls are united in a constant embrace." I'm about to ask her a follow-up question when I hear a male voice in the background. "I've got to go," Dana says. "Namaste."

Acknowledgments

To Elisabeth Weed, who has been my supportive, brilliant agent since I was embarrassingly young and green. She saw something in me before I saw anything in myself. Her sharp eye and literary (and life) advice have kept me afloat for more than a decade.

To Kate Nintzel, my ace editor, who took the first draft of *Soulmates* and made it into a far, far better book than I thought it could possibly be. I am so grateful to have found someone who understands my voice so thoroughly. And to Kate Schafer and Margaux Weisman at William Morrow, whose expertise and help with this book have been indispensable.

To all the colleagues and friends who read early drafts and weighed in, particularly Ann Bauer, who read the first chapter and convinced me it could be a decent book; Hanna Rosin, who did the same; Leah Chernikoff, who provided ongoing Gchat support; and Jason Zinoman, who read the second (or maybe the third?) full version and gave me the confidence I needed to push through the last rounds of edits. To Anne-Marie Slaughter for showing me, by example, that having young children isn't a roadblock to finishing a second novel.

To David Plotz, Noreen Malone, Willa Paskin, Ben Cooley, Jessica Pressler, Emily Gould, Elissa Strauss, Colby Bird, Tatiana Homonoff, Anna Knoell, Thornton McEnery and Kristen Crofoot for providing many things, including but not limited to: literary advice, local entertainment, and occasional toddler wrangling.

To Lena Dunham and Jenni Konner, who have been incredible boss ladies at *Lenny* and have given me the opportunity of a lifetime. I never thought I would go back to a staff job after freelancing for years, but I never imagined the feminist utopia they created was possible. Their work ethic is an ongoing inspiration. To Laia Garcia, who has been an amazing partner in running *Lenny* and makes me laugh every damn day.

To my parents, Richard and Judith Grose, for encouraging my creativity ever since I wrote a satirical play at age ten about Henry VIII and his six wives called *Ouch!* To my brother, Jacob Grose, and my sister-in-law, Anna Magracheva; and to my in-laws, David, Charlotte, Wendell, and Judson Winton, Meghan Best and Noah Pritzker, for their love and support.

And finally, to Michael Winton, my life and my heart. Thank you for doing long weekends of child care without complaint so I could work on this book, and for being such a true partner. Our daughters are as lucky to have you as a father as I am to have you as a husband.